MARC JOHNSON

REAWAKENING

THE PASSAGE OF HELLSFIRE
BOOK 3

Third Edition, 2013

ISBN 978-0-9834770-8-2

Longshot Publishing

CHAPTER 1

I'M IN A DIMLY *lit room. It's hard to make out my surroundings; all the light is drawn to Krystal, on the other side of the room. She looks as if she's glowing. She turns to me and smiles, her violet eyes glimmering with playfulness. She poses with her hands on her hips, enticing me to come to her. I can't resist. I never could.*

I rush over to her, grab her hands, and spin her around. Her lighthearted laughter brings a warmth to my soul. Our hands lock onto each other and we spin around and around, laughing all the while.

I stop spinning and reel her in toward me. We begin to dance, our bodies getting ever closer to each other. I'm not a good dancer, but it doesn't matter. What matters is the fact that we're having fun, and the heat from her body flows into mine. Our feet stop and our eyes meet. Krystal is almost as tall as me, so I barely need to tilt my head down to kiss her. Our lips connect perfectly and we devour each other.

That's when I start killing her.

Krystal's smooth, beautiful face dries out and her veins blacken. She clutches me, and her scream nearly shatters my ears. I try to keep her from falling, frantically casting spells of healing, but my magic has no effect.

"Hellsfire..." she says with her dying breath.

I cradle her lifeless body against mine, wishing I had been able to save her. But I couldn't. No matter how much magic I had, I was powerless against Renak's curse. The curse that I had delivered to Krystal with my own touch.

I had had this dream countless times in the months since I had last seen her. And while I always knew it was merely a nightmare, it terrified me more than any army or monster I had ever faced.

A sharp ache spiking through my head tore me from my nightmare and forced me back into the waking world, cold sweat drenching my naked body. My web of protection had been breached. There was an intruder in my room. Instinctively, I hardened the air around me so that it would deflect any blow. I turned, scanning the dark room with my wizard's sight. Just in time, I caught the faint glow of an enchanted sword above me. If it were the kind that cut through magic, my air shield wouldn't hold. Instead, I funneled the air magic, using it to push me away from my attacker as he brought his sword down.

His sword sliced through my pillow, barely missing me as I was flung backward off the bed, crashing into the stone wall beyond. I released a portion of my flame, setting my bed ablaze. The flames attacked my intruder but the magic on his sword lit up, keeping them at bay.

I rose, staring at him, the light from the flames dimly illuminating his features. The fiery bed burned between us. His sword's magic seemed to lower my flames, and I had to fuel them with more of my magic to keep them burning. He circled, and I moved to keep the bed between him and my naked self.

He feinted left and I went right, thinking about how I was going to defeat him. His sword, like many enchanted weapons, appeared to be designed to work against magic.

He feinted right this time, and when I went left he headed directly over my fiery bed. The blade cut through my fire, and it almost died out. I reached out to my tattered, burned blankets with air magic and gave them a pull, tripping him and sending him tumbling across the bed onto the floor.

I sprinted to the dresser, where I kept my pouch, and dug for a potion. My assassin was up again and he ran toward me, yelling in rage, his deadly sword sheathed in a hint of bright blue. Before his sword's tip could run me through, I ducked aside and threw the small vial near his feet. The glass exploded.

Thick, dark smoke rose from the remnants of the vial, blackening the air around us. I gagged, cursing that I had put too much salamander's blood in the experimental potion. Vines shot out from where the vial had broken and wrapped around my would-be killer. He dropped his sword and crashed to the stone floor.

I had to make this quick. My potion might not hold him for long.

I kicked his sword away and summoned a portion of my inner flame to my hand. I bent down, using the fireball to guide my sight. I gasped when my fire's light illuminated his face.

My assassin couldn't be more than sixteen—a few years younger than me. His eyes held such rage, yet his face was so young. I stilled my hand, unsure of what to do.

"What are you waiting for, Hellsfire?" he asked, anger and defeat laced in his voice. "Kill me and get it over with."

I brought my fiery hand closer to his face. He cringed, struggling to move, but he couldn't with the vines binding him in place. Yet his hatred toward me didn't vanish in his fear; it only intensified. I didn't recognize him from my time in Northern Shala, or here in Tyree.

"What did I do to you, to make you hate me so?" I asked.

He didn't say anything for several long moments, but rage-filled tears ran from his eyes. "You killed my family, you bastard! They did nothing to provoke you!"

Staring at him, feeling the emotion he radiated, I wondered if his words were true. Since I had become a wizard, I had killed far too many people. It had been in self-defense, or in defense of those I loved, but that wouldn't matter to their loved ones.

He narrowed his eyes. "You don't remember, do you? You wouldn't."

"Why do you think I killed them?"

"My family died when you ended the war, incinerating everyone I loved until they were nothing but ashes. You don't remember them because they were nothing to you, wizard."

I shook my head. That wasn't it at all. I was still haunted by all those people I had killed to end their invasion of my homeland. But it had to be done.

I'd tried to make up for it as I helped repair the land in Tyree after the war, but I knew it wasn't enough. It never would be.

To make matters worse, the dark power I accessed to stop them still whispered to me. It promised me that it could end Krystal's curse and do anything else I desired. If it wasn't for Krystal, I would have burned everyone in that final battle, including her and my friends.

"No," I said, finding my voice. "It wasn't like that. You don't understand what I had to do, or what I went through to bring the barrier down."

"My older sister and brother were in the army you killed. They roasted to death when you unleashed your spell. And I wasn't there with them." The anger in his voice was still there, but it wasn't directed at me. It was pointed at himself.

I brought my hand closer. I knew it would be safer to kill him because while he may have lacked experience, his youth gave him great determination. One look into his eyes told me he wouldn't rest until I was dead.

I sighed and lowered my hand. I used my fire to burn away the vines that held him.

"What are you doing?" he asked.

"I'm letting you go. I know you don't believe me, but I never meant to hurt you or your family."

He slowly scrambled away from me and rose. He backed away, never taking his eyes off me. He reached for his sword and held it, never sheathing it. I clenched my fists, my magic lying below the surface, ready to come at a moment's wish. The dying fires on my bed swayed in anticipation of what he would do. I would kill him if I had to, but I would let him make the first move.

"Don't think that sparing my life today will make me forget that you murdered my family." His fierce eyes met mine and he pointed his sword at me, his hand trembling with rage. "I will see you again, Hellsfire, and I will make you pay for what you've done."

My assassin stormed out of the room. I watched him go, wondering if I had made a mistake, and if one day I would find that sword of his embedded in my belly.

CHAPTER 2

I EXTINGUISHED THE FIRES on the bed and summoned air magic to blow the smoke out the window. No guards, wizards, or servants had come up here to see what caused the commotion. I didn't expect them to. It was the middle of the night and my room was located well away from anyone. Or perhaps they had sanctioned the attack against me?

I had been in the old wizards' school in Fairhaven for almost a month now. The school had been closed and devastated nearly a thousand years ago when war first broke out between the members of the Elemental Council. It had been empty ever since. With the council reunited, they wanted to reopen the school. They said that they wanted to help train and guide wizards again. I hoped that was it, but I believed it was more likely that those six wanted to rule from their place of power once more. Before the war, Fairhaven was one of the biggest and most important cities in Tyree.

Whatever their reasoning might be, for the past two months I had been helping the council to take down the defenses of this capital city and get things in working order. My former master, Stradus, had told me stories of the wizard school and his time training there. I didn't know if the school would ever be restored to its former glory or even if it should be, considering that the council had started a war, and could do even more damage with wizards they had handpicked and trained themselves. But there should be a place where young people could learn to use their powers. With the Great Barrier down, I hoped that one would also be established in Northern Shala.

I also needed to build a working relationship with the council, lest they try to invade my homeland again. I wasn't sure if they would, but they had their own motives I couldn't begin to understand. I also helped with Fairhaven because of Krystal.

Since I'd been down in Tyree, I'd been trying to find a cure for Krystal's curse. I'd had no luck in the matter. Neither wizard nor witch, sorcerer nor seer had been able to help. The curse was created by one of the most powerful and feared wizards who ever existed—Renak. But Renak had been dead for centuries. It was another wizard who'd used it to hurt and nearly kill my beloved.

Premier.

He had killed Stradus, and had somehow twisted Renak's spell to hurt me. Instead of killing me, it had almost killed Krystal. Only the magic from the necklace I had given her had saved her.

I had spent the first few months searching for that bastard so he could fix what he'd done, or at least, so I could make him pay for it. But after my brief run in with him in Romenia, he had just vanished. That worried me more than anything. Whatever Premier was planning, it would bode ill for all of us.

I took my purse that contained my potions, a book of spells, and a few supplies, and left my room, traversing the quiet hallways. The small fireball in my hand was my only light. I glanced at the shadows, preparing myself in case my assassin lurked in the dark, or if he was just the first wave of an attack.

I had helped take down the wards on the school in hopes that it would contain some sliver of information to help me break Renak's curse. But the school had already been ransacked ages ago. I knew that, but I stayed, hoping that I would find something the council and their armies had overlooked. People were slowly trickling from all over the land, not just from Tyree but from Northern Shala too. There was always a chance that one of the visitors would have the knowledge I needed.

The school, while no longer dangerous, was still in shambles. The third-floor dormitory rooms I resided in were at the top of one of the few sections that still stood. The eastern side of the building had collapsed, ravaged by time, and the underground rooms had caved in.

I ran my finger over a fallen and faded painting, my finger picking up a thick trail of ancient dust. I sniffed it, and it tickled my nose, my body sensing a tinge of dead magic in it. My ears heard childish laughter down the darkened hallway as feet ran across the stone floor. My mind filled with images of children chasing each other, laughing while they cast magic.

What would that be like, I wondered. To be taught magic openly, with others, at a younger age? Would I have made the same mistakes, or would things have been easier, if I had the support of others?

I shook my head, clearing it of cobwebs, unlike the corridors. The school might have been abandoned for ages, but its memories and ghosts remained. No matter how much power I had, I couldn't change the past.

I continued my journey downstairs. On the first floor, toward the back of the grand building, was an old workroom that was once used to teach students how to make potions. The door opened directly to the garden and a large window allowed the light to shine through. The garden had become overrun with weeds and the ground was rough and hard. It was going to be some time before much-needed plants could grow there. I wanted to work on the garden, but it wasn't a top priority. And I wasn't even sure how long I'd stay in Tyree.

I went to the rotted workbench in the back. On top of it were a pestle and mortar, plants and flowers I had gathered, and small vials to pour the potions in. I had been restocking my potions and experimenting with a few, but there was one I was hesitant to make. It was the one I was going to make now—a maleika potion.

Years ago when I was an apprentice, I had made a maleika potion against my master's wishes. Maleikas can be used to spy over great distances, and I had desperately wanted to see my mother, as I longed for home. The maleika I summoned wasn't a normal one, and nearly killed me. If it wasn't for Stradus intervening, I would have died. This time I would have to summon one alone.

I took out the small book of spells Stradus had given me and reread the maleika ritual. I didn't need to study it intently, because after my first summoning of one, I wasn't likely to forget it. But Master Stradus had taught me I had to be more careful, even though it was a hard lesson to learn.

When I was finished, I carefully cut, chopped, and ground up the plants I needed. The grinding of the pestle echoed in my ears against the stark quiet of the dead school. The magical presence of the school never left me. I felt the long-gone teachers and students watch me as I prepared the ritual, wanting to make sure I did everything right.

As I heated up the plants, my mind kept wandering back to Krystal. I could have summoned a maleika months ago. The urge in me grew every day, as I missed her more. But I'd never summoned one until now. I didn't want to invade her privacy and spy on her. She would never forgive me if she found out I had. I was also terrified that she had moved on to someone else, and I would see that too.

None of that mattered now. I had to know if she was all right. I knew in my bones that she never would be completely all right as long as she was inflicted with that curse, but I had to see how badly or how well she fared. The maleika was the only way, since Alexandria was so far away.

The potion finished cooking and I stirred it and poured it into a vial. While I waited for it to cool, I placed candles on the floor in a wide enough circle for me to sit in. Before I lit them, I spent time casting a spell into the candles. It should be strong enough to immobilize, then kill, that malicious maleika if I ran into it. But neither Stradus nor I ever understood where the maleika had gotten so much power from, or why it had wanted to kill me.

By the time I finished my trap, the potion had cooled down. I lit the candles and the flames blossomed. The undercurrent of magic I put in them lay in wait to be sprung.

I sat down cross-legged in the circle of fire and reached out to each of the six manas that resided in all life. In the ancient language of Caleea I recited, *"Being of the other plane, I call you forth. Being of the other plane, I call you forth. Heed my words. I seek a maleika to come into this world and be my ears and eyes. Come, oh maleika."* I downed the potion, ignoring its salty bite, and spit it back out. *"Come, maleika, and obey me!"*

I stared at the place where I'd spat the potion. It shimmied and vibrated, the small puddle of liquid moving faster with each passing moment. Wisps rose from it like steam, carrying a sour smell into my nose. The liquid solidified, pulling itself together as it rose above the ground. A misshapen head appeared, like a grayish haze of fog. I'd always thought that their ghostly state was how the maleikas were able to travel to nearly anywhere, but no one knew for sure. It floated above the ground, waiting for me to instruct it on what to do.

I glared at it and squeezed my hand, reaching out to the magic hidden in the candles. As its face came into focus, I saw that it didn't have a scar where its left eye should be. It was just an ordinary maleika. I exhaled, letting myself relax.

"What would you wish to see?" it asked, giving me the standard response.

I closed my eyes and visualized Alexandria, the great city to the north. I pictured its throngs of people all packed into one place, how its sky-piercing towers watched over all, and how its soldiers were the Guardsmen of Alexandria and protected Northern Shala from the creatures of the Wastelands. But those thoughts didn't stick with me and weren't good enough for the ritual.

As much as it pained me to do so, I let my memories of Alexandria flow from me, and focused on Krystal.

I remembered a time when she surprised me with my favorite sweet, honey bread. We stood away from prying eyes in an alcove's shadows. She lifted up the bread to my face. I opened my mouth wide, thinking she was going to feed me. What she actually did was rub it into my face. I almost licked it off, but decided against it before reeling her in and kissing her hard and sloppy, getting as much honey on her face as I possibly could.

And there was this one spot she showed me in the southern tower. You had to climb a multitude of stairs, and it was hidden in a storage room behind an old bookshelf. You had to crawl through a hole in the wall, and it opened up to a small room. There was a tiny window that overlooked the entirety of Alexandria. Old blankets were kept there and we'd often lie in that room that was barely big enough for both of us, and stare at the beautiful landscape. We couldn't go there often because the princess was a busy woman. When we did, we'd snuggle and she'd allow herself to be taken into my arms with her head resting on my chest before she fell asleep.

She also had this mole right above her waistline that I'd dance my fingers on ever so lightly. She always shivered when I did that.

My eyes stung at the memories. Gods, how I missed her.

"I see it now," the maleika said, and vanished.

With the maleika gone, I was forced to deal with the persistent thoughts I had been ignoring the past few months. The irritating silence did nothing to drown them.

The last time I had seen and spoken to Krystal, I told her I loved her. Her face lit up with a grand smile but then faded. She hadn't said the words back, just left me and rode toward Alexandria. I had written to her every week, giving her reports on what had changed in Tyree, how things were progressing with finding her a cure, and how I'd tried to track down Premier. Every month, I'd send a courier into Alexandria with all those letters. I always wanted to end the letter by saying how terribly I missed her. I only just stopped myself. Instead I asked her how she was and said that I hoped she was doing well. A different courier would come back the following month and I always asked him if he had a letter for me.

I never heard back from her.

The maleika shimmied back into view, and in place of its ghastly head was an image. It was Krystal's bedchamber. Candles were burning low, and she was lying on her gigantic bed.

I couldn't help but smile at the sight of her, and my heart lightened until the image sharpened and I saw the state she was in. As if sensing my thoughts, the image of her grew closer.

What drew me and others to Krystal, I'm sure, was that she had this abundant energy about her. With that energy, she was tenacious and always fought for her kingdom and the people she loved. That strength overflowed from her. I felt it from the moment I met her and was touched by it every time I was around her. I still didn't understand that blazing white aura she possessed that I had glimpsed with my wizard's sight, but I believed it had something to do with her strength.

That intensity was now dimmed by the sickness that had overtaken her. Her skin was pallid and beads of sweat dripped down her forehead. Her breathing was shallow and erratic, as if someone suffocated her.

"Krystal," I said, reaching out to her. My hand disrupted the image. I was afraid I had killed the ritual, but the maleika returned a moment later.

I extended my magical senses to try to see what was wrong, but there was nothing to sense. She was hundreds of miles away. While the maleika allowed me to view things, I couldn't interact with them, magically or otherwise. All I could do was watch in horror as she suffered.

Krystal's body jerked and she cried out in pain. Through the blankets piled on top of her, I glimpsed a glowing green light. It was the necklace I had given her as a token of my love. I bit down on my lips, praying to the gods in silence that the necklace's magic would hold against Renak's curse.

A hand came into view, placing a damp towel on her forehead. I expected it to be one of the healers, but the image pulled back and it was Ardimus. He was a warrior from the Burning Sands, and her protector. More importantly, he was like a second father to her.

"Rest, princess," Ardimus said.

He lifted the towel and stifled a yawn. The warrior looked haggard—exhausted beyond recovery—but I knew he would never quit in his duty to her.

"Enough," I said. The image of Krystal and Ardimus vanished, to be replaced by the ghostly face of the maleika.

As much as they tried, Ardimus and the healers wouldn't be able to help Krystal. She had been afflicted by a magical curse, and it was magic that would help her. Alexandrians didn't look too kindly on magic. Their city was founded to not only defend Northern Shala from the vile creatures in the Wastelands of Renak, but they also guarded any magical artifacts found in the area to keep them out of the hands of wizards. With Premier taking over Alexandria and almost destroying the city, and me almost killing their beloved princess, they were going to be even less accepting now.

Still, I had to do something. There was a death sentence hanging over my head if I tried to return to Alexandria, but I had to try to help Krystal. Yet, my power lay strongly with fire. It wasn't known for healing and life.

There was another I knew who was a master in such things. Asking him would come with a price, but it was a price I was willing to pay. I banished the maleika and went to go meet him.

I had two hours until dawn broke. As soon as that happened, I was going to do something I didn't want to do—ask the Elemental Council for help.

When the council had split, right after the War of the Wizards, they had fought another pointless war for nearly a thousand years, devastating Tyree. I had crippled the councils' armies when I stopped them from invading my homeland. I had ended the war, but if it wasn't for me bringing down the Great Barrier in the first place, they never would have had the opportunity to spread their war beyond Tyree into Northern Shala.

I had good reasons for bringing down the barrier at the time. Renak's essence had told me of a war between the gods, and how there was an imbalance that he once tried to deal with. I had listened to Renak and brought down the Great Barrier because of those reasons, and because the barrier spell was slowly destroying Northern Shala. In time, Northern Shala would have become as desolate as the rest of the Wastelands.

I had stayed in Tyree to try to learn if Renak was right about a war between the gods, and to find a cure for Krystal. The council tolerated me and in return, I shared with them the information I had learned while in the Wastelands, and I explained to them what Northern Shala was like. I helped to rebuild the land from its war-torn devastation. Even while I did all of that, I did most of it alone.

There were a few who weren't angry, but most wizards and soldiers still blamed me for killing their friends and family. Still, they worked with me, and I did my best to try to work with them. But it was going to take a long time before such wounds were healed. Unfortunately, wizards tended to live long lives and have even longer memories.

By the time those two hours were up, I had already packed my supplies and gotten my horse ready for the long ride up north. Time was of the essence, and I had to hurry for Krystal's sake.

I sent word to one of the council's pages as soon as I could. She gave my message to Ardonis, the master of white mana. If there was anyone that could help me, it would be him. Dawn was breaking as I stood by the door to the council's rooms. That section of the school had been repaired the fastest, as the council wanted to be in the place they once ruled. One of the goblin soldiers eyed me while I paced in front of him, anxious to get in.

No matter how long I stayed in Tyree, I still couldn't get used to the goblins and ogres in the land. They were completely different from those in the Wastelands. The creatures here spoke well, were well-armed and dressed, and their odor wasn't as nauseating. From my battles in the Wastelands and the childhood tales I'd heard growing up, though, I still didn't completely trust them.

I kept eyeing the door, wondering when it would open up again. I had seen pages, servants, and soldiers come and go, and while I had considered barging in and demanding to see Ardonis, that wouldn't get me what I desired.

The door opened and as always, I glanced in to see who it was. The young page who I had seen earlier looked at me. "Master Ardonis will see you now."

I almost said, "Finally," but stopped myself. "Thank you."

I passed the goblin guards and slipped through the doorway. The page had left to return to her morning duties. I didn't need her anyway. I had been to the council's chambers before.

Their section of the school was designed differently from the rest. It had only one floor, and past the door the goblins guarded, it branched out, opening into a large chamber with seven doors. Behind the large double door was the place where the council met and ruled on matters of magic. The other six doors split off like a web, one for each of the six wizards on the Elemental Council. I hadn't visited all of the councilors' chambers, but the ones I had were drastically different from each other.

Protecting the six doors were guards that I had only seen around the council. They were garbed in chest and leg armor, over long black flowing fabric. Their helmets were thick, with only one long slit to see through, so I couldn't see their eyes. Each of the soldiers' armor was colored to match the mana of the master they protected. They weren't all massive soldiers with gigantic swords, either.

The soldier protecting Nairi, the ancient master of Earth, was a surprisingly short woman with a long pike at her side. Helios, the young master of fire, had a thin, wiry man with a flail for his weapon. Ardonis's guard was a massively large man with a long broadsword. His huge hands flexed as I stared at him.

What made soldiers like these different from the others was that they radiated magic. As far as I knew, they couldn't cast it like a wizard, yet it was more than just their enchanted weapons and armor. It was like they were touched by magic. Not by the gods, but by the Elemental Masters themselves.

When I was in the presence of the council, their magic shone from them. It was as if their bodies couldn't contain the powerful mana inside them. Their eyes reflected that, as they were without pupils and constantly swirled with their respective colors. I could feel that same power here, even though it was toned down.

I had always wondered what these guards, otherwise known as the Council's Champions, could do. Luckily, I'd never faced them, but I had heard stories of them in battle. They were ferocious, and imbued with the council's powers for a reason. Oddly enough, they were always human, and there was only one at a time for each master.

I couldn't see Ardonis's champion's eyes, but I felt them as I opened the door and walked by him.

As tense as passing those champions was, I was even more nervous when I stepped inside. Ardonis was kinder than some of the others on the council. I didn't know if it was because that was his personality, or because he was the master of white mana and of life. Even so, he was still one of those who'd wanted to bring war to my homeland and who wielded a tremendous amount of power—both magically and politically. I was going to have to tread carefully if I wanted his help.

Ardonis's area of rule had a sense of life in it. It was that feeling you experienced when you witnessed a birth of a litter of kittens or watched a seed sprout for the first time. Normally, that feeling was fleeting, but here, it was built into every wall and woven into every fabric. The other councilors' sections, the ones I had visited, permeated with the magic they were masters in. I had never visited Bellona, the master of black mana. But I had always imagined that her lair would be as cold as she and death were.

Even though the council had their section of the school repaired first, there were still a few things out of place. As I traversed the hallway, the long carpet I walked on was far from being lush. Its colors had faded into the background, nearly matching the stones they covered. I almost tripped on a loose stone when I rounded the corner.

When I reached out with my magical senses, I felt Ardonis's presence. The closer I got to him, the stronger it got. The hallway opened up to a small waiting room. There were cushioned seats nearby and I sat in one of the chairs. They weren't exactly comfy, though. There was a small tear in the seat of mine. I bounced up and down and the insides leaked out. However, it was the most comfortable chair Ardonis had in his waiting room. I kept picking at the loose threads on the cushion, trying to keep myself occupied. Every time I glanced at the closed wooden door, I thought of Krystal and how ill she was. The fire within me threatened to swell up and burst at being so helpless.

"Hellsfire." I looked up to see Ardonis standing in front of me, with a confused and concerned look on his face.

I glanced up at the wizard and into his pure white eyes. The master of white mana's body was frail because of his age, but his magic enhanced it. If it wasn't for his pupil-less eyes, I wondered if people would mistake him for just a simple, ageing man with short, frizzy hair and a graying beard? I hoped so, because I was going to need him.

"Forgive me," I said and rose, bowing my head.

"Do not worry," Ardonis said. He stifled a yawn. "It's early and you look like you've been up half the night."

I rubbed my eyes. "Longer, actually."

"Come inside, and let's talk. I take it this must be important."

I thought of Krystal. She always was. "It is."

"I was just about to have breakfast. You can join me and tell me all about it."

Ardonis led me away from his waiting room and to a small alcove near his personal kitchen. He didn't say a word while we walked. I couldn't tell if he was being kind because he could see how exhausted I was, or if it was his way of maintaining some kind of control. As much as I wanted to tell him what was going on and ask—no, beg for his help, I didn't. I held back. Being around Krystal and Prastian had taught me that I needed to play this political game of theirs. Ardonis was bound to ask for something in return. While I was willing to pay any price to save Krystal, he needn't know that.

One of Ardonis's servants laid out a platter of fresh cheese, bread, and jam. It smelled delicious and while I was thankful for the meal, I was happier about the fact that this would be a quick breakfast.

"How are you enjoying your time in Tyree?" Ardonis asked after finishing a slice of bread.

I hesitated for a second too long. "It's fine." I allowed myself a small smile. Despite the fact that it hadn't felt like home, it did have a few things to recommend it. "Tyree is a very beautiful land. The type of magic I've experienced here has been wonderful. I've learned a lot about magic, and for that I appreciate my time here."

"And I appreciate what you've done. I know you've had trouble in your quest to track Premier or find a cure for the princess, but you've helped us tremendously. Both with your expertise about Northern Shala, and with your magic in helping us rebuild from the war." Ardonis leaned forward and smiled. "Now tell me, what's so important for you to come to my doors this early in the morning?"

I put down my half-eaten piece of cheese. After what I'd seen of my beloved, I wasn't much in the mood for eating anyway. I took a deep breath, then told him what I had seen and how sick Krystal was. I knew I tried to not sound desperate and emotional, but I also knew that I failed. This was Krystal's life in the balance, and I had to get to her.

The Elemental Council had tried to help Krystal shortly after I ended the war, but they couldn't defeat Renak's curse. That was then. I had hoped that since all this time had passed, that they might have been closer to finding a cure. Those who specialized in curses weren't able to help me, but Ardonis was the master of white mana. There was no one else to turn to.

When I was finished, Ardonis spoke. "We sent forays to Alexandria shortly after the war ended."

I raised an eyebrow. I didn't understand what that had to do with aiding the princess.

"And while Princess Krystal and King Furlong have been accommodating, their people haven't been as…friendly as I would have thought, when it came to the wizards I've sent with them."

"I warned you about that," I said.

He gave me a wry smile. "So you did. We miscalculated how unwelcome we would be. I'm surprised they tolerate you."

I shrugged. They used to tolerate me. That was before Krystal's illness.

"They're a good people," I said, finding myself believing it. "You shouldn't judge them too harshly. They've been through a lot."

"You may be right, Hellsfire." He sighed. "I hope things will change over time, as we'd like to establish a working relationship with Alexandria."

I perked up. We were finally getting to the point. "And what are you after?"

Ardonis reached for his tea and took a long sip. He finally put the cup down and said, "The Wastelands of Renak. Despite repeated attempts, we've not been allowed access to journey to Masep. We require no resources, guards, nor even guides, yet they still won't let us venture there."

I narrowed my eyes at him. The council wanted access to the powerful magic I had experienced there. If they had their army, the council wouldn't need to ask. But the Wastelands were too far north for such an army to go unnoticed or unchallenged. I was only able to get there because of an unobtrusive spell, and I had help from Alexandria and from my friend, Jastillian.

"We are the rulers of magic, Hellsfire. We do not want to go to Masep to find an ancient and powerful artifact to start another war. We only want to ensure that if there is one, we safeguard it so there won't be another Premier. We've tried to get this point across to King Furlong, but to no avail. If Alexandria had its own wizards, we wouldn't need to take such drastic or direct action. And as wizards, Masep and the Wastelands are part of our history. History we must learn from so that we may never make the same mistakes again."

I sighed. "You want *me* to see if Alexandria will grant you access to the Wastelands."

He nodded.

"You're overestimating my importance there. I have no power. I'm not even from there. I'm an outsider like you. I've been banished and threatened with death." I stared at Ardonis. "Does this mean you won't help the princess unless I can coerce them into complying with your request?"

He leaned back in his chair and said nothing. He didn't have to. His silence spoke volumes. I thought of my other options. There were other healers. Healers that were duty bound to help those in need. There were also witches and sorcerers who dabbled in magic different than mine. None of those had been able to help me. However, Ardonis hadn't been able to find a way all those months ago. Maybe he wasn't the answer either.

I didn't care if he was a member of the Elemental Council. I matched his look with my own. "You don't have a cure. You can't help. You couldn't help months ago. Nothing's changed." I got up from my chair. "Sorry to have wasted your time."

"Wait," Ardonis said. "I may not have found a cure, but I have been looking into it. Now that the council's whole again, I've had access to spells and rituals that may work. There's also a potion that could ease her symptoms and fight off the curse. I cannot promise you that I will be able to break it."

"That's all right. If we can restore her health and ease her symptoms, that will be good enough for me. And I promise you I will try to convince them to let you pass. That's all I can do. But you must promise me that you'll help her even if I fail."

"Agreed." He rose and shook my hand. "Now I assume you have everything ready?"

I nodded.

"I'll need some time to gather my things," he said. "But it shouldn't take long. Also, I'll ask the unicorns to see if they can take us."

"Unicorns?"

"They're the fastest mode of transportation we have. From what I understand, your winters are very rough. They also thrive in cold weather. The problem is their temperament, but I'm sure I can persuade one or two of them to do us this favor."

I bowed my head. "Thank you."

Ardonis rose. "Give me two hours and I'll meet you in front of the school."

I left Ardonis, glad that I had accomplished what I had set out to do. I grimaced when I remembered that I had to try to convince the king to allow the council to send an expedition into the Wastelands. I didn't completely trust the council, yet Ardonis was right. They were the ones that were best equipped to deal with magic. Alexandria would need wizards in the years to come.

If I couldn't convince King Furlong to postpone my death sentence indefinitely, maybe I could convince him to start a wizards' school even if I wasn't the one running it. Alexandria might have an easier time accepting wizards if they had trained them since youth.

I took the supplies from the horses I'd loaded up earlier and waited at the school's main entrance for Ardonis, right underneath the broken archway. My thoughts drifted to Krystal and the trouble she was in. I kept glancing back at the entrance, wondering what sort of supplies he'd bring. As the master of white mana, he must have created some powerful potions over the years.

Near the end of the two hours, Ardonis came out of the school with a bag slung over his shoulder. "Are you ready, Hellsfire?"

I nodded, more anxious than ready.

Just when I was about to ask him about the unicorns, they trotted into view. I marveled at their deeply colored bodies. One was a dark shade of blue and the other was a lustrous purple. Their manes and tails matched the color of their bodies, and on top of each of their heads was a sharp, glistening horn. Supply bags and harnesses were already loaded onto them. For a second, I thought they were well-trained, since they came toward us with no one to guide them, but I knew better.

Ardonis leaned toward me and whispered, "I take it you've never ridden a unicorn before."

"I haven't."

"They're not like horses or pack mules, so don't treat them as such. They're highly intelligent and can understand you."

I nodded, remembering when I had first met one and how it had led me and the others to one of Tyree's cities.

Ardonis lowered his voice even further. "They also despise having others ride them and being loaded down with supplies and saddles. However, there are exceptions, and they understand the urgency in this matter."

The blue one trotted up and stared at me. He read me with his deep blue eyes, but I couldn't understand what he was seeing or what he even wanted.

"Is he acceptable?" Ardonis asked with a hint of a smile on his face. But he wasn't talking to me.

The blue unicorn shook his head and neighed.

"Excellent," Ardonis said. "Hellsfire, this is Windrider."

"A pleasure to meet you," I said, awkwardly bowing to the unicorn.

"He's the fastest unicorn in all the land."

The purple unicorn nudged Ardonis with her snout, threatening to spear him with her sharp horn.

Ardonis laughed. "Windrider is *one* of the fastest unicorns. This is the other, Purpleheart."

The violet unicorn studied me in the same way Windrider had. She scrutinized me more than Windrider, and I wouldn't even be riding her. She whinnied and stomped her hooves.

"Enough with the pleasantries," Ardonis said. "Let's make haste. We have a long journey ahead of us."

I loaded my supplies unto Windrider, but when I tried to climb on him, he moved and I nearly fell. I tried once more, but again, he moved.

Ardonis chuckled. "Windrider, enough. We haven't got all day."

Windrider finally allowed me on, and I could have sworn that I saw the wisp of a smile on his horse-like face.

I forgot about Windrider's jokes, the school, and even the attack on me earlier. There was only one thought on my mind—Krystal.

CHAPTER 3

BECAUSE OF THE UNICORNS, we made tremendous time traveling to Northern Shala. However, once we crossed the Ennis Mountain Range, the weather turned against us. There was a snow flurry, and at first I was glad for it. The seasons in Tyree weren't as pronounced as they were in Northern Shala. I always found that unsettling, as it made it harder for me to track the passage of time. Dusk came sooner and the wind blew more often, but the leaves' colors weren't as vibrant in the autumn, nor did the winter cold bite with as much ferocity.

The air thickened the moment we crossed through the Ennis Mountains. The morning frost lasted longer into the day, and the leaves had withered away. When I was first training on Stradus's mountaintop, I used to have trouble with the cold, but once I utilized my powers on a continual basis and I accepted they were a part of me, my inner fire kept me warm, and the cold didn't bother me. Ardonis constantly tapped into fire mana, and he always rubbed his hands together and breathed into them when we weren't riding. If he felt the cold so much now, I wondered how he was going to handle it the further north we got.

The weather worked against us, the longer we traveled. The snow turned from a gentle fall into a blizzard. I pulled my robes against me and held onto my fire mana as we rode. The wind blew snow into my eyes, but the bleak, white landscape never changed. I expected the unicorns or Ardonis to quit. It wasn't their fault Krystal was in trouble. It was mine. Ardonis could have waited until the weather was warmer, and the unicorns had no duty in this.

But they didn't falter. Not once did Ardonis, Windrider, or Purpleheart say anything about turning around or quitting. I was thankful for their help and their company.

During our travels, I periodically checked in with Krystal through the use of maleikas. While I didn't want to interfere with her privacy, I had to know if she was all right. I had to use them sparingly, because I only had three maleika potions. I was worried I might see a picture of her still corpse, but the first time I used one, she was alive. She seemed so frail as she lay in bed eating soup. The second time I glimpsed her, I saw her sparring with her personal guard, Ardimus. For a brief second, I thought she was better, but when she lunged with her sword, she crumpled down in pain. Ardimus carried her away and I released the maleika. I couldn't watch anymore.

We were still over a month away from Alexandria. Even with the unicorns, the winter weather had nearly doubled our travel time. Another storm had come two days ago. While we waited at an inn for the weather to clear, I decided to cast my last maleika potion.

I was sitting cross-legged in my room at the inn, finishing the final touches on the ritual, when Ardonis barged in and shivered.

"I don't envy you your winters, Hellsfire. Even the fireplace downstairs and all the people crowded inside can't provide enough warmth."

I almost asked him why he wasn't down there now. It might have had to do with all the questions we got about the unicorns—people knew we weren't from around here. At least Ardonis's eyes had pupils again. He had masked his power to disguise the fact that he was a wizard, and to make the people feel easier around him. However, I found it very unsettling. I had grown used to his look, but I could also feel how much of his power he held back in appearing normal.

"That's why travel tends to stop during the winter," I said. "Only the foolish would go out in this weather."

"Or the brave."

I gave him a wry smile.

"Still setting your traps?" he asked, staring at the candles I had laced with magic.

"Always."

Ardonis shrugged. "The maleikas are such harmless little creatures. Just because you had one bad experience with an unusual one doesn't mean you should fret over it so much." His thumb stroked the side of his staff and he glanced at the candles with indifference. "It doesn't take much to kill a maleika."

"You don't know this maleika like I do."

Ardonis stood off in the corner, content to watch me perform the ritual. I summoned the maleika and as it shimmered into view, I relaxed when I saw it had two eyes. As before, it vanished to Alexandria, and I waited in the dim candlelight.

When the maleika returned, I expected to see Krystal's face, wishing that she was better. Instead, there was an image of darkness. I peered closer into it, feeling my heart thump loudly in my chest. There were only a few reasons that might happen. Either the caster couldn't concentrate enough for the maleika to get a clear image, or they couldn't remember the place or person. The other reason terrified me. It was because whatever they were seeking was no longer there.

"Krystal," I whispered.

I focused, letting the fond memories of her race through my mind. The times when we fought in battle together, and the times when she would lay her head upon my bare chest. Yet no matter what I pictured and focused my magic on, no image appeared.

Was the light of my life dead? Was I too late in reaching Alexandria? Maybe Krystal's people were right. Maybe wizards were nothing but trouble.

"*Hellsfire.*"

The voice of the maleika rang through my head, yet I couldn't see it anywhere. My vision began to get hazy. At first I thought it was fatigue, but then I realized that the maleika was attacking me. It had engulfed my head with its ghostly body.

I had no time to banish it. It cast a spell, sending agonizing pain ringing through my head. Ardonis stepped forward to move against it.

"No!" I said. Not even Ardonis could cast a subtle spell quickly enough to defeat the creature without harming me. Besides, this maleika was mine.

I gritted my teeth, letting anger flow through me to block out the pain. This maleika was nowhere near as strong as the one I had been preparing my traps for. I didn't attempt to fight it. Instead, I drew on the magic in the candles.

The magic laced in the candles shot out and ensnared the maleika, ripping it from around my head. My spell bound its hazy form in a cage of lightning, and it squirmed in torment as my power sizzled it. Its scream echoed in my ears.

I glared at it and said, *"You're not the one I want. Give a message to your master."*

I squeezed my hand and the magical cage burned brighter. The tiny blue lightning flared until the maleika vanished in a puff of smoke. The candle flames were gone, and I was in the darkness once more.

Ardonis relit the candles. "It seems you were wise to set a trap for it," he acknowledged, peering at the area where the maleika had been. "I've never seen one act like that before."

I lifted my tired head. "That wasn't even the one I warned you about."

"Do not give up hope, Hellsfire," Ardonis said, placing a gentle hand on my shoulder and giving me a kind smile. "The image the maleika showed you might be false."

I had always thought there was a connection between Krystal and me from the moment I met her. As powerful as I was, there were some magics in the world I didn't understand—like the one between us. I knew that I loved her with all my heart, and I thought that if she died, I would feel it.

"We shall know soon enough," I said.

Ardonis extended his hand and I took it. "Let's go back downstairs and get something warm to drink. I may not care for your winters, but I do enjoy your food and beverages."

The next day the storm finally abated and we rode onward to Alexandria. While I dreaded what I would find there, there was no turning back.

CHAPTER 4

MY CHEST TIGHTENED at my first glimpse of the city walls of Alexandria. We were still a half an hour away. As much as I wanted to convince Windrider to burst into a full gallop, I knew that I had to be smarter and more cautious if I wanted to get into the city.

I turned to Ardonis and looked into his dark blue eyes. "Do you remember the plan?"

"I do, but do you believe lying to the king is a good way to start?"

"Who says I'm lying? You *are* a healer, and I *am* in charge." I couldn't help but smile at the last part. The Elemental Council was used to being in charge, and Ardonis was no exception. After a moment, Ardonis reluctantly returned my smile.

We continued onward and a trio of riders out on patrol rode by us. Thankfully, I had my hood up to conceal my face. I looked away from them when their eyes passed over us. Luckily, a passing gust of wind gave a reason for my slight shiver."Unicorns," one of the guards said. "I take it you must be from Southern Shala."

I perked up at that. How many people had visited Alexandria from the south?

"Tyree," Ardonis said. "It is called Tyree."

"Whatever it may be called, what are the pair of you doing here? Now is not the time to be traveling."

"So we were told. Still, we were paid to come here. With the Great Barrier down, we've been told that the Daleth Mountains have minerals that are common to you, but precious to us."

"Your master must be very rich to give you such valuable mounts," the guard said.

Beneath me, Windrider stomped his hooves and shook his head, and Ardonis struggled with Purpleheart.

"Forgive them," Ardonis said. He leaned forward and whispered, "Unicorns are very temperamental animals. I'd watch my tongue, lest you get skewered by their sharp horns."

The guard did something unexpected—she laughed. "Very well, traveler. Stay warmly bundled, and welcome to Alexandria."

As I listened to the Guardsmen ride by, I let out my stilled breath. I was thankful Ardonis was able to put them at ease with our prepared story. I was never a very good liar, so we'd agreed to have him do the talking until we got inside.

Just when I thought that we'd gotten away with it, another gust of wind blew my hood back from my face. The guardswoman's intense gaze instantly settled on me. Luckily, none of the guards were ones I knew. I hoped that meant they wouldn't recognize me by sight.

"Do I know you?" she asked. "You look familiar."

I thought of lying but remembered how bad I was at it.

I held her gaze. "Maybe. I've been to Alexandria a few times. I was hired as a guide, even though I told him it would be foolish to travel right now. He didn't listen but his coin was hefty."

The soldiers all chuckled, but she didn't seem convinced.

"We have to be going now," she said. "Enjoy our fair city."

I finally relaxed when they rode away. I kept expecting her or one of her soldiers to glance back and remember me. I stared at them until they disappeared back into the white landscape.

"Hellsfire," Ardonis said, "I believe we can go now."

As we rode closer to Alexandria, I glimpsed the guards pacing on top of the city's outer walls. They were too far away for me to make out their expressions.

Even though I had never quite considered Alexandria my home, there was a sense of awe every time I visited it. The city was vast and the castle towers loomed larger the closer we rode. The castle was at the north end of the city, guarding it from the creatures of the Wastelands, and it was there that our journey would end.

We rode through the open southern gate, passing through the short stone tunnel that ran under the city wall. As soon as we were out of it, we dismounted. The way opened up, revealing a busy marketplace. Despite the lightly falling snow, people were going about their day as usual. A weaver showed bolts of cloth to a trio of women. A man carried two chickens trapped in wooden cages. From my favorite stall came the sweet smell of honey bread. The delicious aroma tickled my nose and my mouth watered at it. As much as I wanted to, I didn't stop, lest the couple there recognize me.

People might not have known it was me under the cloak I wore, but they all stopped and stared at our mounts. I had thought about leaving them at the stables near the gate's entrance, but the unicorns deserved to be in a better place. Besides that, word of us leaving such mounts would travel faster to the castle than if we rode there. I had to make it to the castle walls before anyone suspected who I was.

"I'm hungry," Ardonis asked. "Are you hungry?"

"No," I said, annoyed that he seemed to care more about food than the reason we were in Alexandria.

Ardonis split from me and headed to the stall with the honey bread. I stayed back and watched as he approached the couple I had seen too many times.

They were too far away for me to make out what they were saying, so I cast a simple spell so the wind would carry their words to me

"I'm not from around here, as you can see," Ardonis said. "I've heard that you make the sweetest bread, and I would love a piece after my long journey."

"Another traveler from Tyree?" the man said, staring at the unicorn. "It's like you people are invading us." The man crossed his arms. "I hope you or your friend aren't wizards."

"Behave, dear!" his wife said. Turning to Ardonis, she said, "You'll have to forgive him. The cold weather has seeped into his brain."

Ardonis and the man's wife chuckled.

"While we find the markings on your coin strange," she said, "all are welcome in Alexandria."

"Thank you," Ardonis said. "Two please." While the man prepared our snacks, Ardonis asked, "In my travels I heard the most distressing news. Some said your beloved princess had fallen ill." The wizard lowered his voice, and took on a somber tone. Whether it was because he believed his next words or he was acting, I didn't know. "I also heard a terrible rumor that she now walks with the gods. I pray to them that it's not true."

The couple paused. While I was too far away to make out their expressions, I did see the woman briefly look my way. I turned my head and hoped they didn't recognize me.

"Our princess lives," the woman said, but there was an underlying current of sadness in her voice. "But she isn't well." The woman cleared her throat and steadied her voice. "Let's not speak of such things. Enjoy our treats and please tell everyone in Tyree about us."

Ardonis took a bite. "Hmmm, I will. These are the best I've ever tasted."

He came back and handed me the bread. "You weren't lying. These really are delicious." As much as I loved them, I had lost my appetite.

"She's alive," I said.

"But we don't know how bad her condition is."

"Then let's find out."

I took a bite of the honey bread, the sweet, soft treat flooding my senses. For a moment, I felt like I was home. That moment was fleeting as I remembered why I was here, and who made me feel like I was home no matter where I was.

Even though the guardswoman had said that people had come to the city on unicorns before, the Alexandrians still stared and talked about them. I ignored their gawking, gauging how bad a shape Krystal might be in.

I had learned from my time in Alexandria that the people's mood was a reflection of what was going on with their rulers, especially when it came to Krystal. However, they were all bundled up in thick winter furs, which made it hard for me to get a read on them. I gripped Windrider's reins until my hands ached.

I stared out through the throngs of people, searching for Krystal. She wasn't a ruler who was afraid to be with her people. I glanced at the school where she would often go to greet the children, bringing them delicious treats. We rode by one of the smaller squares. On top of the fountain was a statue of children waving and smiling at a gigantic dragon. The dragon reminded me of Cynder, the dragon who had been Stradus's companion for centuries. That overgrown lizard had stayed in Alexandria for a brief time after we defeated Premier. The people of Alexandria were in awe of him, and he even once tried to convince them to erect a statue of him. I told him I thought it was an excellent idea, as the birds could use another place to roost and relieve themselves on his big head. He'd tried to incinerate me for that remark. The statue was another favorite place of Krystal's, but I didn't see her at the fountain, feeding the birds there.

I looked for her everywhere I turned, but I didn't see her anywhere. While we had gotten valuable information from the vendor, I wanted to question the people of Alexandria further. Ardonis cautioned me against this. A stranger constantly asking questions about their ruler was bound to bring up questions. Besides, we knew she was alive, and that was enough…for now.

There was one last building I checked before we reached the castle gates—the temple of the four gods. The squat, rectangular building was as old as the castle. Etched into its pillars were the symbols of magic, and as a wizard, I was humbled by their magical presence. I had only been inside a few times. I wondered if Krystal was in there praying right now. She might be, but if I went inside, I would surely be recognized.

After that, it wasn't long before we reached the castle gates. King Furlong would want to be notified of my presence, and it was only right that he should. In front of the gates was a guard I recognized.

"Jerrel," I said.

He took a few steps closer and narrowed his eyes at me. Recognition finally set in. "Hellsfire." He advanced and I dismounted from Windrider. Jerrel lowered his voice. "You shouldn't be here. If the king finds you here, you *will* be executed."

"I know, but it's very urgent that I see the king." I took a deep breath. "It's about the princess. Is she—?"

"I just remembered where I recognized you from," a familiar voice said from behind me. I turned to see the guardswoman from outside the city's walls. "You don't know me, but on the night when we retook the castle from Premier, I was one of the guards locked in the dungeons."

I tensed, wondering what she was going to do.

She smiled and bowed her head. "I wanted to thank you for what you did that night, Hellsfire. You saved our kingdom, the princess, and the king."

I exhaled and relaxed. "You're welcome. It was the right thing to do."

Her eyes hardened and in a booming voice she pronounced, "Wizard Hellsfire under standing orders of King Furlong, I hereby place you under arrest."

Jerrel shifted uncomfortably, and a few soldiers did the same. Not enough, though, as most had their weapons drawn. On top of the walls, I felt magic on three of the arrows that were trained on me. Alexandria had improved their weapons against wizards since the last time I'd been there.

"Natasha, what are you doing?" Jerrel asked.

"Obeying our orders, and what you should have done."

"Who says I wasn't going to? I always do my duty. This is my station, not yours."

Natasha opened her mouth to respond, but I interrupted her. "There's no need to argue or even ready your weapons. I will go with you. Peacefully."

Despite my reassurance, the soldiers didn't lower their guard.

"Windrider and Purpleheart," I said to the unicorns. "Please go with them."

"I promise you that they will be well taken care of, and no harm will come to them." Jerrel took Purpleheart by the reins. "We've had unicorns here before, and I've always admired their majestic beauty."

"Thank you," I said.

Ardonis and I were flanked by a dozen soldiers, and a few of them had enchanted weapons. Ardonis didn't say a word and neither did I. I kept my head and eyes forward, glancing at the people we passed by from the corners of my eyes. The whispers followed us as we walked up the hill from the castle's gate toward the inner keep, and word of my arrival outpaced us.

Dozens of eyes were on me as we made our way along, making my skin prickle. The soldiers practicing near the barracks stopped fighting, their weapons falling silent. Servants stopped shoveling snow and peered up at me.

We reached the entrance to the keep and I handed over my father's dagger and my purse of potions. I wiped my feet on the thick red carpet and stared up at the dragon tapestry hanging from the rafters. I shook my head, freeing myself of any loose snow, as I wanted to be presentable to the king.

One of the guards motioned for me to continue and I followed him down the hall until we ended up in the throne room. Sitting on the great throne was King Furlong.

The king lifted his head, his piercing blue eyes meeting mine. In an exasperated voice he said, "Hellsfire, I hope there's an important reason you're here, because you've forfeited your life."

CHAPTER 5

I KNEELED. "I understand, Your Majesty. I came here for one very important reason—the princess."

He clenched his hand. "What do you know of my daughter?" A low, rumbling anger was hidden beneath his words.

It was hard to meet his eyes and find my voice now that I was here, but I managed. "I came because I know how ill she is. I haven't been able to find a cure, Your Majesty, but I brought the best healer in Tyree with me to help her."

King Furlong said nothing for several moments as he stared at me. Finally, he spoke. "Guards, seize Hellsfire. He will be executed in the morning."

The guards swarmed in from all sides with weapons drawn.

Ardonis stepped back, making no move to help, and I didn't summon my magic. The king rose from his throne and walked away. As the guards closed in on me, I struggled to break their grasp and yelled at the departing king for him to hear me out. My cries fell upon deaf ears.

One of the guards whipped out a collar. I froze in horror, remembering that those things stopped the wearer from performing magic. The thumping in my heart grew louder and I had a hard time breathing, gasping for air.

I had first worn one shortly after I ventured into Tyree. One half of the Elemental Council had imprisoned me for refusing to guide them into Northern Shala for their invasion.

The collar cut me off from my magic, causing a backlash of uncontrollable pain if I tried to use it. My magic was more than just power. It was who I am, a part of me. Through it, I experienced how the world truly was—how everything was interconnected with an amazing force that guided us. Without my magic, I was nothing, and the world was dull and meaningless.

I had vowed never to be in that situation again.

I clenched my hands and yelled, "No!"

Wind magic exploded from me. It pushed at the guards around me, tumbling them to the floor.

I reeled in my power, staring in horror at the sprawling bodies. They groaned as they struggled to get to their feet. I closed my eyes for a moment and focused on my breathing, trapping my magic within. "I'm—I'm sorry. Please forgive me, Your Majesty."

The king turned and stormed over to me. "My daughter is *dying*, Hellsfire! *Dying!* That curse you brought from the Wastelands is eating her away, and since you've been gone, she's gotten worse. No matter what we've tried, nothing has helped. *That's* how she is. I won't give you the satisfaction of seeing my only child one last time. Guards, seize him! And if he resists, kill him."

This time I did nothing to stop the guards from grabbing my arms. I watched as King Furlong walked away, and with him, his chance at helping Krystal.

"Your Majesty," I pleaded in a tired voice, to his back. "I beg you to listen to me. My life means nothing next to your daughter's. I know that. By the gods, all I ask you is to let us try. Do to me what you will, but at least let me *try*."

Before the guards could clasp the collar on me, King Furlong lifted his hand and the guards froze. I held my breath, feeling a drop of sweat run down my brow despite the freezing weather outside.

"You've done enough, Hellsfire," the king said.

The king was wrong. I had not done enough. I couldn't go back in time and change things, but I needed to at least try to help Krystal if it was the last thing I did. I held my anger down lest the fire get out of control at the king's reluctance to help her.

"However," King Furlong continued, softening his voice, "I will allow you to see her." His voice hardened. "But know this. Even if you do help her, it may not change your fate."

I bowed my head and said, "Thank you, Your Majesty."

"You will find her in her room."

The guards dispersed and I left before the king changed his mind.

Ardonis followed on my heels as I hurried toward Krystal's room.

"That was...tense," Ardonis said. "Are you sure you'll be able to convince the king to allow us to send an expedition into the Wastelands?"

"No," I said, angry that this was what he cared about, despite being the master of white mana. He should care about saving lives "But I never said I could. I said I would try, and I promise you that I will."

"And no matter what happens, I will do my best to save the princess." Ardonis glanced back down the hallway. "No father should ever lose a daughter."

We made it to the tower where Krystal's chambers were. I stood outside the closed door, staring at the handle. I had been in her room once before, and that was to save Alexandria. As much time as we spent together, she usually came to my room late at night, traversing the secret passageways in the castle. There were also secret spots where other people seldom went that she showed me throughout the city, like a rock formation on a hill, outside and underneath the roof of one of the nobles' buildings. I grinned at the memories, feeling my love for her overtake me.

But like a tide that pulled away, my love for her was washed away by fear. Fear of what I would find on the other side of that wooden door.

"Hellsfire," Ardonis said, laying a hand on my shoulder.

"Sorry," I said. I took a deep breath and opened the door.

Despite the sun outside, the curtains had been drawn, draping the room in darkness. The lack of light and air made the otherwise large room feel stifling. The only light in the room emanated from the few candles and the open door behind me.

"Shut the door," a woman whispered and stormed up to me, finger wagging in the dim light. "What have I told you about—" She paused. "Hellsfire, what are you doing here? You shouldn't be here."

"Forgive me, Mistress Shanna. I came to see if there was anything I could do to help with the princess's condition. I brought a renowned healer from Tyree to help her."

Shanna glared at Ardonis and me. "Your magic is the reason she's like this in the first place."

"I know, but I have to try to help her."

Shanna's expression didn't agree, but she stepped aside. "Since the king allowed you in here, very well."

A previously motionless figure stood up from the chair he was slouched in. Even without his enchanted chainmail and scimitar, I knew who it would be.

"Ardimus," I said.

"Hellsfire," he said and smiled, the weariness in his eyes briefly vanishing. He extended his arm and we grasped each other's forearm. "It is good to see you, my friend. I wish it was under better circumstances."

Ardimus looked back at the still figure lying on the bed.

"Me too. How is she?"

"Dying," Shanna said, appearing beside me. "The curse you've caused has gotten worse. She's had bouts before, but this past one seems to be the worst yet. We've tried everything. I don't know if she'll ever wake."

I stepped forward and finally saw the love of my life. Huge blankets smothered her now deathly thin frame. The curves I had known so well were gone, and her bones stuck out like ridges. Her skin was no longer flushed—it was paler than the snow falling outside. Black veins could be seen through her parchment-like skin. She didn't breathe so much as huff for air.

I reached into my bag and put on a glove. I bent down and reached for her hand. Even through the glove, I could tell how clammy and cold it was.

"Krystal," I whispered. "I'm so sorry."

I held her hand for a few minutes, forgetting that everyone was there. I remembered the warmth that normally suffused it and how full of life she was.

"Hellsfire," Ardonis said. The master of white mana pulled me back to the present. "We have work to do."

I used my wizard's sight to peer past Krystal's physical illness and into her aura. With most other people whose auras I'd glimpsed, they were a mixture of colors composed of the six manas that comprised life and death. The dominant color tended to be the mana that matched whatever skill they were best at. Krystal was different. The few times I'd peered into her aura, it was blindingly bright with no traces of colored mana in it.

That bright aura had vanished, replaced by a consuming darkness. Like a thick fog, it smothered all that beautiful light within her. There were only traces of it left, and they shrank with each passing moment.

"The curse is entwined in her aura—deeply," Ardonis said. "That we already knew. But it's grown and spread since the last time I saw her, and I don't know why. What could have caused it to grow so?"

"You're another wizard," Shanna said, making it sound like a curse word. "I thought you were a healer."

"Mistress, not all people who can wield a little magic are wizards. You have the gift of healing. Magic could enhance it. You might be able to use it to see what's truly wrong with the ill. Depending on how gifted you are, you might be able to do more." He finally looked at her. "You should come down to Tyree. There's a lot you could learn there. From what Hellsfire has told me, you're gifted with potions."

"First, I want to see what you can do for Her Highness, and if magic can be used to heal rather than destroy." Shanna's gaze focused on me.

Ardonis took out five potion vials. "Hellsfire, I brought these potions with me in hopes that one of them would help the princess. Her condition is far worse than when I last saw her. I'd hoped that the maleika's images were false, but it looks like they weren't."

"So you can do nothing."

"Although we have been busy, the Council has looked into Renak's curse."

I stared at him, wondering if the reason for that was because they wanted access to Masep.

"Unfortunately, we've not found anything that could break it. However, with the help of Bellona and Nairi, the three of us were able to concoct a potion." He reached into his bag and pulled out one more vial. White and green liquid swirled inside it.

Potions weren't normally laced with magic. I created mine mostly with plants, since that's how Stradus taught me. Potions could be concocted in other, stranger ways, though—a salamander's tail, an eagle's claw, green mold that grew on a rock right above the snow line. If magic was infused into a potion, it was normally weak. Any stronger and the magic might overtake the potion. Ardonis's vial teemed with his white magic, along with Bellona's black mana and Nairi's earth magic.

"This potion is based on an antidote potion used to expunge poison from the body," Ardonis said. "Curses are different from poisons, and are more entwined with the soul than the body. This potion should expel as much of the curse as it can. That's what the magic will do."

"What's the risk?"

"Because this curse is so intertwined with her soul, in a way, it's like the potion is also expunging her soul. Without a soul, a body will die."

"Is this the only way?"

"Right now it is," Ardonis said. "It's the best we've been able to come up with."

I reached out and stroked Krystal's brittle hair. Pieces of it clung to my hand. "I don't know what to do. I don't want to lose her."

"Tell the king and have him decide," Shanna said. "After all, she is his daughter."

"The princess *trusts* you, Hellsfire," Ardimus said. "She has placed her life and her kingdom in your hands before. She would do so again."

"I still think we should tell King Furlong." Shanna turned and moved, but Ardimus stepped to the side to block her way.

"The king already knows that Hellsfire is here and intends to treat the princess. Otherwise he would not be here."

Shanna's eyes shot daggers at Ardimus. "Very well. If she dies or is harmed further, this will be on your and Hellsfire's head."

"It's already on my head…" I said. "…and my heart."

"Hellsfire, I believe you should do this." Ardonis handed me the vial.

I leaned in close to Krystal's ear and whispered, "I need you to fight, beautiful. I'm here with you, and I will give you all the strength you need. Come back to me. I love you."

I tilted her head and poured the potion down her throat. I wiped up the excess liquid and massaged her throat to help her swallow.

"Fight, princess, like I know you can." I grabbed her hand and watched her, squeezing it for support.

After a minute, Shanna spoke. "Did your potion work? Nothing's happening."

"Patience," Ardonis said. "It needs time."

Krystal's grip tightened and her frail hand crushed mine. I pushed aside the pain as her eyes shot open. She yelled in agony, and through my wizard's sight I saw the dark curse rush from her body. The sweat from her hand drenched my glove and the blankets that covered her. Then the strength left her hand and it went limp. She shut her eyes and stopped screaming.

"Krystal?" I softly asked, as if my voice would damage her further.

I reached out with my magic and peered into her aura. I still found traces of Renak's curse in her, but the beautiful bright light that composed her aura was gone. There wasn't a trace left.

"What did you do to her?" Shanna asked, knocking me out of the way. She opened Krystal's eyelids, then leaned into her mouth to hear her breathing. There was none. "The princess is dead."

I was looking at Ardonis to ask him what went wrong when Shanna slapped me so hard I fell backward. I couldn't feel that pain as I stared at Krystal's lifeless body.

"You wizards and your accursed magic!" Shanna yelled. "Always believing you know what's right when you understand nothing!"

Shanna's words were true. I had arrogantly thought I could save Krystal, when it was my fault she was in this condition in the first place. I crawled to her bed and leaned my body over her. "I'm sorry." Even though the warmth of her body was gone, I snuggled up against it and sobbed, the water from my eyes mixing in the blankets.

The fire within me boiled over with anguish. I let it loose as I cried out in pain. The candles in the room blossomed with fire before extinguishing and plummeting the room into darkness. I sensed that my magic wasn't just confined to the room or even the castle, but that it affected all of Alexandria.

"I'll go tell the king," Mistress Shanna said in the darkness.

Before she could leave, light flared from the necklace I had given Krystal. The green light blinded us all. I relit the candles in the room and saw her chest rising again. I laid my head on her chest and heard her heartbeat. The hexagram's green light thrummed in time with it.

"Impossible," Shanna whispered.

I glimpsed into Krystal's aura and saw the hexagram's magic spread into her entire body, fighting back the curse. But it wasn't enough. She was so weak.

Ardonis came over and placed his hands on her body. He summoned white mana until his hands were covered in magic. The power he wielded flooded into her and it strengthened her body. Both Ardonis and the hexagram's magic worked together, revitalizing her.

When he finished, Ardonis said, "Hellsfire, give her another rejuvenation potion, and she'll need a lot of water."

"You're more than just a simple healer, aren't you?" Shanna asked.

"Yes, I am."

I gave Krystal another potion and as much water as she could drink in her unconscious state before she began coughing it up.

"Now all we can do is wait," Ardonis said. "She must wake on her own. We can do nothing more for her."

And wait I did.

King Furlong came by not long after that, and was relieved to see his daughter had gotten better even though she hadn't yet woken. He said nothing of what awaited me, or that I should leave the room. The most he acknowledged me was with a glance, and I took that as a positive sign.

I sat in a chair right next to Krystal's bed and waited for her to wake up. I fed her broth, gave her water and potions that helped strengthen her, and watched her. The most important thing I believe I did, when we were alone, was just talking to her. My words were letters that I delivered in person. I told her of my journey up here and the maleika I ran into. How I had gotten to know Ardonis better in our travels together. I even told her about how I thought Alexandria could open up a wizards' school here, and that I would love to run it.

Even though I spoke to her, I didn't open up about how worried I was about her, and how I feared for her life.

While Krystal was physically getting better, there was no telling how badly damaged her soul was. That's just something that's hard to measure even if you're a wizard. I may have wielded the powers of the gods, but I wasn't a god.

I slept in that chair and while it hurt my back, it warmed my heart to know that she was near me. Four days passed, with me staying at her side and hardly sleeping, just nodding off from time to time.

During one of those times, I was disturbed from my slumber. I snorted awake, feeling a tingling sensation creeping into my left hand. It was dull because my hands were still gloved, but the touch was very familiar. When I opened my eyes, I saw what the cause of it was.

"Hey," Krystal said and gave me a weak smile. She was lying on her side, and had reached out with one of her hands to hold and caress mine. She squeezed my hand and I returned the gesture.

"Hey," I said. Out of the corner of my eye, I caught Ardimus exiting the room, leaving the two of us alone.

"You shouldn't have come here."

I instinctively loosened my grip on her hand, but she held firm and smiled.

"But I'm glad you did."

I squeezed back once more. "Me too."

Krystal let go of my hand and struggled to sit up in her bed. I moved to help her but she waved me off. I knew to let her do this by herself. She gasped for breath and waited to speak until she had composed herself. "That was much harder than I thought."

"You should get some rest, Krystal. You've been through a lot."

"I will, but I have duties to attend to. I've been asleep long enough." She stared me straight in the eye, and despite how disheveled her hair looked and how frail her body was, her violet eyes had that same steely resolve in them. "Now tell me why Ardonis is here with you, and what you promised him."

"Only if you promise to rest afterward."

She grimaced, unaccustomed to being spoken to this way. I would never do it in public, but she was sick and we were alone.

Krystal nodded.

I told her why I'd decided to ride up to Alexandria, and just as I thought, she was none too pleased about me sending a maleika to spy on her. I also gave her the answers she required when it came to Ardonis. I left out my feelings and fears over whether she truly loved me or cared for me as I did her. And it took tremendous strength on my part to not question why she hadn't answered my letters. The king might have me executed, and if I was going to die I would prefer not to know the answers to those questions. Besides, my fate didn't matter. All that mattered to me was her recovery and well-being.

"What do you think?" I asked her when I had finished talking.

Krystal took a few moments to answer. She grabbed a fistful of blankets to steady herself. I gave her a glass of water and she drank all of it. Our conversation was a strain on her, but I knew she wouldn't rest until it was over.

"Thank you," she said. "What you proposed is a good idea. We *should* be working with the council more. They know more about magic than we do, and we all could learn more about the Wastelands and prevent attacks from there. Unfortunately, it's not that simple.

"The council has sent many envoys, but those from Tyree don't understand that ever since the end of the War of the Wizards, we've been tasked with guarding magical artifacts so that they won't be misused again. That, along with the war, has made us mistrustful of wizards." Her breath became ragged as she struggled for words. "Premier taking over the city and your—Renak's—curse have made things worse. I think things could change, but it will take time."

"The council may live long lives, but they're not very patient," I said. "I think they're too far removed from their early years to remember what it was like to live normal lives." I scrunched my face in thought. "Changing the core ideas of your people could take generations, if it could be done at all."

"Perhaps we'll never change, Hellsfire. Gods help us, but we might just be too set in our ways. But tomorrow belongs to the children. Maybe if we establish a school and teach them, they'll be the ones who lead the way."

I stared at my beloved and she had a wry smile on her face. "You heard me."

"Parts of it. You really want to teach?"

I nodded. "I love magic, Krystal. There's nothing like it in the world. It's amazing and wonderful. Yet I also know how dangerous it can be when you don't understand it or have control over it. There are people out there that need to know how to use their gifts. In helping them, I would learn more about myself and my abilities.

"There needs to be a school in Northern Shala. If not, they'll just go to Tyree and the council will use them for their own selfish purposes."

The princess was quiet as she considered it. "We'd have to start small, Hellsfire, and it may not work. People may be against it. We'll also have to find someone young with a magical talent, but we needn't worry about that now. The more pressing concern is Ardonis. You've put my father in a very precarious situation. After what he's done for me, it will be difficult for the king to refuse him."

I met her eyes. "I knew the risk. But any political fallout was worth it to me if it meant saving your life. Besides, I don't disagree with him, Krystal. With the barrier down, Alexandria *needs* a wizard. Gods know what Premier's up to, and there will be other wizards and magical matters you should be prepared for. With Premier gone and excluding Kemek's goblins, the Wastelands may be more volatile than before. I agree that you shouldn't trust anyone who is close to the Elemental Council, but you should have someone. Maybe Malik, or a wizard who wasn't caught up in the war."

Her purple eyes hardened as she scrutinized me. "I will consider your words. But the council is a long way from home. You tell my father who Ardonis is as soon as possible. He must know, and if you wait it will anger him further."

"I understand."

"Good."

Krystal opened her mouth to say something else, but instead her eyes rolled back and she almost fell from her bed.

I caught her. "Krystal!"

Her eyes fluttered open and she said, "Thank you. I'm all right. I'm just more exhausted than I thought I'd be."

I said nothing, but tapped into my magic, reading her aura. That dark curse had come back, still entwined in Krystal's light. It had receded far from what it was before, but it still affected her.

"All right," I said. "Get some rest. You're still not fully recovered."

She scowled, but let me lay her back in her bed before I tucked her in. I bent down and kissed her on the top of the head where her hair was thickest, and her scowl disappeared.

"Hellsfire, go back to your room. No one's been allowed in it these past few months except for me." Krystal stared down at where her feet were as if she couldn't meet my eyes. It was very unlike her. "I'm glad you're back, hero. I've missed you."

I almost questioned why she didn't write or visit, but didn't. "Get some rest, princess."

I walked away and before I could slip through the door she said, "Hellsfire."

"Yes?"

Her violet eyes looked up and stared at me. "I love you."

A burning sensation warmed my heart and it had little to do with my fire inside. I turned back to look at her and saw how fragile Krystal was. It wasn't because she had almost died, but instead had to do with how naked she was. Not physically, but emotionally. There wasn't a trace of that royal mask, as I liked to call it, that she often put on. Her face was full of fear, but also hope. That's exactly how I felt all those months ago when I first told her those three powerful words, and how I must have looked.

Yet as great as I felt that I now knew that Krystal loved me, her curse still loomed over my head. My death sentence didn't matter, nor did Alexandria's future with Tyree. There would be no future without Krystal. I had to make sure that she would still be around.

"I love you too," I said, and smiled at her. "Now get some rest. We have a long day ahead of us tomorrow."

CHAPTER 6

IT WAS TOO LATE to talk to King Furlong after I had seen Krystal. I sent word to him before going to bed. The next day, I was summoned to an early audience with the king, along with Ardonis. Despite Ardonis's reservations, I told him that I planned to tell King Furlong exactly who Ardonis was.

We entered the audience chamber and made our way to the throne. I bowed and when I rose, I looked for Krystal. I didn't see her anywhere. Even though I knew she'd want to be present for this, she might have still been resting.

"Your Majesty," I said, "thank you for agreeing to see me. I know how valuable your time is."

He leaned forward in his throne and asked, "What is it you want, Hellsfire?"

I took a deep breath. The direct approach it was, then. "First of all, I must apologize. I haven't been completely forthcoming with you. The man traveling with me isn't a simple healer. He's on the Elemental Council. May I present to you, Wizard Ardonis."

"Sire," Ardonis said and bowed.

"I welcome you to Alexandria," King Furlong said. According to his expression he wasn't surprised—or he hid it well. "May I ask why the need for secrecy?"

"I had heard about the death sentence looming over Hellsfire's head," Ardonis answered. "I thought it best to distance myself from the possibility of joining him."

King Furlong waved his hand. "Nonsense. His fate has nothing to do with yours. I would like to extend my thanks to you for helping heal my daughter. From what I understand, you're the master of…white mana that's supposed to heal and give life. I had heard that your eyes lose their pupils and become the color of the mana you've mastered, but I see no evidence of that."

"They do. I've just been suppressing my power." Ardonis gave a little smile. "But I suppose the time for secrecy is over."

Ardonis released his power and his eyes flooded white again. I stared at him in awe as the magic he radiated brushed up against me. His power always made me feel more alive. The others felt it too, even though they didn't understand it.

"Amazing," the king said.

I looked enviously at Ardonis. His skill with white mana made everyone feel at ease, whether he did it consciously or not. My mana did not work that way, as my emotions were tied to my power, which my former master would often lament to me about.

"There is one more thing, Your Majesty," I said. "While we're all extremely thankful that Ardonis came all this way through the winter weather to save the princess's life, he did not do so without reason."

"And that reason is?"

"He wants to send an expedition into the Wastelands, and specifically Masep."

"Ah, this again." The king's gaze settled on Ardonis, and I felt Ardonis's calmness waver and his hand tighten on his staff.

"I've received your envoys, Wizard Ardonis," King Furlong said, "and I thank you for the gifts you've sent us."

"And I, in return, thank you for the hospitality you've shown my people. They've enjoyed their time in Alexandria."

"I'm glad to hear it."

King Furlong said nothing as he sized up Ardonis and weighed his decision. None of us in the room said anything. I wondered what the king would say, and what Ardonis would do if the king denied him yet again.

From the eastern doorway, I caught a glimpse of movement and heard the clacking of wood against the stone floor. Krystal used a cane as she limped her way toward her father.

"Forgive my tardiness," she said. "I tried to get here as fast as I could."

"What are you doing out of bed?" the king asked. "You should be resting."

"I've been in bed long enough to last me a lifetime, Father. I need fresh air and to walk around."

"And what does Mistress Shanna believe?" the king said, with a sly smile on his face.

She returned the smile. "I think she would tell you the same."

"All right, but I don't want you out for too long."

"As you wish, Father."

Krystal eventually made her way to sit down next to King Furlong. She did her best to hide her increased breathing, and I watched as droplets of sweat dripped down her face. She had exhausted herself. I had seen her that way before, but only after we enjoyed ourselves. To see her need the help of a cane to walk, looking pale and like she was about to slide out of her seat, pained me.

The king must have felt the same. Yet he allowed her these few minutes because he knew how much her freedom meant to her.

"I have reached a decision," King Furlong said, returning to the matter at hand.

We waited to see what it would be.

"For far too long, the Wastelands have been spreading. The desolate land was nowhere near this close when Alexandria was first founded. As the years passed, the creatures grew bolder as their corrupted land spread. We were no longer able to ride deep into the north as we once had and couldn't return to Masep. But things have changed.

"At great cost, Hellsfire has reversed what was done to the Wastelands, and in turn brought down the Great Barrier. That has created new and old opportunities for us. Even with the Wastelands weakened, their creatures are still a force to be reckoned with. They won't let us return to Masep unmolested."

The king spoke to us all, but looked directly at Ardonis. "We must fulfill the duty Alexander bestowed upon us long ago. As Premier reminded us, Masep is still a danger. But we need help. We should work together with Tyree to venture back to Masep."

Ardonis bowed. "Thank you, Your Majesty."

"But know this," the king said, his face growing even sterner. "We will lead this expedition. You know nothing of the Wastelands, or even of the winters here. As for the spoils—" the king's face lighted, "—that we will discuss. And we will have much to discuss, and plenty of time to do it. The winters in Northern Shala can be long, and we won't leave until winter is over."

"I look forward to our discussions, sire," Ardonis said. "However, I do have one last request."

Krystal glanced at me. I shrugged. I had no idea what Ardonis was after. He had gotten what he wanted...or had he?

"What is it you want?" King Furlong asked.

"I understand that Alexandria has a repository of magical artifacts collected through the years."

King Furlong leaned forward. "We do. What concern of it is yours?"

"Ardonis, what are you doing?" I asked.

He ignored me and stepped forward. "We are the Elemental Council. We rule over matters of magic. Now with the Great Barrier down and the council whole again, it's time for us to resume our duties."

"And what would those duties entail?"

"We need to be able to catalogue and understand what you have," Ardonis said. "What's in your possession could be something as simple as an heirloom, or a dangerous and powerful weapon."

King Furlong said, "And you think I would give that weapon to a war council? You overstep your bounds, wizard. You are far from your home."

"We are *not* a war council. We were founded to guide and train people in the use of magic to make sure that no harm would come to them or others."

"And yet you started a new war, long after the war between Shala and Renak was over."

"Before you say no, I must warn you, sire. While I was able to save your daughter's life, she will require further treatments. Without those treatments, her life will be in danger again."

I glowered at Ardonis and hissed through my teeth. "What are you doing? That's not what was promised!"

When Ardonis glanced at me from the corner of his eye and I caught his expression, I realized I had made a mistake. He had made no promises about what was to happen afterward. I had thought I needed his magic, but I was a fool to trust him with my beloved's life.

The king and Ardonis continued to argue. The king believed that it was none of the council's business what Alexandria decided to do in its own kingdom. Ardonis countered that those items could pose a threat to the city. Ardonis said that with the barrier down, there would be others seeking items that were once considered lost. King Furlong said that they would continue to do their duty as they'd done for a thousand years.

This was getting us nowhere, yet I had no idea how to stop it. As the words grew harsher and bolder, Ardonis's magic spiked. More guards appeared in the throne room with weapons at the ready. I had to do something to stop this. Yet I had no idea what. I might create the very thing I was hoping to stop.

"Gentlemen!" Krystal said, her words sharp like a whip cracking. "I believe I have a proposal."

"What do you propose, daughter?" the king said, softening his words for her, but still keeping his fierce gaze on Ardonis.

Krystal might have kept her composure but it had begun to crack. Being out of her bed, forced to endure this, was taking its toll on her. Her left hand gripped her chair's armrest tighter to keep from falling, and she only breathed through her mouth. Couldn't anyone else see how much trouble she was in, or did they just not care?

"Wizard Ardonis," she said, "your council's reach doesn't extend this far. From what I understand, it never did, even before the barrier was erected. That was one of the problems you had. Do not presume otherwise."

Ardonis opened his mouth to speak, but she stopped him.

"However, you bring up a valid point. We don't have a wizard of our own. Our defenses were put in place nearly a thousand years ago. We don't know whether those spells can, or have, degraded with time. Would an inspection of our vault be sufficient for the council?"

The king looked at his daughter but didn't contradict her. His gaze focused back on Ardonis.

I stared at the Master of White Mana, wondering what he would say. I was already angry at him for not telling me he wanted access to the vault earlier, and even more infuriated that he used Krystal's life as a bargaining chip for it. Because of that reason alone, I wouldn't back him and would fight against him if it came to that.

Ardonis bowed. "That would be acceptable, Your Highness and Your Majesty. Forgive me for my outburst earlier. It's just that...I've seen too many deaths during the war because of people not knowing what they held, or allowing others to use dangerous items without proper safeguards."

"If I allow this, you will cure my daughter?" King Furlong asked, leaning forward.

"I cannot promise a cure, sire. I will promise you to treat her symptoms and make sure she doesn't fall into a coma again, and that I will try to find a cure."

"How can you do that? I don't expect you to have a permanent residence here."

"You're correct," Ardonis said. "If you'll allow it, I will station a wizard here. A former apprentice. He or she will have the expertise to concoct the potion that this requires. I will also send potions of my own brewing to be delivered periodically."

The king nodded. Then he added, "There is one last thing. To protect the secrecy of our vault's location, you will have to be stripped of your powers and drugged before being taken there. Do you find this acceptable?"

Ardonis paused. Finally he said, "I do. Thank you, sire."

The guards in the room relaxed and Ardonis's power dissipated. The king helped his daughter up and led her back to her room. For a second, my eyes met Krystal's questioning ones. I hoped to talk to her later to explain that I'd known nothing about this.

Ardonis and I left the chambers. Once we were out of earshot, I couldn't conceal my anger any longer. I stopped in the middle of the hallway and cornered him against the wall.

"What in the Inferno was that about? You *never* mentioned that you or the council were interested in the vault!"

I expected Ardonis to strike me with his magic, or at least step forward. He didn't move. In a calm, collected voice he said, "Neither you nor Alexandria understand the danger of keeping all that magic locked up in one place. It's like a teakettle about to boil over." I stared into his pupil-less eyes, but I'd forgotten how unsettling they could be. He went on. "They could have powerful and dangerous weapons, or worthless trinkets. If they had a wizard of their own, like you, to guide and help them, we wouldn't have concerned ourselves with this matter."

I exhaled, as I couldn't find words. Gods help me, I agreed with him. No matter their feelings toward me, Alexandria needed a wizard in the upcoming times. Times were changing.

I thought about that future, but then remembered how he'd used Krystal's life as a bargaining chip.

"No!" I said. "You don't get to play games with people's lives. With our power, we're supposed to help people."

"You're a powerful wizard, Hellsfire, but you don't understand that there are forces in play that could have great repercussions."

I eyed him, trying to grasp what he was saying. I had gotten to know Ardonis well in our journey here, but there were still things about him I didn't understand. What repercussions did he mean? His words reminded me of when I heard Renak's essence speak to me in Masep. That dead wizard warned me of a war between the gods. He said if I brought down the Great Barrier, then I would have allowed that war to continue, bringing great devastation and death to our mortal realm.

I'd told the council and other wizards about it, but they didn't believe me. While I was in Tyree, I had searched for signs of this war, but had found nothing. That still didn't stop me from looking. Whatever Ardonis or the council was looking for, I doubted much would stop them either.

"You're right," I said. "I may not understand." My fire bubbled up inside of me. "But what you don't understand is that you don't threaten or bargain with the princess's life ever again, under any circumstances. Or you'll be reminded of how I ended your war."

CHAPTER 7

I **WASN'T ABLE** to see Krystal again before the next day, but I was given a message to be ready the following morning to visit the vault, and where to go to meet the escort. Though nothing was said in the king's chambers yesterday, it turned out that I was going to be accompanying Ardonis to Alexandria's vault.

We had been told to meet at one of the castle's towers, the place where Premier once made his lair. The throng of people going about their duties thinned out as I approached. This time, it had nothing to do with me. Even though Premier had been gone from Alexandria for a long time, and I had cleansed the tower of his lingering magic myself, the people still avoided it when possible.

My stomach growled to me as I walked. I wished I'd had time to eat, even if it was just a light snack. I had learned a long time ago that it was best to eat before a battle. While visiting Alexandria's vault might not involve swords or arrows, I had a feeling it would be a battle all the same.

Ardonis and I reached the tower at the same time. I was still angry at him for what he'd done the previous day, but greeted him anyway. We went inside and followed the voices upstairs. Krystal was already waiting for us along with her personal guard, Ardimus; her close friend and a member of the guardsmen, Rebekah; and about a dozen other guards. The princess looked a little better than the previous day, but still used a cane. One guard cradled both collars that would contain Ardonis's and my magic. Next to the soldiers were two wheelbarrows.

The soldier holding the collars had a wisp of a smile on his face, and his fingers danced in anticipation. I had no doubt that he couldn't wait to use the collars on us. I wondered how many wizards they had tested these collars on, or would we be the first? I shivered like a cold breeze had come into the room. While I had always wanted to see the vault and had gotten banished because of it, I hated the collars. But if I needed one to get where I was going, I would wear it. I thought Krystal might need another wizard in there besides Ardonis.

"Wizard Ardonis and Hellsfire," Krystal said. "Glad to see you have made it. We have made the necessary preparations. Whenever you two are ready."

"We're ready, Your Highness," Ardonis said.

The eager guard with the collars headed in my direction, but Krystal stopped him and took one collar from him.

"I will do this," she said. Krystal limped over to me. "I know this will be hard for you, but I must do it."

"I understand. Thank you for allowing me to visit your vault, Your Highness." I whispered to her, "How are you feeling?"

Krystal unclasped the collar, stepped in closer, and reached up around my neck. "Better." She bestowed a small smile upon me, and I returned it. "But we have a long way ahead of us."

Her smile faded when she snapped shut the collar around my neck.

All the vibrancy of the world faded. As I stared into Krystal's violet eyes, even they seemed to lose a hint of their color. I ached to reach out with my magic to feel life's sensation around me. I knew that if I did that, the collar would shoot agonizing pain throughout my body. Yet it was hard to control the magic. It was like an itch that had to be scratched.

"Hellsfire, are you all right?" Krystal asked, concern in her eyes.

"I'm fine, Your Highness."

She could see right through my lie. "I know this is hard for you, but you'll get through it."

Krystal turned away from me to Ardonis. She paused and so did I. I was just as shocked as she was as I stared at him. Without his powers, Ardonis appeared frail to me, as if he would fall over with one push. He always looked older, with his gray hair and beard, but he seemed ancient now. He stooped as he stood, and his skin appeared saggier and dried out. It was like time had finally caught up to Ardonis.

Those on the council were far more in tune with magic than most wizards were. It helped them in ways I couldn't even begin to understand. Without it, they were mortal.

The shock on Krystal's face vanished quickly, unlike mine. She handed me and Ardonis two small vials. "I need you two to drink this. It'll keep you unconscious long enough to get where we're going."

Ardonis lifted his vial at Krystal and said, "To the beginning of new friendships." He downed the vial.

I drank the contents of the vial, tasting a hint of poppy in it. It wasn't long before Ardonis passed out, and I along with him.

As the world came into focus, I was surprised that my body wasn't as groggy as I thought it'd be.

Krystal leaned over the wheelbarrow I was in and smiled. "How are you feeling?"

"Good. Thank you, Your Highness."

I climbed up out of the wheelbarrow and saw how low the ceiling was. I realized we were in one of the castle's hidden passageways. The only light that shone was the torch in Ardimus's hand. As the shadows closed in on us and the stale, heavy air filled my lungs, I was reminded that I hated small and cramped places. I focused on the task at hand instead of what would happen if the ceiling caved in on us.

Only half a dozen guards remained, and two of them were Ardimus and Rebekah. Ardonis was still unconscious in his wheelbarrow. I put my hand around my neck. My collar was gone.

"Are we there yet?" I asked.

"Not yet," Krystal said. "We've still got quite a ways to go."

I looked around in confusion. "I don't understand, Your Highness."

She gave me a playful grin. "You've only been unconscious for about twenty minutes. Your dose was nowhere near as strong as Ardonis's."

Krystal limped down the darkened corridor while I followed on her heels. The others trailed us, two of them pushing the wheelbarrows. As we walked, I couldn't make out where we were. There was no light shining through the kill holes I had seen in sections of the hallway before, nor did the air feel lighter. It felt heavier and grew staler and more suffocating with each passing moment. At the end of the corridor, it branched off. She picked the middle opening and it gradually sloped downward.

"Because of the wheelbarrows, we're going to have to take the long way down," Krystal said. "I apologize for that."

I looked at her, then back at the others. I didn't want to question her in front of them but something was gnawing at me. I cleared my throat but lowered my voice. "Forgive me, Your Highness, but I have to ask. Why am I awake and Ardonis is not?"

"You were right in your assessment that Alexandria needs a wizard. More and more wizards have been visiting Alexandria."

"I see you've armed yourself with weapons designed to be used against magic."

She nodded. "Yes. We must prepare ourselves. However, Ardonis was right. We don't know what we've collected over the years, and we must know what we have. We might need some of these items in the upcoming years. Officially, Alexandria doesn't have a wizard and may never have a wizard of her own."

Krystal stopped and faced me. "Unofficially, you should know how to get to the vault and what lies in there."

As she stared into my eyes, I knew exactly what she meant. I might not be Alexandria's wizard, but I was hers. Yet, my attempting to venture into the vault was what got me banished from Alexandria in the first place.

"That's very kind of you, princess, but I might not see tomorrow."

"We'll see about that." She continued to lead us. She ducked underneath a low archway. "Watch your head."

As I watched a spider skitter away from the torchlight, I thought about Krystal's words. I remembered the time when Alexandria's people threw rocks at me, and the triumphant looks on some of the nobles' and guards' faces when I was banished. Alexandria might never accept me for who and what I was.

"I'm sorry, Your Highness," I said. "But I don't think I can do what you're asking."

Krystal's back stiffened, and she slowed her pace but she didn't stop. "I understand."

"No, you don't. Alexandria may never accept me. I will protect them from Premier, the council, the Wastelands, or whatever dangers may lie in wait, but only because it's the right thing to do. Know this; I am *your* wizard, not Alexandria's. I always will be, and I will do whatever it is you require."

Krystal turned around and smiled. Despite how sickly she still looked, it lit up her whole face. She had a hard time finding her voice. "Thank you, Hellsfire."

We resumed our journey, but as time passed Krystal moved slower. She had to take frequent breaks to rest. She never once complained and none of her guards dared to do more than give her water. It hurt me to watch her in pain, yet I also did nothing. I cursed Ardonis for putting her through this. She needed to rest, not exert herself with this needless journey.

With our slow pace, it took us nearly two hours before reaching our destination. We had been through at least a dozen doors while making our way deeper into the bowels of Alexandria. This wooden door looked just like the others, except that it had a lock. I assumed it was to confuse people if they made it this far, though that was unlikely. There were plenty of other traps to contend with that Krystal had led us around or bypassed. Krystal leaned against the wall, gasping for air, as I studied the door.

"Hellsfire, what is it?" Krystal asked, watching me. She peeled herself off the wall.

I stared at the door before placing my hand on it. "Nothing, and that's the problem. I thought I would be able to feel the magic in the room long before we reached here, but now that I'm here, I don't feel anything at all. This tells me that whatever wards are in place are powerful and designed to keep magic in."

"This is why we need a wizard of our own."

Krystal took out an ancient key. I didn't sense any magic from it until she used it to unlock the door. Then the key hummed to life with the magic that was imbued in it. When she took the key out, the magic vanished and no one there was the wiser but me.

"Your Highness," Ardimus said. "Perhaps it may be best for Hellsfire to get into the wheelbarrow now instead of in the vault."

"Why is that?"

Ardimus had a tiny smile on his face. "Hellsfire isn't...the best liar, Your Highness. Ardonis might see his reaction and figure out that Hellsfire was brought back to consciousness before he was."

"He's right," I said. "I shouldn't see what's in there until Ardonis does."

"Very well," Krystal said.

I climbed back into the wheelbarrow, looked up at Rebekah and smiled. "Hi."

Try as she might, the blonde woman couldn't conceal a smile. "Hello."

I curled up so that I couldn't see anything except the edges of the wheelbarrow. I didn't need my eyes to feel the intense magic radiating from that room when the princess opened the door.

It was like stepping out of a dark cave, letting the light wash over you and blind you. That's what struck me when we entered the room. I tried my hardest not to peek. Ardimus was right. I was a terrible liar and it would have shown on my face. I had to let Ardonis wake up first and hopefully, he'd be too caught up in looking around the vault to notice anything odd in my behavior.

"Remove his collar and wake him," Krystal said.

A couple of minutes later, Ardonis said, "My aching bones. I'm too old for this."

I stretched and did my best to yawn as I rose. I briefly glanced over at Ardonis but the vault and what was stored there pulled my attention away from him.

The more powerful the magic, the more you can see past its mundane trappings and glimpse its true nature. I glimpsed that now. Through my wizard's sight, rainbows of color floated through the air. The bright, vibrant colors clashed against each other. There was so much that I had no idea what color trail to follow first. Ardonis had the same awe-filled look on his face that I did on mine. We both went our separate ways and started searching the room.

The vault was small compared to most of the rooms in the castle, yet it was also the most cluttered one I had ever been in. It was littered with all sorts of artifacts, tools, and assorted mementos. I walked by a shelf lined with dozens of tiny gemstones. They appeared to be nothing but jewelry, but magic emanated from those gems. On the table next to the shelf was a candleholder. I sensed no magic from the candleholder yet it had to be here for a reason. I wondered if it required a special kind of candles in it, or if any candles would do? In the corner of the room was something with a sheet draped over it. I took it off and found my reflection staring back at me.

I gazed into the mirror and as I did so, a haze overcame it, until my reflection disappeared. It slowly cleared up and when it did, Krystal appeared. I turned around, expecting her to be behind me, but she wasn't. She was on the other side of the room, her hawk-like gaze on Ardonis.

As I turned my attention to the mirror, Krystal rematerialized. She held her arms open. At first, I thought it was to me but then my reflection reappeared and the pair embraced. The Mirror Hellsfire twirled her around and she laughed. He had no problem touching her bare hands. I envied the pair when Hellsfire drew her closer to him until their mouths found each other.

The Mirror Hellsfire disappeared and Mirror Krystal looked directly at me. She smiled in that special way I knew so well and beckoned me to come closer. I knew she was in the room with me, but I could never touch that Krystal again without killing her. My hand was drawn to the mirror. Before I could touch it—her—a wooden staff came crashing down on my arm.

I yelped in pain and withdrew my hand. Ardonis stood next to me with his staff in hand. He didn't look at me, but instead inspected the mirror.

"A Mirror of Desire," Ardonis said. "I haven't seen one of these in ages. Thank the gods, there are very few left." He finally focused on me. "I'd be more careful, Hellsfire. These mirrors can grant you what your heart desires, but not without cost."

"Can you see what's in the mirror?" I knew it wasn't real, but I couldn't tear my eyes away from Krystal's image. That urge within me to touch her grew stronger, yet I withheld my hand, instead focusing on the pain from Ardonis's staff.

"No, it's only for you. The mirror is a gateway and if you touch it, you'll be pulled inside and left at the whims of this creature."

The tip of Ardonis's staff lit up and he rapped it against the mirror's frame. The image of Krystal cried out in pain and disappeared, replaced by a shadowy black creature. It hissed and pounded against the glass. It spoke in a language I didn't understand, but I knew what it wanted—out.

Ardonis covered it with the sheet once more. "Well, that's enough of that." He walked away and I followed him. "This is a prime example of why the council should have what's in here. These items can be dangerous."

"Or they could be destroyed," I said.

Ardonis paused. "We do not destroy knowledge, Hellsfire. We study it and put it to beneficial use if we can. If we can't, only then do we destroy it."

The princess came up to us. "Is our vault satisfactory, Wizard Ardonis?"

He bowed. "Forgive me, princess. In my old age, I am slow. I've not finished surveying the room. I will need more time."

"As you wish."

Ardonis walked away from us and went back to studying the room—specifically, the wards around it.

When he was out of earshot, Krystal said, "There's another reason I wanted you down here. I want you to see something."

I followed her as she navigated through the vault's overflowing shelves and tables. On the floor on the other side of the room, leaning against the wall, was a large painting about four feet tall and three feet wide. Painted on it was a hexagram—a symbol of magic and the gods themselves. Each part of the symbol was in perfect relation to the others and matching in size—a balance.

"This painting was always one of my favorites," Krystal said, standing beside me. "There are other paintings and tapestries with the hexagram, but this one feels more alive." She bent down and ran her fingers over it. "We acquired it centuries ago. The woman called this The Window into the Gods. I never quite understood what she meant until now.

"When I returned from Tyree, I came back here. I knew we might need some of the things stored in here. As I searched the room, that's when I came upon this discovery."

Krystal motioned for me to squat down beside her. She never took her eyes off the painting. "In all the times I've been here and stared at the painting, it's never been moved. Yet, neither dust nor cobwebs have settled across it. The painter created it with such depth and skill. Each of the colors are used with different materials and were all equal." She leaned in. "If you look closer, you'll see that it's no longer like that."

I stared at the colors. At first, I wasn't sure what Krystal was getting at. But when I inspected the painting more closely, I began to see what she spoke of. The elemental gods—green, red, teal, and blue—were fading while the black and white portions were not. Not only that, but the red, which represented the Goddess of Fire, Emery, was a lot lighter than the rest, and the black portion mingled into it.

I sensed an unknown yet very familiar magic in the painting, and while Krystal had no problems touching it, I was hesitant to put my fingers on it.

"You say it wasn't like this before?" I asked.

"No. I had no idea what it meant until I remembered your words. You say there's a war between the gods that will tear apart the land. I'm no wizard nor have I grasped the workings of magic despite being around you and surrounded by this, but I trust you, Hellsfire." She withdrew her hand. "I'm still not entirely sure what this means, but I think it has to do with the gods' war. You brought down the barrier because of what it was doing to the land." Krystal whispered into my ear. "I know you'll end the war before it destroys the land."

She rose and left me. I stared at the painting, wondering if it would give me some kind of clue as to what I should be doing, where I should go. My master believed me to be some kind of chosen one, but would even I have enough power to stop the gods' war? As I glanced at Krystal, I knew that I would if she were by my side.

I left the painting and walked back to Ardonis. He was enthralled by an old book. The tan-colored cover had faded. At first, I thought it was leather-bound, but leather didn't have that appearance when aged.

I gasped when I realized what it was. "Is that...skin?"

Ardonis had no problem touching it, the dry flesh not bothering him.

"What's in it?" I asked.

"That I don't know," he said, turning another page. "It's blank."

"I don't understand."

Ardonis closed his eyes and inhaled. "Can't you feel how powerful this book is? The spells in it must equally be as potent."

"What makes you think they're spells?"

He gave me a wry smile. "What else would they be?"

"Anything." I stared at the dried skin. "This book was clearly created by a madman. He could have recorded his mother's secret quiche recipe, for all we know."

"You could be right." Ardonis closed the book. "And that's the problem. There's so many things we don't know in here. This book could be dangerous, or it could mean nothing."

Ardonis made his way back to Krystal and the others.

"Are you satisfied, Wizard Ardonis?" she asked.

He bowed. "I am, Your Highness. The wards placed around your vault are...adequate. They could be strengthened. A lot of time has passed since they were first created. And these are old spells. We could improve upon them."

"I appreciate your offer, but we would prefer to handle it ourselves."

"Understood."

"Glad you can see it that way." Krystal motioned to one of the guards, and the guard withdrew another vial and got the collar ready. Ardonis and I were collared and drugged once more.

When I awakened shortly thereafter, Krystal took her time as she led us away from the vault. She wanted me to memorize the way there. She pointed out a broken torch next to one doorway, and a hallway that was exactly one hundred feet long. I shook my head. It would take me quite a long time to memorize all these differences I couldn't see, and I would have to frequently return to the vault to do so.

It had taken us longer to return than to go, with Krystal pointing out these landmarks to me, but I believed she did it so that the pace would be easier on her. I almost suggested that she should ride in the wheelbarrow, but thought better of it.

Now that I had access to the vault, my first thought was to see if it contained a cure for Krystal, or could point me to one.

CHAPTER 8

I HAD NO IDEA how long I would stay in Alexandria or if I would even keep my head, but it didn't take me very long to find out.

King Furlong summoned me the following day. The young page did not lead me to the king's chambers as I expected. Instead I was led to a small private room, well away from the king's chambers. The king was seated at the wooden table, a steaming kettle near his person. The ferocious winter wind banged against the shutters behind him.

"Thank you, Charles. That'll be all. Hellsfire, if you please." The king motioned for me to sit across from him in the empty chair.

"As you wish, Your Majesty."

"Would you like some tea? There's nothing better than hot tea on a chilly day."

My mouth became dry, and not from the weather. While I could have used something to wet it, I had to be on guard. I had never seen this side of the king before and it unnerved me more than a death sentence.

"No, thank you, Your Majesty."

The kindness in the king's face disappeared and he became the Ruler of Alexandria once more. That was a person I was used to dealing with.

"Hellsfire, while we're in here, I don't want you to think of me as a king. I want you to think of me as a father. A very protective father."

My eyes widened and my heart stopped. That was worse than him being a king.

"I will try, Your—sir."

"Good." King Furlong cleared his throat. "You should know that my daughter told me everything."

"Everything?"

He nodded, his face darkening with anger. "Yes. She told me how she wanted you to go to the vault, and how she left you awake as you traveled to and from it. I wasn't pleased to hear her words. But what's done is done. I'm not sure if I can trust you with that secret, Hellsfire. But my daughter trusts you. For now, that's enough."

I nodded, still staring at my hands in my lap.

The anger in his voice faded and a great weariness overtook him. "She also told me how she loves you."

I was finally able to meet the king's blue eyes. "I love her too."

The king allowed himself a smile. "I know you do, Hellsfire. I've known you care about my daughter greatly for some time now. The only thing I didn't know until now was if my daughter reciprocated your feelings. My daughter's love is a precious thing. She guards her heart well and she's given it to you."

He poured me a cup of tea. I took it, letting the warmth of it flow through my hands. While Krystal had dropped her guard around me, there were times when she closed herself off. I thought it was because she was a princess and nothing more. I now realized how wrong I was.

"While I hope and pray that you find a cure for my daughter, I'm a pragmatic man. The curse she lives with will be like an ailment. Since you now have access to our vault, you might be able to find a way to break it. If you do so, I will withdraw my objections to your relationship."

"You will?" I asked, barely getting the words out. I wiped my sweaty hands on my wizard's robes.

"Yes. A father always wants to make his daughter happy, and I know that you make her happy. But know this. The people of Alexandria will never accept you as a king. At best, you can be a consort, but you'll have no real power. Even in magical matters, you can advise her, but it will be up to her to decide the outcome."

"I've never wanted power, Your Majesty. All I've ever wanted was to help people, and all I want for your daughter is to live a happy and healthy life. I love her."

He sighed. "I know you do, but things aren't that simple, especially for a princess." The king took a small bite of the biscuit on his plate. "I just hope that you can find a cure for Krystal…or you can get the man responsible."

I leaned forward and clenched my hand. "Premier."

"Yes. I've sent out search parties since the last time you were in Alexandria, scouting the land for him. We've not been able to find him, but we now know where he is going—the Burning Sands." The king put his fingers together, staring directly at me. "He's looking for something called the Jewel of Dakara. With this jewel, he can enhance his powers. He might even regain them. In your battle, you've weakened him considerably. He's still a danger, but if he becomes as powerful as he once was, he'll once again be a threat. Before you came, I was going to send an expedition to retrieve his head, or if possible, bring him back alive. Even though we've acquired weapons to combat wizards, we still don't have a wizard of our own, Hellsfire. Would you like to accompany my soldiers?"

The king reached for his tea and appeared to enjoy his meal while I pondered my decision.

I wanted nothing more than to see Premier pay for his crime. He had brought so much destruction and death, and he had hurt the one I loved. Yet as much as I wanted to bring him to justice and get revenge for what he had done, not even that was more important than Krystal's safety. Within the vault, I might be able to find a cure for her. But that would take a considerable amount of time. I'd have to catalog and test things. Tracking down Premier would also take time, and even though he was responsible for Krystal's curse, it wasn't his magic that had directly caused it. He might not know how to reverse it.

But if there was a chance that I could bring Premier to justice, *and* free Krystal from her curse at the same time, I would risk it.

I nodded. "I'll go, Your Majesty. I'll bring him back to face whatever punishment you decree, if possible. If not, I'll kill him."

"Good. I'll make preparations with Ardimus. He will be leading the expedition. There's a village west of here that's a crossroads of several trade routes. My agents often go there to gather information from travelers of all kinds. Someone there might know where the jewel is, or Premier might even be headed there to find out himself. While my men have been able to figure out what Premier wants, we still don't know where it is, other than someplace in the Burning Sands."

I nodded. "Understood, Your Majesty."

"Ardimus has a contact in the Burning Sands that might know where the jewel is, if you're unable to find out before you arrive there. Unfortunately, that's all the information I can give you. See Ardimus first thing in the morning. You must ride fast and hard if you're to stop Premier."

I stood up, thinking our conversation was over, and bowed.

"There is one more thing," he said.

I stared at the king, fearful of what his next words would be.

"My daughter won't wait forever—she *can't* wait. Krystal's my only heir, and it's her duty and mine to make sure our bloodline continues, especially in light of what has happened to her. You need to hurry; otherwise, I must insist she marry someone else." He opened his mouth to say something, but then paused. "Talk to her before you leave. She should be the one to tell you, not I."

"I will." I wondered what more he had to say, but knew I wouldn't get it from him. I started to bow but then stopped myself. I extended my hand toward the king. "Thank you, sir, for being honest with me, and for rescinding the death sentence."

King Furlong shook my hand. "And thank you for saving my life and my kingdom. Now, go talk to her."

I let go his hand and bowed before exiting the room.

I sent word to Krystal. Ardimus came to me and told me that she wouldn't be able to see me until well after everyone was asleep. He also said he would have everything ready by tomorrow morning, and that he knew of someone that could guide us when we reached the Burning Sands.

Afterward, I went to Ardonis to ask him about the Jewel of Dakara. Unfortunately, he did not know anything about it. Even though he was part of the Elemental Council and had been alive for centuries, his knowledge of anything north of where the Great Barrier once stood was still lacking.

I awoke to a warm body snuggled against mine. Krystal looked up at me and grinned, putting a gloved hand to my face. I wrapped my arms around her body, hugging her like a man dying of thirst.

"Hey, beautiful," I said and yawned. "Sorry, I couldn't stay up."

"It's all right." Krystal leaned closer to me. "I've missed this."

"Me too."

"Now, what did you want to talk about?"

As I held Krystal, she listened to how my conversation with her father had gone. It was only when I got to the end of my story and I asked her about what King Furlong had said, that I felt her body stiffen in my arms.

The princess didn't say a word. Now that I understood her better, I didn't press her for an answer. I wanted one, and I felt I deserved one, but I understood if I didn't get one.

"Your timing, as always, has been impeccable, Hellsfire. A delegation is due from Maera any day now. In that delegation will be Prince Valmont, my once-betrothed."

This time I was silent. I struggled to find the words. "Will this Valmont be your betrothed again?"

"Maybe."

I exhaled. At least she hadn't lied to me. "Is that why you didn't write me?"

"Yes. I was...afraid of what you would think. And I shouldn't break your heart in a letter. I do love you, Hellsfire, I truly do. No matter what happens, I want you to know that."

Tears hovered near the edge of my eyes. "I do," I croaked.

Yet I knew in that moment that our love might never be enough.

Krystal disentangled herself from me and faced me. She wiped the tears from my eyes before laying her head on my chest once more.

"Let's worry about that tomorrow. Tonight, I want to enjoy being with you, hero."

I wrapped my arms tighter around her. "And I you, princess."

While it was great spending time with Krystal again, my heart and mind worried about our future. Even though it was selfish of me to do so, I didn't want her to be with anyone but me even if I couldn't find a cure for her. I didn't voice those concerns or my feelings to her, though. She and King Furlong were right. They did have a duty. I tried to push aside those thoughts and focus on the task at hand, but I knew they would linger in my mind until it was settled.

The next morning Ardimus had our supplies ready. It would be just the two of us. Two of us would travel faster, and we would have more help once we got to the Burning Sands. The king had given us two collars to entrap Premier with. That was all. We only had my magic and Ardimus's enchanted scimitar to fight him with.

I stood outside the keep's walls, letting the winter morning's frost worm itself into my lungs. I watched the soldiers near the barracks doing their morning exercises.

"How long are you going to be staying here?" I asked Ardonis. He had come to the gate to see us off, which surprised me.

"Most likely until winter's over," he said, crossing his arms and rubbing them. He looked at me. "How long will you be gone?"

"As long as it takes. Premier must be made to answer for his crimes. If not, he must die." I finally turned to look at him. "I trust you'll be able to negotiate without me."

He had a wry smile on his face. "I'll manage."

"Good. Sorry I can't stay, but I have to do this."

"I understand. Be careful out there. I've not met Premier, but from what I understand he's crafty."

I returned his smile. "I'll try."

Krystal limped her way over to us, grimacing at the slight incline of the hill.

"Your Highness," Ardonis said, and bowed. I did the same. Ardonis melted away from us and back toward the keep.

I kept my voice low and inched closer to her. "What are you doing here, Krystal? It's too cold for you to be outside."

"I wanted to say my goodbye to you in private, not in my chambers with countless people around." She closed the gap between us until our bodies were touching each other. "And being next to you, I've never felt cold."

The heat rushed through my cheeks, and I turned my head away.

Krystal moved in front of me and pulled down my hood. She kissed me on the cheek, my wizard's robes blocking our skin-to-skin contact. Her head tilted to the side and she smiled. "I love you, Hellsfire. Never forget that. Now go get Premier and come back home to me."

I ached to kiss her and feel her soft lips brush on mine. I wanted to at least hug her goodbye. But I didn't. There were far too many people around and—

I wrapped my arms around Krystal's waist and pulled her closer. Her cane fell to the ground. I held onto her and squeezed as I twirled her around. Her laughter rang in my ears. It felt good to have her laugh and smile this way again. As I looked into her violet eyes, I realized I never should have doubted her love for me. She didn't need to say it with words. Her actions and her looks spoke volumes to me. I just hadn't listened until now. I had no idea what tomorrow would bring, but I knew that for this moment, she was mine and I was hers.

I set her back on the ground and handed her the cane. There was a big grin plastered on my face and I bowed deeply. "Your Highness."

She failed to hide her smile as she said, "Wizard Hellsfire."

I left her and walked down the hill to Ardimus.

"Did you have fun, Hellsfire?" he asked with a slight grin on his face.

Out of the corner of my eye, I glimpsed the nearby soldiers whispering. One of the servants smiled and shook his head as he walked by.

The heat crept up my cheeks. "I'm sorry, Ardimus. I shouldn't have done what I did. It's just—"

"It's all right. The princess needed it. *We* needed it."

I raised an eyebrow. as I didn't understand what he meant. I followed Ardimus's gaze and saw how they all basked in how happy the princess was. Her spirits lightened her people's spirits. I had to find a cure for Krystal, for their sake and hers.

As I led my horse away, I tried not to turn back around to see if Krystal was watching me go. We reached the castle's walls and just as I was looking for Jerrel, a delegation arrived near the gates.

There were eight or ten people, wearing thick winter wolf-lined coats. Their horses were strong and finely groomed. Their emblem was a picture of an eagle.

"Where are they from?" I asked Ardimus. "I've not seen their crest before."

"Maera."

I was about to ask him where that was, but then I remembered.

I moved closer until I caught a glimpse of the one in charge—Prince Valmont. He was a lot younger than I thought he'd be. He had to be the same age as Krystal and I. He was clean-shaven, and his blond hair stood out against the dark wool of his clothes. He laughed with the soldiers. I first thought he was just some well-bred whelp, but then saw the sword hanging on his side.

I had thought the betrothal between Krystal and Valmont was of convenience or to strengthen ties, but what if it was more? What if she did once love him as she loved me? As I watched how at ease the soldiers were around Valmont, I thought that might be the case. I wished I had dug deeper into her past, but she was ill and truthfully, I didn't want to know. What would happen between those two while I was away? Valmont's touch wouldn't kill Krystal.

I turned back to take one last look at Krystal, but she was gone. I clenched my fists and stared at Valmont's back as he headed toward the keep.

"Are you ready to depart?" Ardimus asked.

I wasn't. I wanted to stay and learn more about Valmont.

"Let's go," I said. The sooner we left, the sooner I would get back to Krystal.

We left Alexandria with that light-heartedness in my chest fading rapidly.

CHAPTER 9

AS WE RODE east toward the Burning Sands, I couldn't help but think of Valmont and Krystal and what could happen in my absence. I knew it was stupid and petty of me to feel jealous, but I couldn't control my feelings no matter how much I tried.

I was quiet for that first day of the trip, letting my mind wander in places and possibilities it shouldn't, instead of focusing on the task at hand. The frigid weather did nothing to distract me from my thoughts.

At the end of the first day, we reached an inn. Once in the common room, my hands cupped the mug of steaming hot barley tea as the warmth of it flowed through my body. Ardimus sat back down and we waited for our food to arrive. I stared into the tea, watching the swirls dance around.

"How well do you know Prince Valmont?" I asked.

"Well enough," he said. "I've seen him around Her Highness over the years. I'm sure you know by now that they were once engaged to each other. He is a good man."

Good enough for her? I wondered. "What happened between them?"

Ardimus exhaled and he looked away, into a different time. "The princess was never the same after her mother died. She became distant and colder, and it wasn't long before she ended her betrothal with the prince. Prince Valmont was very understanding of it all. Though I believe he thought she would come back to him once she was done grieving. She never did, though."

But did she love him? I stared into my tea, wishing Krystal had told me all of this. I had lost my father before I was born, so I only knew my mother. If I lost her, it would devastate me too.

"The princess once loved Prince Valmont, Hellsfire. But she never loved him as much as she loves you. Her passion and fierceness when you two are together is multiplied tenfold. Remember that."

I finally lifted my head up and met his dark brown eyes. "I will." I wanted—needed—to change the subject. "What should I expect in the Burning Sands?"

He paused for a moment as if he wanted to say something else. Finally, he said, "From what I've heard, your mother is from the Burning Sands."

I nodded. "She is, but I've never been there. I was born in Sedah. I know very little about it."

Much like Krystal, my mother also had a hard time opening up about her past. Once I realized that, I stopped pressing her about it. She had given me a dagger that once belonged to my father. I carried that with me at all times. Like my mother, it had also come from the Burning Sands.

As I reached for the dagger, feeling that it was still there, I ached to learn about it while I was in the Burning Sands. It was the only connection to my father that I had, and it had saved my life once. It tore a hole in the world and sucked in the little beasts that attacked us when I had no magic, in a swamp in Tyree. The dagger contained magic, that much I was sure of, but it wasn't any I knew of.

Maybe once Premier was taken care of, I could spend a few days in the Burning Sands, finding out about my dagger and my father. Ardimus might even know of people who could help. But I wasn't going to ask him now. Capturing Premier would be my first priority.

"The Burning Sands is named that way for a reason," Ardimus said. "The heat is scorching. Clouds are rare and it rains even less than that." A wistful smile passed his face. "I remember the princess once describing it to me like eating a pie directly out of the oven, and it burns the roof of your mouth. Except that instead of your mouth, it's your skin if you stay uncovered in direct sunlight for too long."

Our food finally arrived. I dug into the plate of steaming vegetables, and the warm bread with butter and honey. My appetite began to subside.

Ardimus took a bite of his stew before continuing. "The Burning Sands can be a dangerous place, Hellsfire. The number one danger is heat exhaustion and the lack of water. Always make sure you're well supplied. Yet there are more dangers than the environment. There are things there that can even rival the Wastelands for danger."

My body tilted forward. "Like what?"

"In the desert, there are safe havens known as oasis. There you can find water and even a few trees. Because of how valuable water is, predators have been known to lurk there. There's this one creature. It looks like a harmless stalk sticking up from the ground. While you can cut certain stalks to eat their roots, if you pluck these, they will sting you. Since we're bigger than their normal prey, it might hurt no more than a bee sting. But the poison will slowly work its way through your system. You will die in excruciating pain without treatment."

Ardimus took a drink and ate more of his meal. I swirled the contents of mine with the fork and took one bite.

"But I think the most dangerous creatures in all the Burning Sands are the sand devils."

"Sand devils?" I asked. I imagined gigantic creatures that rose out of the sand. Their yellow eyes pierced you, and they could reshape any part of their body, making their hands into deadly claws.

"The sand devils are small creatures no bigger than a small dog," he said. "But don't let their size fool you. They hunt in packs and look like small twisters. They don't attack you, but take all of your supplies. In doing so, they might as well leave you for dead."

"Can my magic defeat them?"

Ardimus paused. "I'm not sure that will work. The creatures are immune to any blade or arrow. They might be immune to magic too. The only thing that will work is water. While most consider water to be the giver of life, for them, it burns." His almond eyes stared at me. "We'll also have to get you new clothing. Those robes you're wearing will be stifling."

I glanced at the thick black sleeves of my wizard's robes. My robes had been a gift to me from Stradus, when he had proclaimed me a wizard. They were a part of me as much as my magic was.

"What can you tell me about your contact in the Burning Sands?" I asked.

A smile crept across Ardimus's face. "I've known Serling a long time. You could say he was a mentor of mine. As long as I've known him, he's had an interest in the past, and the items that have come from it. He was the one who gave me my sword and chainmail. If there's anyone in all of the Burning Sands who knows where the Jewel of Dakara is, it will be him. If we cannot find the information we need in Relara, then Falak is our best bet."

"What will he want in return?"

"King Furlong has opened his coffers for this mission. We needn't worry about money."

Ardimus's enchanted chainmail glistened in my wizard eyes. "It's not money that concerns me. You said it yourself, you got your sword and chainmail from him, and that he has an interest in the past. Men like him want more than money."

He paused to think about his answer. "You are right, yet I feel like I know Serling well enough that the price won't be steep. It wasn't easy for me to do so at first, but I trust him, Hellsfire."

I nodded. I didn't trust Serling, but I did trust Ardimus. He was an honorable man, and he wouldn't associate with those that didn't have some sense of honor. Yet it wasn't Ardimus who had to pay the price. It was me. I would do anything to free Krystal of her curse, but that wasn't the plan here. Our plan was to find Premier and bring him to justice.

Ardimus took another bite. His eyes looked wistful, and he seemed to forget I was there.

"Looking forward to going home?" I asked.

"Hmmm?" Ardimus's eyes came into focus. "Home? I suppose I am. It's been a few years since I've been there."

"Family?"

"Yes, I have a mother out there. She will be glad to see me."

I stared at him, wondering how long his duties had kept him apart from his mother and how often he was able to go home. I knew how it was, not seeing my family as often as I'd like. But as I studied the look on his face, there was something else. There was another reason he ached to go home. I ate my meal and mulled it over and when we were just about finished, I realized what it was. It was a woman. It had to be.

I was about to delve into his real reason for wanting to go back to the Burning Sands when he took his bowl and left the table. I shrugged. There would be plenty of time to get to know the man. We had a long journey ahead of us.

We continued on our trek, though the cold and snowy weather did its best to slow us down. The king had suggested we start at this small village, Relara. While the king had found out what Premier was searching for, the Burning Sands was a huge place. He would need to know where to begin. While the village was of no importance, there was an old man there that King Furlong dealt with from time to time. The man and his family had studied magical artifacts from the war for generations.

When the village was in our view, but still about twenty minutes away, we immediately knew something was off. It was too quiet. Even though the snow had smothered it, and most people would be indoors if they could, there were no smoke trails from fires inside homes. We also saw no movement of people.

Our fears were confirmed when we reached Relara. We stared in horror as we saw bodies strewn about the ground. The snow had partially covered and frozen them. Clumps of the snow-covered bodies could be easily mistaken for tiny hills. We got off our horses and bent down to one.

Ardimus pushed the snow off the body. It was an older man, clutching his throat, a horrified look forever etched in his face. We moved to another body. A young woman had scorch marks and burns covering the front of her body. In the rest of the area were another half dozen of the snow burials.

"I don't think they've been dead long," Ardimus said. "We would have heard something at the other villages where we stopped. A week at most." He looked around the village. "Who would do such a thing—to slaughter a village wholesale?"

I clenched my fists, staring at the dead, frozen bodies in anger. I had a very good idea. Someone who delighted in cruelty and who wanted something very badly. "If only we'd gotten here sooner. Do you think any of them got away?"

"Yes, but if they didn't have proper supplies, the weather would finish them off."

We left the outside bodies and went to a small dwelling on the other side of the village—the home of the man we'd come to see. The door was hanging off its hinges. Snow blew into it, filling the home with its white covering. Old, valuable books had been flung off the shelves and scattered across the floor, their pages flapping whenever the wind blew inside. In front of the cold hearth hung a body.

"It's our contact, isn't it?" I said.

Ardimus nodded, his face sad and angry.

A plant had grown throughout the old man's body, its growth clearly accelerated by magic. Through his nose, mouth, and ears small branches poked out. The plant pushed against the body, aching to be free.

There was only one wizard I knew who could—and would—do this.

"Premier," I said, feeling my fire build up within me. "What do we do now?"

"Unfortunately, we don't know if Icheo knew where the Jewel of Dakara is." Ardimus stared at the dead man. "But I'm sure he told Premier all he knew." He stopped to think for a minute.

"For the moment, I don't think it matters whether or not Premier learned the location of the jewel from Icheo," he said finally. "He will head for the city of Kadir, the gateway to the Burning Sands. All travelers pass through it, in order to resupply before setting out across the desert. Whether Premier knows his ultimate destination or not, his path will lie through the city. And if he needs more information, there is where he will find it." He turned to me, his face grim. "If we hurry, we may still catch him before he gets there, or in the city itself."

I raised my hand and let loose the fire inside of me. The mana struck Icheo's unnatural body, setting the monstrosity ablaze. "Then let's go, before Premier hurts more innocent people."

As we traveled to Kadir, it felt as if we moved at a snail's pace, but we moved as fast as our mounts and the weather allowed. I thought about summoning a maleika to check on Krystal, but decided against it. I didn't want to see her harmed again, or with Prince Valmont. I wished I could use one to spy on Premier, but I didn't know where he was, so there was no place to anchor the spell.

The closer we traveled to Kadir, the easier the weather became. The cold weather gradually dissipated. The snowline rose higher and soon settled on the ridgeline of the mountains, instead of in our boots. Rather than trudging through heavy wet air, it was warmer and drier. While the thought of warmer weather should have made me happy, all I thought of were the people Premier had killed, and Krystal dead on her bed. It took nearly a month before we finally arrived near Kadir, the last city in Northern Shala.

CHAPTER 10

WE FIRST GLIMPSED the city from a distance. We'd left the forest, and the land had grown dry, with scrub and coarse grasses instead of trees. From the top of a rise, we could see the buildings of Kadir, shimmering in the bright light. Ardimus had told me about the desert glare—that it could make the air shimmer and even create illusions. Now I was beginning to see what he meant.

While Kadir was a major city, it wasn't as large as Alexandria or Sharald. Ardimus had explained that the land couldn't support enough people for the city to grow any further; there wasn't enough water. It had started out as a way station between the Burning Sands and Northern Shala, but more people had settled there as the years passed, as it was conveniently situated between the cold of Northern Shala and the heat of the Burning Sands. Many wealthy people from nearby lands passed the winter in Kadir because of its mild climate.

For the past few days, I had been trying to acclimatize myself to the warmer weather, but now that we neared the edge of the Burning Sands, it was oppressive. The sun seemed to burn brighter and hotter than it had before. My thick black robes smothered me, and the sweat dripped down the sides of my body.

I glanced up at the sky, watching the sparse clouds float away. I knew it was going to get hotter. I couldn't wait until I changed clothing.

"Something wrong, Hellsfire?"

I looked back at Ardimus, blinking a droplet of sweat from my eye, and smiled. "What makes you ask?"

"Don't worry. I'll get you a proper change of clothes soon."

When we entered the city, I saw the clothes Ardimus had in mind. Some of the people were dressed the way I was used to, in tunics and trousers or leggings. Others wore loose, light fabric that floated around their entire bodies. A few of those wore headdresses.

One thing that caught me off guard was that a majority of the people had far darker skin than I was used to seeing. I should have expected it, since my mother had the dark skin of her Burning Sands heritage, and I was darker than most in Northern Shala. Still, seeing the streets filled with a majority of dark-skinned people—darker than me—was a strange experience. Everywhere I turned, I was reminded of my mother—and father. I hoped that once I had done what I'd come here for, I'd have some time to see if I could find out more about him and his family.

I gazed around as we rode, fascinated by the different architecture in the buildings we passed. A few were built of stone, but many were made of bricks. We rode past a group of very strange buildings, constructed of wood, but instead of being square or made of logs, the wood seemed to have been bent into a half-circle to make a curved shape, and then sanded down until it was smooth as a tree that had shed all its bark. They looked like cave entrances. One such building even had a second floor, looking like another curved house had dropped on top of it. I wondered what it'd be like when we actually got to the Burning Sands. The designs might be the same, but what would the buildings be constructed out of, and would there be far more elaborate ones? Did these designs help keep the buildings cool?

"Some people in Kadir prefer their homes in the style of the Burning Sands," Ardimus said. "It seems they have enough money to get a slice of home."

I noticed that although the city was filled with people from different regions, as well as the occasional dwarf or elf, there seemed to be no obvious tensions between the groups. Well, aside from a customer yelling about how ridiculous a vendor's prices were, and a man staggering out of a tavern and barging into indignant passersby.

We dropped our horses off at the nearest stable and Ardimus led me to the marketplace so we could get supplies for the next leg of our journey. The first stall we went to sold dates, figs, prunes—food I tended to keep with me since I didn't eat meat. I was about to ask the price when Ardimus took the lead.

I watched Ardimus haggle with the vendor in another language, until they reached an agreement and the man had his son carry our supplies away.

I stared after him, but Ardimus was already moving on to the next vendor. "Don't worry, Hellsfire," he said. "I'm having our purchases delivered to the stable where we left the horses. It's easier that way, and common practice for travelers. We're going to need a lot of things to traverse the desert." His eyes scanned the people behind us, and in the crowded aisles between the market vendors. "I've also asked if they've seen a man fitting Premier's description."

"And?"

He shook his head. "There are too many travelers coming through Kadir. They might not remember him, if he didn't do anything to stand out, and hid his scarred face as best as he could. But don't worry. There are many more people we can ask."

I nodded. Even if Premier were still wearing his wizards' robes, they wouldn't necessarily stand out here as they did in Northern Shala. Many people wore robes. "Do people here speak the common tongue, or does everyone in the Burning Sands speak your language?"

"The major cities, like this one, see so many travelers that most of the vendors and many of the citizens speak a number of languages, so you'll be able to get by. However, we'll get better prices in the market if I bargain; once they know you're a native they stop trying to gouge you quite so badly." He grinned. "If all else fails, you'll have me. I will even teach you a few phases and words."

I smiled. "Nothing bad, I hope?"

Ardimus didn't reply, but a small smile curled at the corner of his lip.

We passed by a stall, and the gleam of gold forced my feet to stop. Plates were displayed across the front of the stall, reflecting the light until they shone like the sun. The lamps on the shelf behind them glistened with the same color. Drawings were etched into them. One had stars in the form of constellations, and another showed an oasis in the desert, like Ardimus had told me about.

Ardimus appeared next to me and said, "In case you're wondering, that's not real gold. Looks like it, but it's only brass." He leaned in and whispered to me. "If you're interested in a piece, they'll be far cheaper where we're going, and of a higher quality with far more places to choose from. This place does well because it's one of only two shops in the city that sells these items."

"All right."

We left that fascinating shop and went to another stall that sold waterskins—leather bags for carrying large quantities of water. I still couldn't understand anything anyone was saying, though I paid close attention, trying to piece together words. When we passed by one saddler only to stop at another fifty yards further along, I realized that Ardimus was choosing only vendors of his own people who had the same dark, weathered complexion that he had. He didn't even glance in the direction of those with fairer skin.

"Are we just going to the vendors that are from your homeland?" I asked.

Ardimus paused. "I hadn't thought of that, but I suppose we are. I know these vendors and am able to get us a good deal." He paused again. "And I admit, I am happy to be able to speak in my native tongue again. It's been way too long since I've last been home."

"I thought the princess took regular trips to the Burning Sands so you could return home."

"She used to, but she hasn't in the last couple of years. She's been busy. First with Premier, and now with her illness and the Great Barrier falling, she hasn't had time. Alexandria comes first."

I finally understood that. Even though Krystal loved me, her kingdom would always come first. I looked at Ardimus, feeling a certain kinship with the warrior, I never had before, except when we fought on behalf of Krystal.

We went to a few more stalls and Ardimus taught me a few phrases, though my accent was thick and my tongue was twisted. When we were finished, we still had one more place to go to.

Ardimus finally brought me to the tailor's shop. He was greeted warmly the moment we went inside. When the tailor caught sight of me and what I was wearing, he gasped and elbowed Ardimus aside.

"What it is this?" he cried, rushing to me and plucking at my robes. "My friend, why do you wear such hot and stifling clothes?" I tried to pull away from him, but everywhere I turned he was at my elbow, prodding me. "You are no longer in the icy winters of Alexandria. You are but a stone's throw from the Burning Sands." He smiled. "Good thing you've come to Samir's shop."

I pleaded to Ardimus with my eyes. He just shrugged. As he turned around and walked away, I saw a glimpse of a sly smile across his face.

I was powerless as the tailor cornered me and took my measurements. His fingers were oddly delicate as he poked and prodded me to get my size.

"As soon as Samir is done with you…," the little man said, pausing as he realized Ardimus hadn't introduced us.

"Hellsfire," I said.

He beamed at me. "Hellsfire, with my help you will escape the desert heat's clutches and it will bother you no more."

On the other side of the room, Ardimus chuckled. He leaned against the wall and shook his head.

"Pay no attention to Ardimus," Samir said. "Warriors like him must always be ready for battle. Whereas you and I can dress for the environment." Samir leaned in close and said, "We do not need to be weighed down by leather or metal." He raised his voice. "While the warriors are ready to fight, the blazing bright sun and harsh, desert wind can be an even more deadly enemy."

"Next time, I'll have you make something for me," Ardimus said.

"Bah! Next time, next time. Always 'next time.' Come, my friend. Let us make him jealous of how good you will look."

I couldn't help but smile as Samir led me to a small room. I undressed and cradled my wizard's robes in my hand. My fingers squeezed the fluffy warm fabric, and I knew I was going to miss them. They were more than just clothing. They were my uniform, and in a way, my armor. If had to face Premier, I would have preferred to do it wearing my robes.

Samir stared at me, waiting for me to hand him my robes. His look wasn't impatient. He was a man who knew the importance of clothes to people. I finally nodded and gave him my robes. He gently folded them and laid them down on a nearby table.

"My friend," Samir said, "are you ready?"

I nodded.

Samir handed me white robes to put on. They were far lighter than my wizard's robes. I thought they might be too sheer for my tastes, but I couldn't see through them. I spun around and chuckled as the floating fabric made me look like a butterfly. A slight breeze floated through the clothes and onto my body, and I knew that Samir was right. I would remain cool in these clothes. I tugged on the sleeves. While I was used to long sleeves, these nearly reached my knees.

"Do not fear," Samir said. "I will fix that for you."

Samir quickly altered the fabric, wielding the needle and thread like I cast magic. He shortened the hem and the sleeves, and took in the seams so that the garments weren't quite so flowy. I slipped my hand in the opening at my chest and found I could easily reach my purse and my father's dagger. I would be able to access them quickly if I needed to.

I looked to Ardimus. "What do you think?"

He pursed his lips and put a long finger to them. "It's missing something."

"Ah yes!" Samir said, snapping his fingers.

He disappeared and returned with more fabric. He wrapped it around my head until there was only a slight opening for my eyes.

Samir clapped his hands. "Perfect!"

I tried to say something, but my voice came out muffled, as I kept inhaling the cloth around my face. I pulled on it until my mouth was free again. "I don't like this."

"But it is necessary, my friend," Samir said.

"He's right," Ardimus said. "You want as little of your body exposed as possible. You'll be burned if you don't wear it."

I folded my arms across my chest. "You don't know what it's like." I scratched my head. "*You* have a bald head." I couldn't stop scratching. It's not like the fabric was made out of wool, but I had let my hair grow out these last few months. It was tight against the headdress, trapping the heat and making my scalp itch.

Samir reached up and loosened the headpiece. I sighed in relief. "Better?"

I smiled. "Much."

"Good! I'm glad you like it unlike that other man with the black robe."

My ears pricked up and I glanced at Ardimus. Could he mean Premier? "What man was that?" I asked.

Samir said, "The other man with robes similar to yours. I've never seen fabric like this before, so unusual. I was outside my shop when he passed by and tried to get him to come inside and buy more suitable clothing, but he wouldn't let me anywhere near him. In fact, I thought he'd kill poor Samir." He laughed. "All over clothing."

Ardimus stepped forward and his fingers went to his sword's hilt. "Samir, what did this man look like?"

The tailor rubbed the back of his neck. "I don't understand. What do you want with this man? Do you know him?" When he saw the look in Ardimus's eyes, Samir described him to us. "Like I said, he wore robes like Hellsfire's, but he kept his hood up around his face. When I approached him to help him take off the suffocating clothes and try on his new ones, I nearly stumbled over my tongue. He had a terrible burned face."

Ardimus's tone was low. "How long ago was this?"

Samir scrunched up his face in thought. "A little over a week ago? He had many supplies he was carrying, as if he were planning a long trip into the desert."

"Did you hear where he was going?"

Samir shook his head. "He talked to no one except when he had to. Even then, he was very mean." The tailor stroked his chin. "With all the supplies he bought, if I had to guess, he might have enough to make it as far as Amir or Falak."

"Thank you, Samir," Ardimus said, relaxing. "If you see this man again in the next few days, send word to me. And stay away from him. He's very dangerous."

"I have no doubt that's true, if you're looking for him." Samir went to the back and returned with a folded-up headdress, giving it to Ardimus. "Give the princess my regards. And to my newest friend, 'May the desert gods be kind to you.'"

"Thank you," I said.

Ardimus and I left Samir's shop. When we were outside, I said, "So Premier was here a week ago. Can we catch up to him?"

Ardimus was silent as he thought about it. "Maybe, if he's headed for Falek, as I hope he is."

"What if he's headed for Amir?" I asked. "It's much further south. By going to Falek, we might be increasing the distance between us."

Ardimus sighed. "We have three choices," he said. "We can head for Falek, or head for Amir, or we can stay here and make inquiries, trying to find out which way Premier went."

I nodded. "Maybe we should talk to some more people."

Ardimus said, "We could spend days doing that and come up empty. Or we may find that Premier was headed for one city but told people that he was heading for the other, to throw any pursuers off track."

"He doesn't know we're following him, though." I pointed out. "So why would he feel the need to throw us off track?"

"He destroyed a village," Ardimus said. "And he's a very devious, suspicious, and cruel person. He's probably made plenty of enemies that he wants to avoid." I nodded at that. Premier definitely had a talent for making enemies.

Ardimus went on, "Falek is my home city. I have a network of contacts there. If Premier passes through, I'm much more likely to learn about it there than in Amir. More importantly, Falek is where Serling is. If he can tell us where to find the Jewel of Dakara, we don't have to track Premier. We just have to go to the jewel's location and wait for him. And if we get there first, and take it, then he'll come to us."

We walked toward a nearby inn, as it was getting late. The next day, we went to one of the local stables. We had enough money to buy horses bred in the Burning Sands. Those horses were bigger, stronger, and faster than anything in Northern Shala or Tyree. It had to do with how their muscles were trained to move in the shifting desert sand. After that, firm ground and grass must seem like a luxury to them.

However, to my surprise, Ardimus didn't choose horses for our journey. He chose an animal that my mother had told me about when I was younger. I had never truly believed her stories; I always thought she was exaggerating or making things up to amuse me.

These...camels, she and Ardimus called them, were far larger than any horse I had seen. I gawked at the two large humps of what looked like fat on their backs. I petted one of the beasts, surprised at how thick the fur was that covered his body. How was that supposed to help him survive the desert heat?

Ardimus chuckled at the expression on my face. "I take it you've not seen camels before."

I shook my head. "No, but my mother told me about them. I didn't believe her." I ran my fingers through the camel's thick fur. "I don't understand. How are these going to help us? Wouldn't horses be faster? Every second, Premier gets further and further away from us."

Ardimus fed the other one oats while he talked. "True, but remember how I said a desert can be an even worse enemy than a sword? If Premier pushes himself hard enough, the desert might finish him off for us. Camels are slower than horses, but they can travel great distances and carry far more than a horse ever could, requiring less food and water. We will ride hard, but not to the point of exhaustion. Agreed?"

"Agreed."

We loaded our supplies onto our camels, and as Ardimus had said, they didn't even flinch. We left Kadir and traveled west toward the desert city of Falak.

CHAPTER 11

WITH EACH PASSING moment, the sun burned brighter and the ground became harder and drier. After two days, the earth became sand. It slowed the camels down, and to me it was like we moved through molasses. I ached to spur the camels onward. Time was working against me, both for finding Premier, and curing Krystal.

But neither the camels nor the desert cared about any of that. The camels strolled across the rolling mounds of sand, taking their time and frustrating me with every hoof impression in the sand. Despite the clothes I had received from Samir, the heat still seared me. I now understood the need for the headdress, as there was no place to hide from the sun. The clouds had vanished, taking not only my meager shade but a piece of my hope.

During the day, the sweat dripped down my body, only to be instantly devoured by the dry air. It amazed and surprised me how sand could get everywhere. It embedded itself in my boots, hid in the strands of my hair, and settled itself in cracks and folds of my body that I didn't even know I had.

As suffocating as the blazing heat was, the nights were lovely and weren't anything like I had imagined. When we camped, I would gaze up at the flashing stars, watching their silent chorus. The cool breeze, while bringing more sand into my crevices, was a welcome reprieve from the day's smothering heat. Still, as I lay back and stared up at the stars, I wondered if Premier was watching the same stars. How far were we behind him?

Ardimus also stared up at the night sky. But unlike me, he didn't gawk at the view, and marvel at being in such a strange and different land. He studied the positions of the stars and planned the next day's direction from them. He even showed me how, or tried to.

While I knew of the brightest star in the sky, called Mind's Eye, and had navigated using it before, I had trouble telling the other stars apart. Ardimus pointed out the stars to me, telling me that one group of stars was a scorpion, and another a camel. Sadly, I didn't see any of that when I gazed at them. I only saw bright lights scattered over our world.

The Burning Sands were just as deadly as the Wastelands of Renak, but their dangers were far more subtle. The desert threatened to kill you with its suffocating heat. I ached to down the contents of my waterskin and soothe my parched throat, but Ardimus taught me to ration our water with nothing more than a capful.

The fourth day we were out in the desert, I had a scare. A large black critter fell from my boot when I was shaking the sand from it one morning. I jumped back and scrambled away as the scorpion ran across the desert sand. Ardimus laughed and told me if I was going to take my boots off that I should turn them upside down.

I didn't take off my boots again.

After nearly two weeks of travel, I stared into the horizon like I normally did, searching for Premier and questioning how much longer it'd be before we reached the city. The wind picked up and howled. I tugged the headdress tighter around my head to try to keep the sand from shooting into my eyes.

Ardimus tugged back on his camel's reins and stopped. I rode up beside him and asked, "What is it?"

He was silent for a time, scanning the landscape. "Could be nothing or it could be a sandstorm. If it is, we'll have to take cover, and quickly."

I nodded and began thinking of ways to use my magic to help against the sandstorm. I had tried to use my magic against the sand once, but the environment hammered at my spell until it buckled. It was a waste of energy and in this dry climate, I couldn't afford to waste anything.

Ardimus came to a stop. He slid down his camel and put his hand on his scimitar.

I slid off my camel and readied my magic. "What's wrong?"

"Look."

On a low hill fifty feet away, small whirlwinds appeared, blowing in our direction.

"What it is?" I asked.

"Sand devils."

More twisters appeared behind us and to the sides. They all spun toward our location.

"Remember my words," he said.

I did. I squashed the fire mana that came to my command and tried to summon water. However, it didn't come easily. I couldn't draw it from my environment, and because of the horrible outside heat, my body was reluctant to give it up.

A dozen sand devils surrounded us and gave me no time to concentrate. Their wind-like movement blew sand in our faces, and I turned away. I summoned my magic to force the winds to disperse. Nothing happened. Whatever these sand devils were, they might have looked like wind, but they weren't.

"Protect the camels!" Ardimus shouted as the animals bucked in fear.

I fought my way through the sand devils' wind to grab the camels' reins. The tiny storms grew in strength the closer they got to us, and since they surrounded us, it was like we were at the center of a huge, intensifying storm.

Ardimus attacked the twisters, his sword swinging through the air like a bird in flight. It was strange seeing him attack the wind, as the little whirlwinds twisted and dodged his blows.

From the corner of my eye, I saw one of the whirlwinds stop on the other side of the camels. The wind near the camels ceased, and a three-fingered hand grabbed at one of the camels' reins. Two more whirlwinds appeared, and then their wind vanished, to be replaced by little brown creatures smaller than goblins. Rocks and sand covered their scaly bodies, blending with the environment, and tiny horns protruded from their heads. They ignored me, grabbing at our belongings. One managed to break the straps and our things fell to the ground. They scrambled to steal what was ours.

While I might have had trouble summoning water, surely these creatures couldn't be completely immune to magic. With my free hand, I used magic I would never have trouble with—fire. I created a simple fireball and hurled it at one of them. It crashed against the creature and dispersed. It was as if the creatures were enchanted against magic, like Ardimus's armor. How much magic could those little creatures deflect? If I increased my power, could they withstand it?

I cast a thermal blast, and its long flame splashed against one of them. I pumped more magic into it, its body turning crimson as it heated up. With a little more time, I knew I could reach its breaking point. But while I was focusing on one, the others stole more from us. One such creature took all it could carry and twisted away.

I couldn't waste any more time. I took the water from my body and used it to fuel my water spell. The moisture in my skin and mouth evaporated. My head spun, and I held onto the reins to keep from collapsing. I needed water, and one of the little devils was about to make off with our skins. The water coalesced into my hand, swirling until it became a ball. I used my last bit of strength and slung the waterball at the devil.

Unlike my fire, the water breached the sand devil's defenses. It struck the creature and he shrieked in pain. His scaly, rock-covered body burst into flame. The water melted away his covering, exposing bloody flesh. He glared at me and hissed. He broke off one of the sharp rocks on an undamaged part of his body and wielded it like a weapon.

Another sand devil leapt onto the top of the camel and peered at me. His dark brown eyes widened in surprise and in Caleea he said, *"A wizard! We must retreat."*

The burned one brandished his sharp rock and glowered at me. *"But he struck me!"*

The other hissed at him. *"You know the rules. We're not allowed to go against wizards. Leave everything."*

"But—"

"We honor our agreement, even if they do not honor theirs."

His fierce eyes met mine before he leaped from the camel's back onto the ground. He grabbed the one I had injured and they twisted away, transforming into whirlwinds once more. The others dropped what they had taken and headed back into the desert.

"What just happened?" Ardimus asked, looking in the direction the sand devils had gone. "I've never seen anything like that before."

"They left because I'm a wizard."

"No," he said. "It's more than that." He sheathed his sword and paused. "There was an old story I heard when I was a child. 'The twisters are numerous and quick as the eye can see. They'll steal your belongings, leaving you to die as they flee.' That line obviously talked about the sand devils, but there was another line I've never given much thought to until now. 'They were an ancient race who once almost died. Until they escaped their fate and the Great Divide.'"

I waited for Ardimus to continue. He didn't.

"And?" I asked.

"That's it. That's all I can remember of it. It wasn't an epic poem. We don't know much about the sand devils. No one's been able to find out where their lair is or where they even come from. We know they're somewhere out here, deep in the Burning Sands, but that's it."

I thought about what the sand devil had said. They had an agreement with wizards—with us.

"No," I said. "It's something more. Do you think wizards were…responsible for changing them into what they are?"

"I don't know." Ardimus reached down and picked up a skin of water. "Drink all of it."

I shook my head, but still took it. I tried to stop after a couple of sips, as usual, but my body wouldn't allow me to. I had used too much of myself in such a simple spell.

I wiped my slimy mouth when I was finished and stared off into the direction the creatures had gone. I wondered what wizards were out here besides Premier, and what they were up to. Before I brought the Great Barrier down, wizards were few and far between north of the barrier. Because of the

War of the Wizards, after the war was over, a lot of wizards were blamed and persecuted. The few left were either killed or went into hiding. While I hadn't heard any stories of the remaining wizards when I was living in my small village of Sedah, that meant very little. They hadn't been doing nothing all this time, and with the barrier down, who knows what they might be up to? Who knows what else I might be responsible for?

"Let's gather our things," Ardimus said.

Ardimus and I went around the area, scooping up the belongings the sand devils had scattered. Not all of our supplies were there. From what I could tell, about half were gone.

"How bad is it?" I asked.

Ardimus's eyes briefly stared at the empty water skin I had just drunk. "We have enough to make it to Falak. We'll have to ration our food and water even more, but we'll make it."

I hoped so. I hadn't come this far to die in a desert.

CHAPTER 12

WE PUSHED ONWARD toward Falak, trying to outrace our ever-dwindling supplies. We cut back on rations and gave what we could to our camels. Ardimus gave me most of his supply of water. He never once complained about the heat or his thirst, but no matter how much I drank, my mouth was never satisfied.

My thoughts wandered to Premier. Was he half dying of thirst like we were? Part of me hoped so, but the other half wanted him to pay for his crimes. And I wanted to be the one to dole out justice.

Through the suffocating heat, thoughts of Krystal and a future with her were what kept me going. Though I knew it was a bad idea, I had to check up on her. One night, when Ardimus was fast asleep, I decided to summon another maleika.

I was well away from our encampment. For previous maleika summonings, I had always tried to build traps in case that one-eyed monster showed up, but I was too exhausted from the desert sun and the effects of our ever-shrinking supplies. It wouldn't be long, I told myself. I only needed to see if she was all right and that I wasn't too late. What were the chances of summoning that same maleika again?

Since our run-in with the sand devils, we had been talking less to conserve water. I was barely able to finish the ritual, as I had a hard time opening up my sticky mouth to say the words.

I blinked my heavy eyes to bring the maleika into view. The night sky covered its blemishes, and its ghostly body blended in with the desert behind it. I focused on where I wanted to send it and the maleika disappeared.

My body was weak from the day's journey. I needed more water than we were rationed, and a day's rest that didn't involve the sun, sand, or wind.

An image appeared in front of me, but I could barely see anything in the dim light. I expected or hoped that Krystal would be lying in bed, getting some well-deserved rest. Instead, as I forced the maleika to give me a better view, I found Krystal kneeling in front of an altar. Candlelight danced around her and she prayed in front of an altar to Emery, the Goddess of Fire. Krystal's eyes were closed and her mouth, was moving though I heard no sound.

As I watched her, my heart lightened at how healthy she looked. She had regained some of the weight she'd lost and her skin looked healthier. I reached out to stroke her cheek, noticing that it wasn't as hollow as it was the last time I'd seen her. I stopped myself, remembering that she wasn't really there, and that I couldn't physically touch her.

Before I was ready, the image of Krystal shimmered and faded, to be replaced by the maleika. As it came into focus, there was something about it that looked familiar. That's when I was finally able to see that it was missing one eye.

I instinctively summoned my fire as a barrier. The creature spoke in a deep and dark language, and it froze my flames. Its spell then froze my entire body, and I couldn't move.

"I've had time to study you, Hellsfire," it said in Caleea.

I struggled against his magic with my own, but every time I tried to fight it, its spell sapped the heat from my fire.

It glared at me with its good eye. *"Predictable, as always."*

I figured out what he meant and stopped fighting his magic with my fire. I needed to try a different spell, but my energy was so depleted. It had nothing to do with the creature and everything to do with the desert. I tried to cry out for help, but the maleika stopped me.

"I've never understood the love you humans have for each other. You're as bad as the fairies." The maleika floated closer to me and hovered around my head. *"I've*

killed many wizards that were foolish enough to summon me over the years, but I'm going to enjoy this. Your kind has enslaved and abused my people for centuries. One day, wizard, we will have our revenge. But first, your *master cost me my eye. I'm going to take another apprentice away from him."*

The maleika floated toward my head and I knew what it was going to do. The last time I had run into it, it had drained away my magic. That must have been where it got all its magic from—from dozens or maybe even hundreds of wizards slain over the centuries.

My fingers twitched from all the non-fire magic I had summoned. The colors of mana swirled in my hands, but I wasn't able to focus it into a simple blast. The magic within raged against me. With no way to release it, the storm fought against my body. My eyes wanted to burst and blood trickled down my nose.

The maleika grinned at me in delight and anticipation, knowing there was nothing I could do to stop it. Its ghostly form reached out to me, trying to absorb my power.

A blade sliced through the air and into the maleika. Ardimus's scimitar shone with magical energy as it passed through the creature. The maleika's magic had been severed and I was able to move again. Ardimus's weapon also cut loose the spell I had used to summon the creature here.

I brought my hand up and unleashed a fury of energy at it, illuminating the night sky for miles. My magic struck it and it howled in rage before its ghostly head faded from existence.

Ardimus's hand reached out to me. "Are you all right, Hellsfire?"

I took a deep breath and shook my head. He helped me stand, but I wobbled against him.

"Here, have some water."

I looked at him. We didn't have much left. He pushed it into my hand and I drank it. "Thank you."

"What were you doing?"

"I...I was summoning a maleika. I had to check on the princess."

"And how is she?"

I nodded. "She looks better than when we last saw her."

"Good. I suggest we get some rest. We still have a long journey ahead of us." Ardimus walked back to the encampment.

I didn't move. I stared at the spot where the maleika had been. What did the maleika mean when it said it had been studying me, and how could that have been possible? It either performed its own rituals in the Netherrealm or...

My eyes widened as I realized my mistake. Just as I was using the maleika to spy, it must have used its fellow creatures to spy on me. I could no longer summon maleika without giving it any more information.

Days continued to pass. We walked our camels so that they could take brief periods of rest, but we grew too tired from doing even that. We clung onto them for life while they carried as across the desert. With our lightened supplies and even lighter bodies, they didn't seem to mind. Yet with each passing day, I felt their fattened bodies get thinner and their pillowy mounds of flesh recede.

After a fortnight had passed from our encounter with the sand devils, Ardimus spoke.

"Finally." His voice was raspy and dry. He may not have complained about the lack of water but he needed it as badly as I did. Maybe more since I drank more water than him.

I lifted my tired head up from the camel and glimpsed something off in the distance. Near the horizon, were the outlines of a city. I didn't get my hopes up, as I didn't trust my sight. For weeks I had seen images near the horizon—a small village, trees, a castle, Premier even, but none of them were true. As I chased them down, I had learned the hard way that they were nothing but mirages. They were tricks brought on by the heat, my desires, and lack of water. This time, though, I might not have trusted my eyes, but I did trust Ardimus.

He perked up in his saddle and the corners of his mouth curled up in a smile. His gaze never once turned away from the horizon. It was then that I knew that we had reached our destination.

"Thank the gods," I managed.

I had grown up in a small village, but when I was set upon my path to become a wizard, it had taken me to faraway places and huge cities. And while I had grown used to enormous buildings and crowds of people, there was always a sense of wonder and awe when I visited a new city for the first time. Falak was no different in that respect, but compared to the other cities I had been to, it was very different.

Falak was surrounded by the bleak desert landscape for miles and miles. As we rode closer, the first thing I noticed was the lack of hard stone or wooden structures, like I was used to. The buildings were all constructed from brick.

I soon realized why. Brick could be made from the surrounding earth; it was the only building material they had that didn't need to be imported. Ardimus told me there was a river northwest of Falak, which provided water for the city as well as for mixing with certain kinds of earth to make their bricks. In Kadir, only some of the buildings were circular. In Falak, almost every building had that circular design. Yet very few of the buildings were higher than two stories, and those were usually set off from the others, as if owned by very wealthy people who could afford a bit of land. The majority of the buildings were densely packed. There were roads between the clusters of buildings, but even those were only wide enough for two loaded camels to travel side by side. Despite how close the buildings were, I noticed quite a few narrow alleys someone could squeeze through.

It felt like an eternity before we reached the stables. I almost collapsed as I slid off my sweat-soaked camel.

"Stay here," Ardimus said. "I'll be back."

I nodded. I took deep breaths, watching the puddles of sweat build up in the sand beneath me.

"Here," Ardimus said, returning and handing me a skin of water. "Drink."

I stared at him, rubbing my throbbing forehead, thinking he hadn't been gone that long. Right near the stables, a vendor had set up shop. Underneath his tented cover, I spotted a devious smile on his face as he played with the coins in his hands.

I didn't care about any of that right now. I gulped the water, letting the cool liquid dribble out of my mouth and down my throat.

"Easy," Ardimus said. "Easy. We'll have plenty of water now." He waited patiently as I sat on the ground, using his shadow for shade. When I finished with the entire skin of water, I looked up at him. "Ready?"

"Yes."

Ardimus helped me stand. "Good. According to the man who sold us the water, a man fitting Premier's description was last seen in the city two days ago, and he's still wearing his robes, even in all this heat." He looked toward the marketplace and the throng of people there. "If the gods stay with us, we'll find him before he can get the Jewel of Dakara. Even Premier has to sleep, eat, and resupply. He'll also need to find out where the jewel is, if he hasn't already. Serling might know where it is, and we can cut Premier off before he reaches it."

"What if Premier goes to Serling to get the information on the jewel?"

Ardimus's cheek muscle flexed, but he didn't say a word. He didn't have to. We knew what would happen if Premier found Serling.

Yet we didn't head directly toward Serling's place. Ardimus said he kept to himself, and it was unlikely that Premier would hear of him, even if he made inquiries about people who studied antiquities. His home was all the way on the other side of Falak, and Ardimus thought it best we start from the marketplace—or bazaar, as he said it was called. Someone there would have seen Premier, and there was a small chance we'd run into him there now.

I stayed behind Ardimus, watching as he conversed in his own language. A few of the vendors greeted him, but didn't remember seeing Premier. They dealt with a lot of different people each day. Others weren't in the mood to be bothered, as they were too busy working. This was just what Ardimus told me. I had a feeling, though, there was more to it than he said.

While Ardimus talked to the vendors, I scanned the crowds, looking for Premier. His robes would make him stand out. Why didn't he change clothes? Was it because those were a wizard's robes he wore, and there was a bond between him and the robes? I missed my robes, but I didn't feel as if I was missing a part of me.

I drifted away from Ardimus, when something in a nearby stall caught my eye. The attractive vendor held out a brass necklace. A large, bright green stone was attached to it and a black swirl ran across it.

2

She spoke in Ardimus's language, but it was far too fast for me. She saw the trouble I had and said in a language I could understand, "You like? You should buy for pretty girl."

"How much?"

Before she could respond, Ardimus came back to the stall. "Kalila, still selling jewelry for your parents?"

"Still employed by Alexandria, Ardi?" The thick accent in her voice almost disappeared and her words cleared up. "We all do what we must." Kalila peered past our heads. "Where *is* the princess? I see no delegation from Alexandria. It's not time for one of your visits, though you've not had one in quite a while."

Ardimus folded his arms. "I'm here of my own accord."

"As I was saying before you rudely interrupted me...," the woman said, turning to me, "Young man, would you like to buy some jewelry? A handsome man like you must have a woman at home. This exquisite piece would win her heart even more."

I glanced to Ardimus for advice.

He shrugged. "It's up to you, but I wouldn't bother with this piece. She already has a necklace. And Kalila, please don't show Hellsfire the little trinkets you sell other travelers. Show him a piece I know you're worthy of making."

She cocked her head, with an expression that doubted whether I had the coin or not. "Very well."

Kalila set aside the necklace on the table and reached behind her. She pulled out a chest, unlocked it, and turned it to face me. She leaned in close and whispered, "She'll love this, and more importantly, she'll love you for it."

While I thought the necklace she had shown me earlier was an interesting piece to buy for Mother, I wasn't believing the sweet words she kept whispering in my ear. Nor did I think she had anything worthy of a princess.

Yet when Kalila lifted the lid, I gasped stifling my surprise too late. A shining gold garland had been crafted into a crown. I recognized a few of the images that decorated it, such as a lizard and scorpion, both creatures I had seen in my journey here. But there were others I didn't recognize. I lightly traced my fingertips over those images. One had a bottom half made of a whirlwind of sand. But the top half was humanoid and very angry.

"Ah," Kalila said, "that's Amrath, one of the gods of the desert. And that mortal woman next to him is Chira." She lowered her voice and I leaned forward to hear her. "One day, Amrath fell in love with Chira. It wasn't her beauty that won him over, but her kind heart. Amrath was an angry god and yet, Chira was able to soothe his temper, like all women do for men. For a time, they lived happily and he gave up his powers to live as a mortal with her. Yet, all was not well. The gods grew jealous of the life Amrath led. While they knew they couldn't kill him, they could strike at Chira.

"After a hard day of hunting, Amrath came home to find his beloved Chira dying. He rushed to her but despite all of his power, there was nothing he could do. Before Chira died, she whispered for him to let it go. But he couldn't. His rage and grief consumed him so much that he became the sandstorms in the desert."

She leaned even closer and whispered. "On those days when Amrath remembers his beloved, those are the days when it's best to find shelter." Kalila smiled at me, and I couldn't help but smile back.

"Kalila was always able to weave quite the tale," Ardimus said. I suddenly remembered he was there. "However, she does also excel in her craftsmanship."

"Do you think she'll like it?" I asked.

"She'd love it!" Kalila said, clasping her hands together. "Any woman worth her sand would."

I lifted the diadem up and marveled at how detailed the pieces carved into it were. I knew it would set me back a lot, but I believed Krystal was worth it and that she would love it.

"Kalila may be right," Ardimus said. "Unfortunately, the princess would not be able to wear it in public, no matter how lovely it looks."

I frowned and set the crown back into the box. "Thank you for showing me this, and for telling me a wonderful story."

She took the chest away and locked it up. "Very well. It was nice to meet you..."

"Hellsfire," I said. When I said my name, her smile stiffened. "And the pleasure is all mine."

"Kali, your shop is set up in a prime location. You can see all those who enter Kadir from the west. Have you seen a man? He—"

She grinned and twirled the ends of her thick, dark brown hair. "I see a lot of men coming to the city. Jealous, Ardi?"

"This is serious. This one you wouldn't forget. He was here not more than two days ago. He'd be traveling alone, wearing thick, black robes, his skin blackened and burned."

Kalila caught her breath. "I remember."

"Good. I need you to send word to the others to track him if he's still in the city."

"Ardi, I remember being wise enough to stay away from him." Despite the hot desert air she shivered. "I thought he was dangerous, and if you're looking for him, now I know how dangerous he is."

"He's a wizard," Ardimus said. "If he's still in the city, I need to find out where he is. Tell the others to stay away from him if they find him, and send a few people to guard Serling."

Kalila barked a laugh. "Still giving orders? And you think Serling needs protection, even from a wizard?"

"I'm serious, Kali."

"So am I." She gave a high-pitched whistle, and a little girl who was begging on the corner, ran over to us. Kalila spoke in her native language before handing the girl coin.

"Still using children?" Ardimus asked as he rolled his eyes and sighed.

"You underestimate them," she said, watching as the little girl scampered away. "People believe them to be nothing but street urchins, but they're the eyes and ears of the city. Your brother knew that."

Ardimus was silent for several moments while his expression became slack. "Maybe. Thank you, Kali, for your help."

Her eyebrows rose.

"Before I go, I'd like to buy that necklace for my mother."

"Oh, you mean this little trinket I showed your friend?"

"Did I say trinket? I meant exquisite piece of art."

That and the money Ardimus handed Kalila was enough for her to be satisfied. Her eyes gleamed in the sunlight. "Just like old times, Ardi."

Ardimus didn't say a word. The two gazed at each other and I felt like an intruder. I took a step back and Ardimus finally spoke. "It was good to see you again, Kali. It's been too long."

As he pulled away, she brushed her hand over Ardimus's. He gave a brief smile, one I had never seen on him before.

"Our people—Kali's people—will find Premier if he's still here."

"All right…Ardi," I said and smiled.

He shrugged. "It's a childhood nickname."

As we walked away from Kalila's stall, I couldn't help but wonder about the man called "Ardi." We had gotten to know each other well in our search for Premier, but I had a feeling I would learn more about him while we were in his hometown.

We headed for Serling's place, but it was on the other side of the city. It was going to be a few hours before we got there.

Music rang through my ears. The more we walked, the louder it became, and its fast-paced rhythm drew me. The narrow, dusty road opened up to a city square. Three other main roads connected to it. In the center, a crowd had gathered. I pushed my way to the front of the crowd.

The drummer sat on the ground, banging his hands on the drums. His head bobbed with each passing beat and he smiled at the crowd. To his left, a woman played the violin. She closed her eyes, swaying her body with each rhythmic note. She never once opened her eyes, as her brow furrowed and sweat dripped down her face. If she did, she might break her concentration.

The last of the trio was a slender woman who danced in the small space granted her. She swirled with a bright pink sash strung across her back, connecting her arms. Her light feet never faltered as she contorted her twisting body, and she never stopped smiling at the crowd. In between her fingers were small cymbals, and amazingly, she even played to the beat the three of them created. Her dark brown eyes soon found mine. She must have seen the stunned look on my face, because she gave me a brief wink before turning back to the crowd.

Ardimus stepped to my side. I was about to give the musicians a coin, but Ardimus dropped a silver coin into their copper jar. The drummer's eyes met Ardimus's then moved deliberately to the left. At the edge of the crowd, a hooded figure turned and walked away. Ardimus and I left the entertainment and followed.

The hooded figure moved faster. Ardimus and I did the same. The throng of people thinned out as we reached the edge of the square. The figure hurried down the road, sliding past people. I gathered my magic, ready to cast a spell. The figure turned left and squeezed into a narrow alleyway. Ardimus and I ran to it, but when we reached it, the figure was gone.

We squeezed into the alley, and that's when the figure dropped down from the low roofs behind us. Daggers hung on his waist. He glared at Ardimus, speaking in their native tongue. I readied my magic, but waited to follow Ardimus's lead.

Instead of reaching for his sword, Ardimus threw back his head and laughed. I dropped my guard as the man went to Ardimus and they hugged. The pair conversed for a minute, with me only understanding every tenth word or so.

Ardimus seemed to remember I was there. "Forgive me, Hellsfire. This is Rasul. He said that living in Northern Shala has made me soft, if he got the drop on me." He clasped the man on his shoulder. "He also told me that they've found Premier."

Rasul spoke again.

"All right, thank you." Ardimus said.

The pair hugged once again. Then Rasul turned to me, put his fingers to his forehead and bowed. I returned the gesture. He scampered up the side of the building and back to the low rooftops.

"Premier has frequented the old part of Falak. It's a place where people go to hide, to sell illegal goods, and seek information."

"That was quick," I said.

"Words can travel faster than the wind. Let's go."

We continued down the alleyway, heading deeper into Falak. It was getting late and the low buildings were starting to block out the twilight. While I was thankful for the shade, the shadows could hide all sorts of things. Ardimus told me that because of how densely packed the city buildings were, there were people like Rasul who would traverse the city using the low rooftops. Wealthy people hired rooftop guards, but where we were going there would be none.

I expected to hear feet thumping above us, but I didn't hear any. That didn't stop me from feeling as if we were being followed.

"Ardimus," I said, glancing over my shoulder. "I—"

"I know," he said, never looking up. "It could be an enemy of mine, a friend, or even a spy."

"Do you think Premier knows we're coming for him?"

"Possibly. You've said Premier has lived centuries. His travels may have taken him even to Falak, and he may know the city as well as I do."

We finally reached the area where Rasul said Premier had been spotted. The buildings in the older part of Falak were dirtier, and many were cracked and crumbling. The throngs of people we had seen earlier in the bazaar were nowhere to be found. The few people in the streets were either hurrying home, or huddled together in tight groups.

We passed near a group of six and a sly smile crossed one's face. He took one look at Ardimus and his smile vanished. Ardimus was a hardened warrior, that much I knew, but I doubt his sword and armor was what kept them away.

We rounded a corner just in time to see a person with thick black robes at the end of the street. I couldn't make out his face, but I could sense the power he wielded.

"Premier," I said.

There was a sheen of magic around him. He must have been using it to keep the stifling heat from affecting him.

I took a step closer, but Ardimus touched my forearm. "Wait. I have another idea."

I followed him as he led me to an alley. At the bottom of the building was a thin hole, like a slot. He reached into it and pulled out a small ladder. He leaned it against the building and we scrambled up. On top of the roof, he paused with his hand on the hilt of his scimitar. If we were still being followed, I didn't see or sense anyone, but that didn't necessarily mean anything. The buildings might not have been tall, but their curving shapes made plenty of small crevices for the shadows to blossom, and for people to hide in, even under the bright night sky.

Ardimus traveled across the rooftops, barely making a noise. He reminded me of the way the elves moved in a forest. My feet weren't as sure, and I thought Premier might hear my heavy footsteps. I had a hard time keeping up with Ardimus, and I couldn't use my magic lest Premier sense it.

Ardimus was perched near the edge of a building. I finally caught up to him, trying not to breathe heavily. We watched as Premier disappeared into another building.

Ardimus inhaled.

"What is it?"

"That's one of Rasmera's storehouses. You do not want to cross her path. The fact that he's allowed into it unchallenged means she's let him in."

"Does she know anything about the Jewel of Dakara?" I asked.

"She knows a lot, and has her hands in almost as many things."

"Can you get us inside?"

Ardimus leaned in closer and said nothing for several moments. "Yes. But we must be as quick as possible."

"Understood."

I wondered what this Rasmera had done to Ardimus to make him fear her so, but now was not the time for that.

~ **117** ~

We crept across the rooftops until we reached the one Premier had gone into. I guarded and scouted the area while Ardimus picked the lock. When he was finished, we crept inside. Clay pots and crates were everywhere, with a few wooden crates sprinkled in between them. Could one of these containers hold what Premier was looking for?

I followed Ardimus as we snuck downstairs. The dim light shining through the windows was the only light in the building. Yet I knew we were headed in the right direction because I felt Premier's magic. The closer we got to him, the more I felt how different it was from mine. He didn't use magic to protect him from the weather. He used his robes to protect him from the weather.

How did he do such a thing? I remember learning that a wizard's robes were more than clothing. That they would become part of the wizard. Had Premier mastered that? What else could his robes do?

We watched him as he rummaged through one of the clay caskets. His back was to us, and I didn't sense him raising any sort of magical defenses. I could easily attack him, or even kill him, before he knew what was happening.

Killing him was tempting. Premier had no mercy and no conscience. If he escaped, there was no telling what terrible things he would do in the future. I could try to capture him, but even if I succeeded, it was unlikely that he'd tell how to cure the princess. I felt the black fire wanting to rise up in me.

I shook my head. That wasn't my way. Even though Premier had killed and hurt countless innocents and deserved to pay for his crimes, I couldn't kill him from behind with no warning. I had killed before, and would do so again, but never that way. I wouldn't be able to live with myself if I did, even if it was Premier.

I motioned for Ardimus to come closer. "I'll capture him in bonds of air," I whispered. I reached into my bag and drew out one of the binding collars. "I may not be able to hold him long, but it should be long enough for you to put the collar on him. Stay alert, though. He's tricky."

Ardimus nodded and took the collar. I reached out with my power and struck.

It didn't come. I felt a small, steady outflow of power, almost like he was maintaining a web or a shield, but not quite. What was he up to? "Premier, I'm only going to give you one chance," I said. "Surrender to the collar, or die where you stand."

Premier sighed. The bonds of air flexed and pushed back—not as if he were trying to break them, but as if he were trying to make room to move inside them. Why?

Premier said, "Why is it always you who troubles me? The gods must hate me for cursing me with you. Now, I know you couldn't have tracked me here to Falak alone. Who is with you?"

I heard Ardimus unsheathe his sword. "I am," he said.

"Princess Krystal's lapdog, of course."

Premier turned slowly to face us, although my bonds should have held him fast. Two hate-filled eyes glared at me. His skin had been burned, and spots of his face had that unnatural shine and smoothness from being healed over. I realized that my bonds of air still encircled him, but he was managing to hold them a few inches away from his body, so he could move a tiny bit. Instead of being ropes binding him, they were more like a tight cage. I wondered why he didn't fight me harder. His power had never been the same since the day I had burned him with my hellsfire, but I had learned not to underestimate him because of that. Premier had lived a long life, and he knew spells that I couldn't even imagine.

"Whatever you're trying, it won't work," I said. "We know what you're after. You're not getting your hands on the Jewel of Dakara. I promise you that if you surrender now, you will face a fair and swift trial, and a merciful death."

"Is that all?" he asked.

I gathered in all the power I could, ready for Premier to make his move. I sensed no magic building up in him, but I never turned my gaze away from him.

He went on in that same bored tone. "As annoying as you've been over the last couple of years, boy, you have become rather predictable."

Inside the cage of air, Premier's hands moved like lightning. Reaching into the folds of his robes, he pulled out a potion and smashed the vial onto the ground. A gray haze of smoke rose among the broken pieces, quickly moving out into the room. I summoned air to blow it away from me with one hand, holding onto Premier's cage with the other.

"Collar him!" I called to Ardimus. "Quick! Before his potion can affect me!"

I heard Ardimus striding down the steps behind me. The wizard smiled triumphantly, and I knew something was wrong. "I admit, I had no idea if you would be coming for me, boy," Premier said. "But I did know that if one person was going to catch up to me in this desert wasteland, it would be him." Premier looked over my shoulder.

I turned in time to see Ardimus's scimitar slicing through the air toward me. I dodged the blow, but in doing so, my grip on the air magic holding Premier loosened.

"Ardimus, what are you doing?" I gasped. But as I asked the question, I already knew the answer.

The potion Premier had cast covered Ardimus's weapon and chainmail. His items had been enchanted by magic, and had been used against magic many times. Instead of fighting against them with magic as Premier had done before, he'd twisted them to be controlled by his magic.

Ardimus's muscles bulged and strained as he struggled to put his sword down or back away. "I'm sorry, Hellsfire, I can't control myself."

Premier crept forward, pushing against my bonds, and I backed away from him and Ardimus, gathering my power once more. I was acutely aware of how small Rasmera's storeroom was. Premier's dark power built. Could I take them both? Even if I could, I didn't want to hurt Ardimus.

"I'm going to enjoy this," Premier said. His power flexed, and the air bonds slipped out of my grasp. He advanced on me, his hate-filled eyes nearly glowing. "And once I'm done with you, the proud warrior shall fall on his own sword."

A shadow flickered in the background. A lithe, hooded figure raised a dagger, aiming for Premier's back. Ardimus countered the blow, deflecting it.

"Ardimus, what are you doing?" The figure pulled back its hood, revealing a tall, slender woman. She brushed aside a lock of her curly red hair.

"Wynna!" Ardimus gasped. "Stay…back."

"No," she said. "You must stop this madness!"

"I…can't."

"Enough talking," Premier said. "Kill her."

He forced Ardimus to attack her. She parried and dodged his blows, using her agility and speed. She was quite nimble, but made no move to counterattack. She clearly didn't want to injure Ardimus, though Premier wasn't giving her much of a choice. Her being here gave me the opportunity I needed.

With Premier keeping Ardimus on strings, and him already weakened from when I first defeated him, I wondered if he could take me one on one. I glanced at the collar on the ground. If I could defeat Premier, there would be no more need for it.

Subtlety was never my strong point, and I needed something powerful to break Premier's concentration on Ardimus. I conjured my fire and shot it at Premier. It coalesced into a fist, smashing into him.

I let my anger fuel my spell, remembering how Krystal had been nearly dead when I arrived in Alexandria. He had no regard for human life. Everyone was just a thing to him, to be used for his purposes. He would throw people's lives away like they were table scraps.

Premier's defenses buckled against my magical onslaught, the flames smothering him. In the back of my mind, whisperings of the dark fire I once used promised that it could finish what it started. It was hard to fight it because I wanted to extinguish Premier's life more than anything.

Suddenly, my fires receded. It wasn't Premier, it was Ardimus pushing against my magic. His sword held my flames at bay, and he pushed them back as he advanced toward me. I cut off the fire and stared at the potion clinging to Ardimus.

"Wizard!" the woman yelled. "How do we break the spell?" She still had her daggers out. Blood trickled down her forehead.

There were plenty of ways to neutralize the potion without harming Ardimus. Those would take time. There was a fast way to do it, but it might injure Ardimus.

"Water," I said.

Wynna moved, heading toward one of the clay pots in the storeroom. Premier raised his hand and a bolt of lightning shot out from it. She twirled just in time just for it to miss her. She pulled the lid off the pot and flung it at

Premier, forcing him to duck. While he was distracted, she heaved up the pot and threw its contents at Ardimus.

The water drenched him, washing the potion away from his armor and sword and severing Premier's connection with him. Sizzles of energy streaked across his chest and raced up his arm. Ardimus screamed in pain, and his body collapsed to the floor.

"Ardi!" Wynna yelled. I could see she wanted to run to him, but she kept her wary gaze on Premier.

"Impudent wench!" Premier shouted. He used air magic to seize her.

I countered his magic, loosening his grip on her and dropping her to the floor.

Premier rolled up his sleeves and his power rose. "Enough tricks." He turned to face me.

Before he could unleash his magic, Wynna scrambled to her feet and drove one of her daggers into his upper back. Premier roared. The energy he had summoned struck out wildly at her, sending her crashing into the wall. A whole shelf of clay jars broke, leaking their contents on the floor.

Premier ripped the dagger from his shoulder. I could feel his power diminishing with each passing moment. He glanced at me, and then at Wynna as she rose from the ground. Premier knew he couldn't take us both on. Not in the condition he was in. I could sense him using his magic to heal himself.

He narrowed his angry eyes at me. "Until next time, boy."

A gust of wind shot up from the floor, blinding me with sand. Premier then aimed his magic at the level above us. The building shook and the floor above us buckled right above Ardimus. The floor cracked and everything that was stored up there came piling down.

I wove wind magic over Ardimus. All the items above crashed into the protective barrier I held over him, the heavy objects stopping just a foot from crushing him. I grunted, feeling the objects strain against my own body as my magic held them at bay. Chests and containers crashed and broke around him, slicing him with their sharp edges. I couldn't do anything about that.

When I turned my attention to the man responsible, he was gone.

Wynna rushed to Ardimus and pushed aside the fallen objects, pulling him from beneath my spell. When he was clear, I let go of the spell, my body dripping with sweat and my muscles sore.

"How is he?" I asked.

"He's alive, but I'm not sure what's wrong with him."

"Give him this." I reached into my purse and gave her a stabilization potion.

Wynna gave it to him then glanced to an open hole in the wall. "We've got to leave before Rasmera finds us here. Can you carry him?"

The strain of the spell made me sore, but I would help him. "I can."

"Good. I know of a place we can take him."

Wynna grabbed Ardimus's sword, and I lifted him. We departed the storehouse, and I followed Wynna as she led us deeper into Falak.

CHAPTER 13

WE MOVED WITH purpose through the city, ignoring the passers-by. I needed to see what exactly was wrong with Ardimus and how to help him, but we couldn't stop until we had a safe place to rest.

Three blocks later, Wynna led us to a building surrounded by a small wall. She took out a key and opened the gate to an open courtyard. She moved to the door at the end of the courtyard, but before she reached it, the door cracked open and an older woman peeked out.

"Wynna?" The woman's mouth dropped when her dark eyes settled on the man I was supporting. "Ardi!" She flung the door open and ran to him. She babbled off words too fast for me to understand, but I got her meaning.

She bustled into the house. Wynna and I funneled in after her, carrying Ardimus, me ducking under the low archway. Instead of chairs, her home had big, fluffy, bright-colored pillows surrounding a low table not more than two feet high. The woman gathered the pillows and lined them up. She pointed to them, and I gently laid Ardimus on top of them. I rubbed my sore arms.

"Is he...all right?" the woman asked me.

"I wish we had a healer," I said. "I'll need time to figure out what's wrong with him."

"Serling might be able to help, Mina," Wynna said.

The old woman grimaced. "You'd put my son's life in that coot's hands?"

"It may be the only way," Wynna said. She didn't wait for an answer, but slipped out through the door.

When Wynna was gone, I used my wizard's sight to peer into Ardimus's aura. The potion had tugged at his life force when it was washed away, desperately wanting to cling to Ardimus. I carefully cast my magic, coaxing Premier's potion, trying to pull it away from Ardimus. It was slow, and as I worked, Mina stood by me the whole time in silence, watching her son.

When I finished forcing Premier's magic out, I breathed a sigh of relief. Ardimus would recover, given enough time and rest. But that was time we didn't have. Premier would no doubt be heading for the Jewel of Dakara as soon as possible.

"He's all right, mistress," I said. "It might take a few days or even a week, but he'll recover on his own."

Mina breathed easier and finally broke her stillness, putting her fingers to her forehead and whispering a word of prayer in her language. "Thank you. Please call me Mina." She bent down and adjusted the pillow underneath Ardimus's head. She kissed him on the forehead. "You must be the wizard Ardi has told me about in his letters. And where is the princess, Hellsfire?"

I stared at her, wondering how much Ardimus had told his mother. "She's not here."

"Ah." Mina rose and gave me a wry smile. She left and came back with a faded green cup. A thick, blood-like liquid floated inside. "Here, drink this. You look exhausted."

I sipped what she gave me, not wanting to be rude, and the sweet juice tickled my tongue. I gulped nearly half of it. "Thank you."

"It's called jallab. Ardi told me how you enjoy sweets, and while it's too sweet for me, I find you young people enjoy it."

I smiled. "It was delicious."

"I'm glad to hear it." Her smile faded as her eyes settled on her son. "This isn't the first time I've seen Ardi in this condition in my home. There is less blood this time, though." The small woman looked to me. "Has my son told you about his past?"

I shook my head. "Very little."

"That has always been his way." She walked to a large, round, green cushion. "Come, sit."

I obeyed her and sat on another green cushion. I leaned against it, allowing the cushion to suck me in. This was far better than any wooden or stone chair I had sat in, or even most beds.

"My Ardi was once like you," she said.

I stared at the motionless warrior on the other side of the room. This was a man who had been in battle many times, who knew how to wield a sword, who never complained about the heat or lack of water, who was always stoic and quiet. With the exception of our love for Krystal, he was nothing like me.

"He was?" I asked, raising an eyebrow.

She nodded. "Oh yes. My Ardi was an angry child. He got into many fights, and then because of his brother, he joined a gang. For a time, Ardi and Omar ran the streets, doing things I never approved of, getting into trouble and even running afoul of the sultan. Through it all, Ardi used his anger to fight whatever got in their way."

Mina fell silent and a teardrop fell from her eye. "That rage almost consumed Ardi when his brother died. Don't mention this to anyone, but I believe Serling gave him a purpose I never could."

She looked to me. "Ardi's told me of your battles. When he sees you fight, he knows you're doing it for the right reasons, but he also knows you're using your anger as a weapon. He believes it to be a far deadlier weapon than magic."

Ardimus was right. I did use my anger as a weapon, and every time I did so the dark fire's call grew stronger.

"Why hasn't he said anything?" I asked. "He's never mentioned any of this to me."

"He believes a man should find his own path."

"What do you believe?"

She smiled. "I believe men should listen to the women in their lives more."

I smiled back. I couldn't argue with that.

"I'm back," Wynna said, opening the door. She glared at the open door behind her. "I'm sorry. If someone would hurry up, we would have gotten here sooner."

I rose from the cushion just in time to see a long dark wooden staff coming through the door, followed by a man wearing sheer white robes much like I wore. He gasped for breath; his long white ponytail was damp with sweat. He leaned on his staff, panting.

I sensed an aura of magic around the older man. I had never sensed this form of magic before, not even while I was in Tyree. It was faint and it didn't seem like he was gathering in energy for any sinister purpose, but that didn't mean it wasn't dangerous. He might not have been a wizard, but this Serling was something. That much I was sure of.

"Forgive me," he said. "I'm not as young as I used to be."

"Serling," Mina said, her voice low with menace.

"Mistress Mina," he said, and bowed his head. "I thank you for inviting me into your home."

The older woman's chest was thrust out as she stood and pointed a finger at Serling. "You are here for *one* reason—my son. Wynna believed you would be of some use, but Hellsfire has already saved my Ardi. As always, you are useless."

Serling limped closer to Ardimus. He looked behind him, but no one was there. "Sandstorms, where is that blasted girl?"

A teenaged woman, about two years my junior, came through the door. There was a streak of white through her brown hair. Her arms were filled with a huge bag, wider than her thin body. She wobbled, trying to balance her load, but she didn't ask for help. She dropped the bag on the floor, the sweat dripping from her. She opened the bag and began riffling through it.

"Hellsfire," Serling said. "Wynna told me what you three went through, but how is Ardimus now?"

"I was able to counteract what Premier did to him. Given time, he will recover."

"But you don't have time."

"No," I said. "The wizard we're chasing is very dangerous. He must be stopped or he will hurt more people. Every second that passes, he gets further away from us."

"Very well. Alyssa, stop rummaging through that and make yourself useful."

"But we brought all this for a reason," she said, looking up. "To help him."

"He's afflicted with magic. The herbs, potions, and poultices we brought may not help him. You can. Remember what I taught you."

"I will." The young woman inched her way closer to Ardimus, hesitant. I remembered once being like that.

Mina blocked Alyssa's path. "What are you going to do to my son?"

"She's going to try to help him," Serling said in Alyssa's defense. "I know you don't trust me, but I promise you that Ardimus will come to no harm."

Mina's gaze clearly unnerved Alyssa, and the young woman glanced away. Serling, however, returned Mina's stare. Mina stepped aside and returned to me.

"You'll watch them?" she asked.

I nodded.

Alyssa rolled up her sleeves and furrowed her eyebrows. Magic began radiating from her. I perked up; that magic felt familiar. I had been around it before in Tyree. It wasn't magic I'd experienced from other wizards, though. It was magic that I only felt around a witch or sorcerer.

A wizard's magic primarily came from the four elemental gods—fire, wind, water, and earth. But we were able to tap into more than just that magic, including life and death, and the strands that connected all the magics. Those four, however, just came naturally to us.

While I didn't know any witches personally, I had been around them enough to know that the magic they used consisted of strands that interwove the magics together, and they could perform magic that I could only access with a ritual or potion. It wasn't better or worse than mine—just different.

Alyssa gathered in her magic then released it at Ardimus. The others couldn't see it or feel it, but there was no subtlety to it at all. Instead of being a whisper-like healing magic should have been, it was more like a scream. It slammed into Ardimus and his eyes and fingers twitched. I held my magic at the ready in case I had to break her spell.

Alyssa closed her eyes, clasped her hands together, and began chanting. A cocoon of light enveloped Ardimus. His body stiffened and Mina stepped forward. I grabbed her hand before she broke the spell.

The magic ceased, and Alyssa collapsed to the ground. I went to her and bent down to her.

"Take deep calm breaths," I said. "You expanded too much magic. I'm not the greatest at healing, but unless it's an emergency, you should be as careful and subtle as you can. Take your time."

She lifted her tired head, staring at me with wide eyes. "Thank you."

I reached out my hand and she took it.

"My son still sleeps," Mina said, hovering over him.

"It…could take some time," I said, glancing at Alyssa. She bit her lip as she watched Ardimus. I didn't tell Mina all the things that could go wrong with someone as inexperienced as Alyssa performing such magic on Ardimus. I didn't want to worry her.

I faced Serling, still sensing a trace of that unusual magic of his. "What are you? Ardimus told me you weren't a wizard. While I believe him, you *are* something."

Serling limped closer to me. "I'm much like the item you have on your person."

His intense blue eyes studied me. I followed them until I found his gaze resting on my waist. I wondered what he meant. It could be any number of things: my book of magic, my potions, my…and that's when I realized what it was—my father's dagger.

I had taken my dagger to others before, and they didn't understand the magic that it contained. It had saved my life once when it tore a hole into another world. Neither I nor anyone else had ever been able to duplicate that effect, but there was a rare group of people who could.

I narrowed my eyes at Serling. "You're a crosswalker."

"What's a…crosswalker?" Ardimus asked.

"You're awake!" Wynna rushed to Ardimus and kneeled next to him. "How are you feeling?" She took his hand into hers and kissed it.

A huge smile spread across his face. "Firebird, I thought that was you tracking us in the city."

"Good thing I did, otherwise that wizard would have killed you."

His hand squeezed hers. "For our sake, I'm glad to see you've retained your old ways."

Mina left my side and stood next to Wynna. "My son."

He struggled to sit up, despite a silent protest from Wynna. She went to sit beside him. Ardimus said, "Mother, forgive me for coming to you like this."

She gave him a cup of water. "Drink. It's all right. Hellsfire told me everything that happened."

"I'm glad you two have met."

"He is a fine young man. Now how are you?"

Ardimus took a deep breath. "My entire body aches, but I'll be all right. As you know, I've been through far worse." His eyes wandered to Alyssa. "I thank you…"

"Alyssa," she said.

"I felt you work your magic, and I'm grateful for it."

The young woman turned her head and blushed.

"It's good to see you again, Serling. I'm even more impressed that my mother allowed you to come into her home." Ardimus gave a brief smile, but then it vanished. "I've known you for many years. For a time, with all the things you knew, I thought you might be a wizard. Until I met Hellsfire and others, I didn't realize how wrong I was. But you are something. What exactly is a crosswalker?"

Everyone stared at Serling. Ardimus and Wynna had curious looks on their faces, but it surprised me that Alyssa did too. She clearly could perform magic, yet Serling hadn't told her what he was. Mina scowled at Serling with a mistrustful look on her face.

While I knew what a crosswalker was, I had never met one, not even while in Tyree. Magic moved through everything, yet wizards, sorcerers, and witches were rare. A crosswalker was even rarer than those.

Serling rubbed his leg, but Mina didn't offer him a cushion to sit on. "A crosswalker is a person who can break the barrier between this world and a world called the Netherrealm. It is from there that we draw our power. It's wondrous, with treasures to satiate desires both subtle and gross. But it's not for the timid." A wistful grin passed over his face, as he no doubt thought about his home.

"Why aren't you there now?" I asked.

Serling's eyes became distant and when he spoke his voice was flat. "My powers have been bound from crossing over in a particularly cruel punishment. Death would have been preferable, as the memories of that place still haunt me." His sigh spoke volumes. "I would be there now if I could."

Mina crossed her arms and grunted.

"We need your help," Ardimus said, leaning up against Wynna.

"You need rest," Mina said.

"There's no time for that. Premier must be stopped. He's very dangerous." He looked to Serling. "He's looking for the Jewel of Dakara to increase his power. Do you know of it? Do you know where it might be found?"

Serling looked thoughtful. "The Jewel of Dakara is legendary. There are many stories of it, but most say it was lost in the Ruins of Naeena, a thousand years ago."

I said quickly, "Do you know where these ruins are? Can you find us a guide?"

Serling said, "I know the ruins—in fact, no one knows them like I do. I've been there plenty of times. But in all the times I've been there, I've never encountered this jewel. If it was ever there, it's likely to have been looted long ago."

"All the better," I said. "If it's not there, then Premier can't get his hands on it. But if someone is looking for the jewel, is that the most likely place they'd go?"

"Almost certainly," Serling said.

"Will you guide us there, old friend?" Ardimus asked.

Serling didn't answer directly. Instead, he turned to me. "May I please see the magical item that I'm sensing?"

I hesitated. Who knew what a crosswalker could do with my dagger? I nodded and freed my dagger, handing it over to him.

Serling lifted the dagger to eye level, his eyes sparkling with desire. "The most powerful crosswalkers were able to imbue objects with their crosswalking powers, using the objects to reach the Netherrealm. That's what this dagger can do—tear a hole from this world into the next. But there is a drawback. If you lose that object, you'll never be able to travel into the Netherrealm again. That's why I never did it. In hindsight, I wish I had."

The crosswalker stopped staring at my dagger and his eyes met mine. "However, with this dagger, I may be able to return home. Where did you get this?"

"It was my father's." I perked up, curious for the answer to my next question. "Did you know him? His name was Elden Niall."

I studied Serling's face, desperate to see any sign of recognition. Since my father died before I was born, I knew very little about him. He was always a painful subject for my mother to talk about. Now I wondered, where did he get the dagger from, and was he a crosswalker?

Serling shook his head. "I'm sorry. I can't say I've ever heard of him. I will help you, Hellsfire, *if* I can use the dagger when we are finished."

"Serling, what are—?"

The crosswalker put his hand up, stopping Ardimus. "I cannot promise you that I will find the Jewel of Dakara or Premier, but I will guide you through the ruins as best as I can. And I guarantee you; no one knows anything more about the ruins than I."

I glanced at Ardimus and balled up my fist. I didn't like being pressured like this. I knew very little of Serling. There had to be a reason he was banished from the Netherrealm in the first place. For all I knew, he was a criminal, and giving him a chance to return home would cause problems—problems *I* would be responsible for.

Yet Ardimus seemed to trust him, and more importantly, I had promised King Furlong that I would capture or kill Premier. If I couldn't stop Premier now, he would cause even more trouble.

I held my hand out. "You have a deal, crosswalker."

Serling took it. "Good. I will have supplies ready by morning. The ruins are only a few days' ride from here. If the desert gods favor us, we'll find out what secrets these ruins contain together. Come, girl!" he shouted at Alyssa, jolting her. "Pick up my belongings and let us be off. We have much to do and my leg hurts." He disappeared out the door.

The frail girl struggled to pick up the sack, and I went to help her.

"Thank you," she said. "It was a pleasure meeting you, Wizard Hellsfire."

"Just Hellsfire. It was nice meeting you too. May the gods walk with you in magic."

Alyssa smiled at me before following Serling.

"I always knew that old coot was hiding something," Mina said, her face full of triumph as she stared at the door. "I would love for him to go back to wherever he came from."

"Mother," Ardimus said.

"Wynna, make sure Ardi gets his rest. I will prepare meals for your journey. Hellsfire, would you please help me?"

"Of course."

I followed her into the kitchen. The cold hearth was in the corner of the small alcove with wood stacked in a hole next to it. I was putting fresh wood into the hearth when Mina came and stood over my shoulder.

In hushed tones, she said, "Hellsfire, I need you to watch over my Ardi. I do not know what a crosswalker is, and I know not of magic, but I understand this—Serling cannot be trusted. He hid what he was, and he has always been after something. I haven't figured out what it is, but I have no doubt in my old bones that sooner or later, it will be at odds with what you or Ardimus wants." She glanced back to her son. "Ardi's admiration for Serling may blind him. I need someone who can see clearly."

I nodded. "You have my word that I will watch out for your son."

Mina gently patted my shoulder. "After you start the fire, I will find you a place to sleep. You will need your strength in the days to come."

Early the next morning, Mina woke us. She had enough food for all of us, except Serling. We left a few things we had brought with Mina so that we wouldn't be loaded down. We needed to catch up with Premier as soon as possible. One of those things we left were my wizard's robes. I had gotten used to the sheer desert robes I wore, but I was still going to miss them.

We left Mina's house, and outside her small courtyard stood Serling with three horses, far bigger and stronger than those I had seen in Northern Shala. Of Alyssa, there was no sign. We loaded up the food Mina had made us the night before.

"How do you feel?" Serling asked.

Ardimus secured one of the straps to the large beasts. "Better."

Mina came over to me and held out a folded tortilla. I ate it, my mouth burning from the spicy eggs. As hot as they were, it was delicious. "Thank you."

She reached up and pinched my cheeks. "You're a good boy. Take care, Hellsfire."

"You too, and I will do as you ask."

Mina went over to Ardimus. Mother and son hugged each other and he kissed her on the forehead.

"Try not to get yourself killed," Mina said. "Wynna, take care of him as you always do." She switched back to her native language and spoke so fast I couldn't follow.

Ardimus chuckled. "Yes, Mother."

We departed Mina's and left Falak, riding across the desert sands once more. As we rode, Ardimus told me that the ruins were once a small settlement called "Naeena" that had been destroyed long ago in a disaster. Serling, however, had a different story.

The crosswalker spoke of a great and malicious monster whose power defeated all those who confronted it. Yet, it fell in that spot because one of its own kind turned on it. Ardimus and Wynna smiled to themselves in amusement, but I wondered how much truth was in that embellished story.

Though we couldn't track Premier in the desert sand, we knew exactly where he was going. In the middle of the second day, we finally reached our destination.

"There it is," Serling said when we were still miles away. He pointed to a large, spiral object that rose out of the desert, reaching for the stars.

CHAPTER 14

THE RUINS OF NAEENA were miles from any settlement or city. As we rode closer, I realized I could only see part of the structure, as it was half-buried in the desert sands. From a distance, it looked like a bent tower of a castle, but the closer I got, the more I could see how wrong that impression was.

From Serling's stories, I had thought that the ruins might have been like a carcass of a great beast. In manner of speaking they were, but it wasn't like the armored shell of a turtle or even the dried-out husk of a dragon. It was something far different.

The whole structure was made of rusty metal. The rust alone showed how ancient it must be; in the dry desert air, rust was slow to grow. Sunlight sparkled off the areas that had been scoured shiny by years of sandstorms. Directly in front of us was a large hole torn into the metal that offered a way in.

We spotted tracks in front of the opening. Ardimus and I exchanged glances. It appeared that Premier was here ahead of us. There was only one set—heading in—and they came from somewhere on the other side of the ruins.

"Everyone, be on your guard," I said. "And go quietly. It appears that Premier is inside, but he may have removed some of his tracks magically. I want to take him by surprise if we can."

We followed the tracks back toward their origin. On the other side of the ruins, where a piece of metal had tilted downward to create a shady spot, was another horse. It was tied to a metal pole sticking out from the ground. It was scrawny and still lathered with sweat, and only carried two small saddlebags. Premier must have pushed his horse hard to beat us here.

"He hasn't been here long," Wynna said quietly, giving Premier's horse a handful of grain and checking to make sure he had left water for it. "We can catch him if we hurry."

After a short discussion, we left our horses tied near Premier's. It was a risk, because if he escaped us, he could kill them or let them loose, stranding us here. On the other hand, there was no other shade nearby, and leaving them in the broiling sun indefinitely could kill them nearly as quickly.

When the horses were secure, we rushed back to the entrance hole. Before letting the others enter, I stood in the entrance, casting my wizard's senses as far as I could. I could sense something was amiss, but I wasn't sure what. Holding up my hand to indicate that the others should wait, I walked up to the ruins and reached out toward the rusted wall. Although I couldn't sense anything specific with my wizard's senses, my instincts told me not to touch it. I hesitated, hand out. Nothing happened.

"Hellsfire?" Ardimus murmured.

"This is ridiculous," I muttered to myself, gathering my courage.

I laid my hand on the rough metal, and a small surge of power coursed through it. I lost my breath for a moment. It didn't hurt me, but it felt like a dog lying in wait, tensing to attack.

"Hellsfire, are you all right?" Ardimus asked.

"I'm…fine."

While that power was faint, I sensed that it had once been strong. It was also very familiar—a magic I had only just learned of in the past few days. I turned to Serling to say something, but he cut me off.

"You feel it too, don't you?" he asked.

"Yes."

"Ardimus was wise to come to me. I have been to the ruins many times, over the years."

"To find a way home?"

"Yes. But I found nothing. The only thing I learned is that Netherrealm magic is embedded in these ruins. For what purpose, I do not know."

I stared at Premier's fresh footprints in the sand. How deep did the ruins go, and was Premier here for Netherrealm magic? "Has anyone tried to dig out the ocean of sand around them, to see what's buried here?"

Serling nodded. "A long time ago, I convinced a group of treasure hunters that if we could dig up the ruins, it could be worth a lot of money."

"I take it you didn't succeed?"

He shook his head. "We made good headway the first day, but the next morning the sands had covered the ruins again. We thought it was the wind, but at the end of the week, we had accomplished nothing. Not one foot of sand had been cleared from this place."

"I remember hearing that," Wynna said. "I also remember them being very upset with you at the lack of profit, since you found nothing inside the ruins."

Serling's face turned even redder, and it had nothing to do with the sun. "Yes, well, things don't always go as planned."

"How long will it take to search the ruins?" I asked.

"The inside's a lot bigger than it looks. If I knew where Premier was going or where the Jewel was, we could reach him by the end of the day. Searching for him could take days."

"I need you to narrow it down to sooner than that."

"I will."

"Good."

"We have a problem," Ardimus said. "Look." He pointed off in the distance, where the sand was swirling around as if of its own accord.

"A sandstorm," I said.

"We may get lucky," Ardimus said. "It may not pass this way. At least we have shelter. I'll go and find a better place to secure the horses, in case our luck doesn't hold."

With the encroaching sandstorm, it seemed that this…thing I had with Premier was going to finally come to an end. There was nowhere for him to run.

I chafed at the delay, but it wouldn't help us to defeat Premier only to be stuck out here without horses. When Ardimus returned, we stood in front of the entrance, and I stared at dark interior. The bright light seemed to vanish inside it, and it reminded me of a large mouth waiting to devour me. Instead of having a tongue, the inside of the mouth dipped downward. I despised cramped, enclosed places. I always felt like they would suffocate me. With how ancient and decrepit the ruins were, thousands of pounds of sand could crush us at any moment.

"Is something the matter, Hellsfire?" Serling asked, staring at me.

"No," I said, a bead of sweat dripping down my temple. "What are we waiting for? We're wasting sunlight."

We followed as Serling led us into the Ruins of Naeena. Stale air swirled through my nose, and there was nothing but darkness ahead. A pile of old, discarded torches lay near the entrance. I reached for one and lit it with a tiny portion of my magic before handing it to Serling. I didn't want to use my magic unless I had to. Premier might sense it.

Serling peered at the torch in his hand. "I think I used this one the last time I was here."

The light held the shadows at bay, but the deeper we crept into the ruins, the more the shadows encroached upon us. Dust and sand covered the place. Here and there a trickle of sand fell through the roof, making small piles in the hallways. The metal had clearly lost its battle with time, but a few spots felt smooth to the touch. I wasn't a blacksmith or armorer, but the way the building was constructed reminded me more of plate armor than any kind of building I had ever seen. Except that it was armor the size of a giant city.

What was the point of Naeena? It was designed this way for a reason, but the reason eluded me. I thought back over the legend that Serling had told us. I've always found that even the grandest, most unbelievable stories held a kernel of truth, but I couldn't see how the legend of a great monster was tied to this strange place. I was about to ask Serling more about the ruins when I glimpsed an engraving in the floor.

I wiped the sand away, revealing a rune about the size of my hand. I brushed away more sand and found there were runes everywhere, carved into the entire floor. I had no idea what they stood for, but I did know one thing—runes were used in very powerful spells and enchantments. They heightened, reinforced, or bound the magic.

What bothered me was that after all this time, despite the condition of the ruins, the runes themselves were pristine. It was as if they were etched there yesterday. What's worse was that they were imbued with that same crosswalking power. And it was still active.

"What are the runes for?" I asked Serling, still crouched over.

"I haven't been able to figure that out yet. Maybe we'll find the answer together."

Serling was a bit further down the hall, staring at other runes that had been recently uncovered—but not by any of us.

"Premier," I said.

I could see the marks where he'd brushed away the sand with his hands. At first, the uncovered runes seemed random, but as we moved through the ruins, they were clustered in groups of three or four, purposefully rather than randomly.

"We can't decipher the runes," I said. "But what if Premier can?"

"They might be leading him to Jewel of Dakara," Wynna said.

"Then we'd better hurry," Ardimus said.

"At least he's left us a trail to follow," I said. "Which may mean he's not expecting us."

Serling limped faster, and we continued deeper into the ancient ruins. I tried to use my magic to sense Premier, but either he was already far away, or he masked himself well. This abandoned and desolate place reminded me of Renak's tower, deep in the Wastelands. I couldn't help but feel a presence watching over us.

"I know these two don't believe me," Serling said as he paused in front of a split tunnel. "That these ruins were once a great beast, but you feel it, don't you, Hellsfire? You feel the watchful eyes of a predator, aching to strike once more?"

I did.

"Over the last few days, I've been thinking about this Jewel of Dakara. You say Premier's looking for it to regain the power he's lost. I don't know of the Jewel of Dakara, but I did remember a story about a jewel from this very region long ago.

"Back when Naeena was a town instead of the ruins it is today, there was once a beacon of light. The power it contained could banish any darkness within miles. The shadows were terrified of it."

"We could use its power now," Wynna said.

Serling chuckled. "We could, but this light might blind us. Before you or I were ever born, roaming the area of Naeena was a great and terrible monster. It lurked in the shadows and only struck at night, feeding on those foolish enough to be out of town and away from the light the small city could provide.

"One brave young girl had grown weary of the monster and had sworn to put an end to the terrifying beast. She remembered the story of the beacon, and knew she could use its light to banish the monster forever.

"Watch your step." Serling stepped over a fallen piece of jagged metal. "After a long and hard struggle, Riera, I believe her name was, succeeded in recovering the beacon. One dark night she confronted the monster. While the light did help her, little did Riera realize how powerful the monster was. The beast swallowed her and ended Riera's life."

"What happened next?" I asked.

Serling paused and smiled. "Unfortunately for the beast, the light's power devoured it from the inside out."

"I don't get it," Wynna said, scratching her head. "How did Riera recover this powerful beacon?"

"And how did the beast become the Ruins of Naeena?" Ardimus asked. "I thought it was another monster who was responsible for this place."

Serling shook his head. "Sometimes a story is just a story. Besides, I thought the story of Riera *might* be related to the Jewel of Dakara. It was just a theory."

"Ever since I've known you, you've had this unhealthy fascination with monsters," Ardimus said with a wry smile.

"That's because I've known a few monsters in my time."

We entered a large chamber. I had thought it would be stark and empty like the rest of the place, but the torchlight glimmered off something embedded in the high ceiling.

"What is that?" Wynna asked.

She broke from our group and peered upward. She motioned for Serling's torchlight and he illuminated the upper part of the room.

It was filled with some type of gears. Like the rest of the ruins, they were slowly rotting with decay. In the corner was a piece of one gear that had fallen off. I picked it up and inspected it, wondering what it could be used for.

"Those gears are scattered throughout Naeena," Serling said. "We'll see more of them. the deeper we go. I've been able to find that a few of them move sections of the walls to open passageways, but I haven't a clue as to what the majority of them do. There is no machine inside here that I've ever found. The Ruins of Naeena are oddly empty, as you've seen so far. Yet the gears do something...or once did."

"Maybe the machines that they were a part of were taken out," Wynna said.

"Perhaps." But I could tell that Serling wasn't convinced. "I believe I know where Premier is going now, though I don't understand why. It's a dead end..." He cocked his head. "Or is it? I know of a shortcut that will lead us to where he's going. With luck, we'll beat him there."

We left the chamber, heading deeper into the "belly of the beast," as Serling called it. The narrow path we took was littered with gears. As we squeezed through the hallway, I peered inside one of the walls whose sides had crumbled. There were all sorts of little gears lying around, even in there. I couldn't help but wonder what the purpose of the gears was, since there was nothing of note inside Naeena.

Also, in the back of my mind, I had started to doubt Serling. Was he leading us to the right place? While the gears were fascinating, there were no more signs of Premier. No more revealed runes, no more footprints, no more tracks. For all I knew, with each passing moment Serling was leading us farther and farther away from Premier.

Serling halted. In the side of the hallway was a small passageway. The sand around the edges had been cleared, as if it had been opened recently. I quieted my mind and sensed that magic had been used to create the opening.

The crosswalker inspected the doorway. "We've arrived at the section where I thought Premier might be. He has been here. This doorway wasn't here before. Unfortunately, I have no idea what's down here. My knowledge of this place ends here."

I stepped in front of him and took the torch. "It's all right. I appreciate what you've done so far. I'll take it from here. You can leave if you want." I gave him a wry smile. "Premier won't go quietly."

"I'm not going anywhere."

Serling limped to the back of the group. Ardimus and Wynna both flanked my sides, as much as the ruins allowed. I wanted to reach out with my magic to see where Premier lurked in the ruins, but I didn't. He might feel it. Instead, I let the magic flow to me, but it limited me. I would only sense anything magic if it was very close, or very powerful.

As we ventured into this previously unknown passageway, I glimpsed more and more of the runes. The thrumming crosswalking power was stronger here, and with each step, the power grew. While I didn't know what the Jewel of Dakara's power might be, and I didn't understand a crosswalker's power, I knew that both the jewel and Premier would be in the direction I was heading.

"I sense something I've not felt in many years," Serling whispered. "It feels like the residual effects of a crosswalking portal. It's faint, but it's there."

I continued to let the crosswalker magic call to me like music, following its melody into the ruins. Its caress was all around me, and I knew it wouldn't be long before I would see where it originated. Suddenly, the music-like feel left me, to be replaced by an icy cold feeling I had felt before.

"Get down!" I yelled.

The shadows melted together as one, and the light that emanated from my torch all but disappeared. The shadows peeled themselves from the walls and leaped out to attack us. I grabbed onto what was left of the torch's light and pumped magic into it. The torch in my hand exploded, shining light into the darkness. Before the shadows could reach us, the light shredded them, driving them back.

The shadows returned to normal, and I fed my torch magic, keeping it lit. At the end of the corridor were two hateful eyes glaring back at me.

"Premier," I said, gripping the torch tighter.

Wynna and Ardimus both drew their weapons, and I gathered in my magic. I gasped when I saw a shiny red gem cradled in Premier's hands—the Jewel of Dakara.

We stared at each other for several long moments. His head was raised and his cold, flinty eyes glared at me. I watched him for any sign of trickery, like in Falak.

Finally, he spoke, "Boy, you're a dog-ridden flea I can't shake."

I reached into my bag to the magic-binding collar. My fingers felt the cold metal, but I stopped myself from taking it out. Premier didn't deserve a chance to surrender. He had shown time and time again how devious he was, whether in a combat situation, or in playing me. He would find a way out of the bindings, and he would never undo the curse he had laid upon Krystal. He had to die so that others could live.

"You're awfully quiet, boy," Premier said. His eyes widened and his tight-lipped smile looked wrong on his burned face. "You're finally learning."

"You're no match for us, or for me," I said, clenching my fists and letting the magic within me rise. What surprised me is that I knew it to be true. Without any tricks, deception, or confusion, Premier's power was no match for mine. Not after what I had done to him.

Premier's nostrils flared. "You may be right, if I didn't have this precious gem here. When I was in Tyree, I learned of the Jewel of Dakara. And do you know why I wanted to retrieve it?"

"To regain the power I took from you."

His eyes lit with rage. "In time I will. No, the Jewel of Dakara can devour a person's essence from within them. Allow me to enlighten you!"

I raised my magical defenses, but the magic Premier had been gathering in was not released at us, as I thought it would be. He funneled it into the jewel. It flared, the bright red light illuminating the entire chamber.

The jewel's magic slammed into my shield. The Netherrealm magic lurked inside the jewel, and Premier used it to power his own spell. I was about to counteract his magic with my own, when a hand clasped my shoulder.

"Don't fight the spell!" Serling said. "Netherrealm magic doesn't belong here."

I nodded, understanding his words. Instead of attacking the spell directly, I shifted my focus to Premier's own magic. I hammered my magic into his, cutting it off. That was all it took for the jewel's magic to stop working. Its anchor into our world was gone. It lessened with each moment, its magic flowing back to the jewel.

The jewel's light had dimmed and disappeared. Premier's power began to grow again, but I wasn't going to give him the time to cast another spell with the jewel. Premier's eyes blackened and the shadows returned. This time, the torch in my hand exploded with power until it extinguished, plummeting us into darkness.

I relit the torch, to see a cloud of darkness where Premier had been. He was hidden inside it. His spell wasn't as good as it could have been, because I caught a glimpse of his robes as he turned and ran. We chased him through the ruins, following the trail of darkness that surrounded him. But he had had time to learn the passageways, and he started to outdistance even my long stride.

I summoned my fire to the surface. I sent the torch's fire streaming forward in the tunnels, hoping to catch Premier, or at least slow him down. The shadows around Premier lessened as he countered my spell, and the back of his robes peeked out from the darkness. The magic he'd used to cast his spell was diminishing with each passing moment.

I conjured enough power for a thermal blast, a spell that was fast, easy, and powerful enough to shatter whatever defenses he could muster. When I was about to release my spell, Premier's power spiked. I knew it wasn't enough to fight my spell. The Jewel of Dakara came hurtling back at us, pulsating with Premier's power. In mid-flight, the light from the gem exploded with power.

We were blinded, and even shutting my eyes didn't keep the light from penetrating my skull. The pressure almost brought me to my knees, and I remembered Serling's story of Riera.

A couple of seconds later, my head lightened. When I opened my eyes, the Jewel of Dakara lay on a pile of sand. It had lost its light, and a huge crack streaked through it. I couldn't sense Premier's power anymore.

"Firebird, with me," Ardimus said. "Serling with Hellsfire. We'll split up and find him. He couldn't have gone far, and there was no way he got past us."

I handed the torch to Ardimus and clenched my fist. He was right. Premier couldn't have gotten past us, but that meant nothing. He might have found another way out of the ruins, or he might try something else. Serling reached for the jewel, and fire blossomed around my hand. We headed down one part of the corridor, while Ardimus and Wynna went the opposite way.

I continued to keep a lookout for Premier or any hint of magic. Serling, however, kept staring at the Jewel of Dakara in his hand.

"This power feels familiar," he said. "And that crosswalking portal I felt is close by."

"Could Premier have used a portal to leave?"

"It's possible, though if one had been activated, its effects would be a lot stronger." He pointed toward a door at the end of the dim hallway. Judging from the markings on the ground, it had been opened recently.

I reached out with my magical senses, trying to see past the door. I pulled my hand back. Tremendous power lay within, along with that strange power Serling wielded. He got behind me while I opened the door.

I scanned the room, searching for Premier. He wasn't there, but the magic was. This room was far different than the sterile, if damaged, passageways we had seen earlier. It looked like the inside of a dried-out tree trunk or a dead husk, and was just as hard and ridged. Trails of luminous color floated in the air—wards. In the center of the small room lay a pedestal. There was nothing on top of it, but there looked to be a small hole, as if something had once belonged there.

REAWAKENING (THE PASSAGE OF HELLSFIRE, BOOK 3)

I didn't dare step into the room lest the wards turn deadly, and there wasn't time to examine and disarm them. I turned to step away, but the crosswalker continued to stare at the room.

"We don't have time for this," I said. "We must find Premier."

He ignored me and stepped inside the room with no concern for the wards.

"Serling!"

The wards reacted to the crosswalker, brightening before swirling and brushing across him. They settled back into place after touching him.

"They're harmless, Hellsfire," he said, not looking back at me. He continued to look at the pedestal.

"Maybe to you and your magic."

"Premier was in here, I'm sure of it, and he's not a crosswalker. This magic is far too old to be his doing." He finally turned around to look at me. "You'll just have to trust me."

"Fine. You stay here, and I'll go search for Premier."

With his lame leg, I didn't need Serling slowing me down anyway.

I ran from the room, heading in the direction I hoped led to the surface. Premier was looking for a way out, that much I was sure of. All the metal corridors looked the same as I zoomed by the gears and runes. I couldn't tell if one hallway with a pile of sand leaking from the corner of the roof was the same as another. Or if those five runes were the same five runes I'd passed by earlier.

The only thing I knew was that I was headed up, but Premier could be anywhere. I kicked a mound of sand in frustration, and that's when an explosion of magical power tugged at me. Premier. He was close.

I sprinted at the end of the hallway and found a small staircase that I recognized. There had been an opening in it, but now the hole was far bigger than when we originally passed by. Sunshine streamed in from the outside. Through the hole I could see Premier's black-robed figure running away from the ruins.

"Premier!" I yelled.

I squeezed through the hole, ignoring the biting cut of the metal into my skin. I plopped onto the warm sand, and got up and gave chase.

The sandstorm Ardimus had seen earlier was nearly upon us. I trudged through the slippery sand, doing my best to run after Premier. The shifting sand kept pulling at me and I kept falling. The wind whipped sand into my eyes, and I had to shield my face. Even though he was older than me and moved slower, Premier kept pulling away from me and the Ruins of Naeena. Yet his horse wasn't out there in the desert sandstorm.

The sand stung in my eyes, and I slipped and crumpled to the ground. "PREMIER!"

The man in black paused and turned to face me before the sandstorm engulfed him.

CHAPTER 15

I STUMBLED MY way back to the protection of the ruins, breathing easier when I was finally inside. I slumped back against the metal walls. The wind blew more sand inside and I watched as it struck the metal with its musical chord.

I rubbed my forehead with my palm. I couldn't believe Premier was gone, perished in a sandstorm. I hadn't thought it would come to this. Yet, I wouldn't rest until I saw his body, even if I had to dig it out of the mountains of sand myself. I got up and left before I was buried in a pile of sand, and headed back toward Serling.

By the time I trudged back to Naeena's inner chambers, Ardimus and Wynna had arrived too.

"Hellsfire, we didn't find him," Ardimus said. "We...what happened to you?"

I lifted my tired head, dusting off the sand that still clung to my hair. "I found him." I told them all that had happened.

"No one can survive in a sandstorm without shelter," Wynna said.

Ardimus and I looked at each other. "Premier is a wizard," I said. "He doesn't have his full power, but he may have enough to protect himself from the storm. I won't believe he's dead unless I see it for myself."

"That must wait until the storm is over," Ardimus said. "Where is Serling?"

I indicated the chamber where I had left Serling, and we stepped up to the doorway.

"Stop!" Serling said, when he saw us. "Hellsfire, you may enter. Wynna and Ardimus, stay out there. If you come inside the chamber, the wards will kill you."

I stepped through the doorway, and the wards reacted to me. They brushed up against my skin, then went back to hovering harmlessly in the room.

"I overheard you, Hellsfire," Serling said. "We'll have to ride out the sandstorm here. Hopefully, it won't take long. While you three were out searching for Premier, I've been studying this place."

"And what have you found?"

Serling never looked at us. He kept staring at the pedestal and the jewel, which he had placed on top of the pedestal. "The Netherrealm magic's strong here," he said. "I wish I had my powers."

"Serling," Ardimus said from outside the chamber, "we need to go see how bad the sandstorm is and how long it will last."

"Forgive me. You're quite right. Let's go."

Serling and I were heading out of the room, when the torch went dim. A loud moan echoed throughout the chamber. The temperature in the room dropped, and a cold chill crept up my arms. I glanced around using my fire to illuminate the shadows, searching for the noise.

The rumbling moan sounded again—deeper, louder, and more guttural. I thought it might have come from the hole beneath the jewel, but the noise echoed throughout the entire ruins. It was as if we truly were in the belly of a beast, and it had awakened.

A ghastly green fog dripped from the Jewel of Dakara like the morning fog creeping from a forest. I held my breath, not only out of fear of choking, but out of fascination. The outline of a smiling face appeared in the fog as it drifted underneath the jewel and into the hole.

"What was that?" I asked him.

Serling shook his head. "I don't know, but the energy was familiar—ancient, powerful, and dangerous." He stared at the jewel. "Something's wrong." The crosswalker limped to the jewel and yanked it from the pedestal.

We left the room, standing directly outside the chamber. While I was glad to be out of that eerie room, we didn't want to stray too far from it. The problem was either in that room or with the jewel.

"Those felt like growls," Ardimus said.

"It might have been—"

Before Wynna could finish her sentence, the door behind me slammed shut. Runes we hadn't seen before appeared across it, and lit up. The four of us tried to push the door open, but it wouldn't budge. A sheen of magical energy covered it.

"Stand back," I said, rolling up my sleeves. I released waves of elemental fire at it. The fire splashed against the door, not cracking the seal in the slightest. Brute force wasn't going to cut it. I needed more time to study the magic guarding the doors, but I didn't get it. The ruins began to shake.

I did my best to hold onto the doorknob. The shaking intensified as my body fought against this unforeseen force. I tried to use wind magic to steady myself, but kept getting jostled.

"We've got to leave," Ardimus said, grabbing Serling so he wouldn't fall.

"We must get back inside that chamber," Serling said. "Whatever's the cause of this lies in there."

Sheets of metal peeled from the roof and crashed to the ground near our feet.

"Come on!" Ardimus said, tugging on my sleeve. "We've got to get to safety. We'll come back later. I promised the princess nothing would happen to you."

We ran through the corridors, dodging fallen debris and sand all around us. Ardimus carried Serling, and the crosswalker didn't object. I did my best to shield us from the chaos, but even with my magic, the sand got in my eyes and small pieces of the falling metal sliced into my skin. I blinked and wiped away the blood that trickled down my forehead.

As we ran, the rumbling chorus was joined by a screeching sound. I glanced above at the exposed gears, and they were now moving, after years of neglect. The loud noise vibrated throughout the halls and into my head. The tremors increased, and we could no longer run. I stumbled as if I was drunk, and staggered from one wall to another.

The tremors suddenly stopped. We froze, trying to get our bearings. The gears also quieted down but they didn't stop.

Wynna looked around. "Is it over?"

Before anyone could answer, the floor tilted, and we were lifted off our feet as if the rug had pulled out from under us. I hung in the air for a moment before falling face first to the ground. I tried to get up, but was shoved upward. I cried out as my back hit the ceiling, a piece of metal digging into it. I was pinned against the ceiling, trying to tear myself free, when my weight shifted and I dropped. I grunted, sand seeping into my mouth as the cold floor greeted me.

The whole building went mad. The floor beneath us tilted once more, and we tumbled down the corridor. More sand rushed in through the open cracks in the ceiling, hastening our slide. I tried to control our fall, but my spell wasn't strong enough and I didn't have the concentration for a stronger one. Somewhere along the way, our torch went out and we were plummeted into darkness.

We were without light, yet at the end of the long hallway was a spot of brightness. It was hard to tell since my face kept hitting the floor, wall, or ceiling, but I thought I could see the blue sky and desert sand. The air was also fresher, which meant that we were above ground, but how could that be?

When I hit what I thought would be the floor, I reached out with my arms to steady myself. I hit the surface with my chin, and my hands were bloodied, but it worked. I skidded down the floor, watching the sky come into view through the large hole in the ruins.

I didn't understand it. How were we now clearly above ground, when we had been beneath it? Those thoughts were fleeting, as more immediate concerns came into my head. How was I going to stop my fall?

The once long hallway had now shrunk, and the end was coming closer. I gathered in as much wind magic as I could. Before we fell through the hole, I summoned a gust of wind.

I jerked backward a bit, but that was all. With no wall at the other end, my spell had nothing to push against. I hoped the sand would soften our impact, but judging from how high we seemed to be, I doubted that would happen. I hoped I'd have enough time to conjure a spell as we plummeted to our doom.

Just when my face hit the outside air, I was yanked backward. A firm hand grabbed my leg, fingernails digging through the light clothes and into my flesh.

"Gotcha!"

I looked up and saw Wynna hanging onto my leg. She held onto Serling with her other hand, and he in turn held onto Ardimus. Ardimus had grabbed onto a small hole in the rusted wall. He grimaced, holding on to his life and ours. Blood trickled down his arm as the sharp metal bit into him.

None of dared to move or speak, lest Ardimus lose his concentration. Serling's eyes were tightly closed as he tried not to lose his grip on Ardimus. Wynna hid her worry behind a smile at me. We were like a dangling vine, and if any of us moved a bit, Ardimus might lose his grip and we would all fall.

Thankfully, I was a wizard and I didn't need to move to cast my magic. Even so, my spell had to be subtle lest it sway us and cause us to fall. I closed my eyes and gathered in energy. As I did so, I tried to figure out ways to use it. Ardimus couldn't hold us forever, so I needed to lighten his load somehow.

Before I could cast my spell, my body tilted again. I opened my eyes and watched as the ruins leveled out. Wynna pulled me back inside before rushing to Ardimus. I exhaled, taking a moment to feel the solid floor beneath my back. The tremors had lessened, but a slight, rhythmic vibration could be felt against my back. I was the last to get up.

I walked over to Ardimus, spotting the torn wall near him. Those once quiet gears now spun. I focused my attention back on the warrior, slumped down against the wall. Wynna was busy bandaging his throbbing hands, but the blood kept soaking through them.

"Give me a minute, and I'll be ready to go again," Ardimus said. He did his best to hide his pain, but I saw him grimace.

I leaned down to him and gently placed my hands on his. "Thank you for saving me—us. I don't know how you did it."

"I promised the princess I would watch out for you."

"Hold still. This might feel a little weird."

I summoned white mana, letting it flow through my hands and into his. The life mana restored his hands, clotting his blood and sealing up the cuts and gashes he had received. When I was finished, I let go of his hands and saw there were scars left on his skin.

"Sorry," I said. "It's not my best form of magic." I didn't tell him how much my own sores and aches were now amplified because of the magic I'd used.

Ardimus flexed his hands. "It's all right. The ache in them has disappeared. I'm sure they'll heal on their own, and if not, it's just one more scar on top of others."

A relieved look passed over Wynna's face as she helped him up. "Still amazing after all these years."

They both shared a smile.

"By the gods," Serling whispered. The crosswalker stood near the gaping hole, peering outside. We all walked up to him.

"Serling," I said. "What is—?"

My mouth hung open as the words left me. The huge hole in the side of the wall was more of a window now. Instead of being underneath the ground, we were now hundreds of feet in the air, and moving. The source of the tremors became clear. The ruins of Naeena had risen from the sad, and were walking across the desert.

CHAPTER 16

I LEANED OVER to get a better look, still clinging onto the edge of the wall lest I fall out again. The exposed gears turned with each step of the huge legs, and gigantic arms swayed from its sides as this monstrous place walked. The runes that were once quiet were glowing with the power reanimating it.

"Serling, what *is* this place?" I asked. I did my best to keep the accusation out of my voice.

Serling continued to stare through the hole. He sighed and turned back toward us. "I don't know. I thought these were ruins left over from the War of the Wizards. I never imagined it was a machine of some sort."

"It looks like it's heading toward Falak," Ardimus said. "This machine will destroy the city unless we stop it."

"How do we do that?" Wynna asked. "Rip out every gear in here and pray it stops while not falling over and crushing us?"

"Hello?" a voice said. "Hello?"

We paused and looked at each other, seeing if any of us had spoken. None of us had.

"Can you hear me now?"

Wynna bent down to the Jewel of Dakara, which was in Serling's hand. "It appears to be coming from the jewel."

Serling lifted up the jewel. I summoned my magic, fearing a trap, or something even worse than the walking ruins we were in now. I didn't sense Premier's magic, but that meant nothing.

"I've been trying to reach you ever since you released her," the gem said, pulsating with each sentence it spoke.

"Her?" I asked.

"Be careful, Hellsfire," Ardimus said. "We should not trust this gem."

The Jewel of Dakara flashed darker. "I'm the only one you *can* trust. You've already released your enemy—a far deadlier enemy than you've ever encountered before."

"And who *are* you?" I asked.

"I'm Kreezakalash, wizard, but most call me Kreezak since you humans tend to butcher my name. And you are?"

"I'm Hellsfire."

"I also sense there's a crosswalker and one with enchanted items."

"That's Serling and Ardimus."

Wynna cleared her throat.

"And the one who you sense nothing from is Wynna. Now that we're all acquainted, can you tell us what's going on?"

"All right," Kreezak said, "but first you need to know what you're up against. I take it you humans know of Shala and Renak and their war?"

"Of course," Wynna said.

"Good. I don't know how long I've been trapped in this jewel, and I don't want to explain everything. While you may know of their war, you may not know of the monstrous creations they built, and we are in one now."

I remembered the gears, and how the ruins rumbled as they awoke.

"Say what you want about Renak, but that wizard's imagination knew no bounds. He thought a machine the size of a small mountain would easily crush

Shala's forces. He knew it'd take him years to build it, and he also knew that the war would drain his resources. Instead of using his entire army to work and control the machine, he thought it best if it could work itself. And that's when he came up with the idea to infuse this place with the essence of another.

"Nothing in this world worked—human, centaur, wizard, golem, or even dragon. More than one essence, and things got a little messy. To get what Renak wanted, he traveled to the Netherrealm—and captured a demon."

There was silence, as we all stared at each other.

"I thought those were just stories," Serling said finally. "Rumors that scared people into leaving the Netherrealm and coming here."

"No, crosswalker. The story is true."

"What was the name of the demon he took?"

"Tashiannaeen."

Serling gasped. "Tashia! She's the most ruthless and powerful demon that has ever existed. The stories I've heard of her are legendary."

"And well-deserved," Kreezak said.

"I thought the fairies imprisoned her, since they couldn't kill her?"

"They did, but Renak freed her."

Serling emitted a low growl, then turned and walked away. He was still within earshot, but clearly frustrated over something the fairies had done.

"Renak made a deal with Tashia," Kreezak said. "I don't know the details, but it was enough to persuade her to submit to his ritual. Instead of merely summoning her into this world with her own body, her spirit would be bound to this construct.

"Shala learned of this, and he tried to stop the construction before it was too late. But his sneak attack failed horribly. Instead, to counteract Renak, he hastily built his own construct and crosswalked into the Netherrealm for help. Unlike Renak, Shala wasn't offering power or riches, and there was only one demon foolish enough to help Shala. He wasn't the strongest demon in the Netherrealm, but he knew Tashia well."

"You," I said.

"Yes, but my body didn't last long. Renak's forces nearly destroyed it before it was completed, and Shala didn't have the time to build a body as powerful as Tashia. And Tashia was…Tashia." I caught the hint of a smile in his voice. "I like to think I put up a decent fight, but who knows how history has judged me?"

I stared into the jewel, remembering the tales I had learned while growing up. "You and Tashia are the great summonings that created the Burning Sands."

"Burning Sands?" Kreezak asked.

"The area we're in now," Ardimus said. "The story goes that this vast desert was created by two battling monsters. That in their fury, they destroyed everything until it was a desert wasteland."

Kreezak laughed. "Crude. We did destroy a lot of the land, but this place was always a desert of sort. The land wasn't the most fertile to begin with, but both sides soon stripped the area dry of resources because of the war. It wasn't just me and Tashia who were responsible."

"How did you stop her, since she was more powerful than you?" Wynna asked.

"The Jewel of Dakara. Its magic is powerful enough to rip the essence from someone and store it here, if you know how to use it."

Premier was right. The jewel could be used to steal someone's essence, but what could he have wanted it for?

"How did you use the jewel against Tashia?" Serling asked.

"We risked an all-out attack instead of the hit-and-run tactics we had been using. We knew she would destroy my body, but it was our only chance. Before she could kill me, Shala transferred me in here. They fought their way to Tashia's heart—the place where you found the jewel—and forced her out of her body and into this jewel."

"Why not kill her when you had the chance?" I asked.

"You don't understand. She's far too strong. She couldn't be killed here. The plan was to crosswalk into the Netherrealm and deal with her there."

"What happened?"

Kreezak paused. "I don't know. I've been trapped in here since that day, with no way of knowing what was going on in the outside world."

"Dear gods, no," Ardimus whispered. He stood near the edge of the hole in the construct, staring out of it. I squinted to see what he was looking at. "A caravan—and we're heading straight toward them."

When I was a toddler, sometimes I would stumble across a trail of ants. I took a perverse joy at stomping my foot down on them, watching them scatter from my little might. I thought of those times again, feeling horror instead of joy at what I did to those poor creatures. I couldn't help but wonder what Tashia felt.

The tiny dots scattered across the desert sand. I prayed that Tashia didn't see them—that they were too small for her to notice, and that she might only accidentally kill a few of them. That notion vanished when she veered toward them. She lifted her mighty leg before stomping down on them. Her body shifted toward another group. The construct heaved, and I held on as one of her feet dug into a mound of sand. Her foot flung the sand hundreds of feet, along with the people that were once on top of it. Sand scattered throughout the air and when it was clear, the bodies of the people were stilled.

A deep, horrific laugh echoed throughout Tashia's construct, shaking my bones.

I let out a sigh of relief when I saw that there were a few survivors the demon was content to leave alone. Yet when she changed back to her original direction, I knew it would be far worse when she reached Falak.

"We've got to do something before she reaches Falak!" Ardimus said, his hand automatically reaching for his sword.

I agreed. Premier would have to wait. I summoned my magic, letting my power rise to the surface. I stared at the hole in the wall Ardimus was hanging on to, wondering how much damage I could do to its exposed gears.

"Wizard," Kreezak said. "What do you plan to do with your magic?"

"We can't stand here and do nothing. She's heading toward a major city, and thousands will be killed unless we get to her first. I will use my magic to tear her from the inside out."

"Admirable, but more powerful wizards than you have tried to destroy this place. She's gathering power, and once she reaches her full strength, her body will be fully restored."

"Then what can we do to stop her?"

"Go back to the chamber and reseal her."

"The door's shut," Serling said. "Hellsfire already tried his magic, and he couldn't get through."

"Elemental magic won't work against it," Kreezak said. "Use the jewel and the enchanted sword. That should get past her defenses. Once you're inside, place the jewel back on the pedestal. Its magic has already been set to remove her from the construct. The bigger problem is, you're going to have to reseal the jewel. The crack will allow her to leave again. I'll do my best to keep her distracted in here."

"How do I seal the jewel? I still don't understand the magic that's involved." I looked to Serling. "Maybe you can help me study the magic."

"No time," Kreezak said. "There's more than her body being repaired. Her old defenses are reactivating. If you want to make it to the chamber, go now, otherwise you'll have to fight your way through."

The others looked to me. I was the reason they were there in the first place. Even though it was Premier's fault for cracking the Jewel of Dakara, I felt responsible for the people that Tashia had already killed, and those deaths still to come.

"Let's stop Tashia," I said.

We ran back in the direction of the corridor we had tumbled down. As we passed the hole in the wall Ardimus had clung onto, I saw it was slightly smaller now, like it had repaired itself. Tashia's construct was a huge machine. How long would it take for her to have no exposed parts and no weaknesses?

We finally spotted the door to the chamber. The hallway we stood in was illuminated with spots of sunlight that had broken through the cracks. Yet, shadows crept over everything. As Tashia walked, the shadows and light shifted.

At first, I thought it was the shadows playing tricks on my eyes, but there was something slithering across the door. They looked like tentacles, and I could sense that the magic around the door was far stronger than it was previously. Guarding the door stood two gigantic monsters. Their round, hard bodies blended in with the dim shadows. They didn't have eyes like we did—their eyes were glowing yellow lines in their squat heads. Their claws clicked with anticipation.

"What are those?" Wynna asked, describing them to Kreezak.

"We called those 'snappers.' I warned you that Tashia would regain strength. You'd better hurry before more of her defenses come back. I hope you're good at close combat. Those things are tough, and their shells are hard to crack. They're also immune to elemental magic."

"Wynna and I will distract them," Ardimus said, drawing his sword. "While you two work on getting inside the chamber. Ready, Firebird?"

She flashed a smile and drew her daggers. "Always." The pair charged forward, meeting the snappers head-on.

Serling and I held back from the fray as Ardimus and Wynna drew the snappers away from the door. The lovers worked well together, parrying the snappers' claws and blocking those that came too close to the other. They never went for a killing blow, although with the exception of Ardimus's scimitar, I wasn't sure if they could even penetrate the thick armor of the snappers. The creatures were strong, as suspected, but they were also fast, and grew faster. Ardimus and Wynna soon had trouble keeping the creatures' attacks at bay.

Ardimus and Wynna drew the fight away from the door into the side corridor. I ran to the doorway with Serling limping behind me. The thick tentacles had stopped moving and solidified. When I placed my hand on the door, I was met with a backlash of energy.

Serling finally caught up to me and held out the jewel. "Well, demon," he asked. "What do we do now?"

"I told you, crosswalker. I don't know. If you hadn't sent the mortal with the enchanted sword off, he might be able to cut through and—"

I knew my magic wouldn't work on the door, and while I was tempted to use my hellsfire, I still didn't fully trust the devastating magic. I gambled and took the jewel from Serling. Using the Jewel of Dakara's magic against the door, I raised it. The jewel's power flowed through me and I brought it down, slashing at the now hardened tentacles guarding the door. The jewel cut through them, and Tashia's howl echoed through the construct. Black blood squirted on my face and they slithered away.

"Hellsfire!" Ardimus yelled. From the end of the hallway, the snappers had broken off from fighting Ardimus and Wynna. The creatures lumbered back toward me and Serling.

The urge to unleash my magic at them rose, but there was no point in fighting them, since Kreezak said that my magic would be useless. Instead I pushed the door open with the jewel. Tashia's magic buckled as the jewel fought against it, and the door creaked open.

Serling and I leaped through the open door, and I quickly turned around and slammed it shut. I readied my magic, expecting the snappers to burst through the door. Several tense seconds passed, and nothing banged against the door. Either the snappers weren't allowed to enter the chamber, or Wynna and Ardimus were keeping them busy. I didn't have time to worry about the snappers. I had to seal Tashia back in the jewel while I still had the chance. Yet when I turned around, the chamber pulled at my attention.

My feet no longer stood on that firm, dried-out floor that had been there earlier. Instead, they sank into the surface, making squishy sounds when I walked. The whole chamber was damp with moisture. The walls, ceiling, and floor were thick and soft. There was a slight pinkish color, but the more I stared at the walls, the redder the colors became. I reached out and touched the wall. My fingers came back with an oozy substance that stuck to my hand. It reminded me of blood.

I had grown used to Tashia's movements, but the ones in her chamber were different from outside. The floor wavered and moved as if it were separate from the rest of the construct. The lulling rhythm beneath my feet reminded me of a heartbeat. Kreezak was right; this chamber was her heart. If Tashia's power continued to return, would the entire place look like the inside of a body?

"You must hurry," Kreezak said. "The longer Tashia has to bond with her body, the stronger she becomes."

I placed the Jewel of Dakara back on the pedestal, tapping into its ancient magic. A red aura blazed around the jewel. The light shot out into lines traversing Tashia's construct. The rocking movement of the ruins halted. The beating heart of the chamber slowed, until it stilled into silence. A deafening roar erupted through the chamber, and a bright light streamed into the hole in the pedestal. The essence of Tashia was ripped from the machine Renak had built and stuffed back into the Jewel of Dakara.

I released my breath, staring at the crack in the jewel, wondering how in the gods' names I was going to fix—in minutes at most—what took one of the greatest wizards ever years to forge?

The Jewel of Dakara's color darkened from a crimson red to a forest green. It illuminated the chamber, the blinding light striking my eyes. The crack in the jewel widened as its color glowed erratically.

"Seal the jewel!" Serling said. "Kreezak's fighting her as best he can, but she'll overwhelm him and break free!"

But I didn't know how. While I had used the ancient magic in the jewel to activate and force Tashia back inside, I hadn't tapped into any of the Netherrealm magic. That was Serling's expertise. Yet in this realm, he couldn't access it. The magic Shala had used, I didn't understand and needed more time to study. Time I didn't have.

Instead, I fell back on magic I knew by instinct. My fingers danced through the air, sparks of dazzling magic sprinkling the jewel as I wove an intricate web. I used the web to contain the energy leaking from the jewel, hoping that by doing so it would give me time for a permanent solution.

The jewel's blinding lights dimmed and the battle waged between the two demons. Now, I just needed to figure out how to reseal it. Before I could ask Serling if he knew of any spells, or consult my book of magic, the jewel darkened to a midnight black. It shattered, pieces of gemstone exploding everywhere. A shard sliced my face, and lines of blood ran down my cheek.

A dark green wisp rose from each of the jewel's pieces, coalescing until they became a face. Angry, hollow eyes glared at me. "You dare try to imprison me again, wizard?" The magic in her voice made it loud and penetrating, scratching at my insides. Tashia's ghostly head swooped toward me and forced her way through my mouth and nose.

I couldn't breathe. Grabbing at my throat, I tried to conjure my magic, but whenever I tried to access it, a searing pain tore through my head. I could sense the magic within me and around me, but couldn't grasp it. Tashia kept blocking me by sending waves of pain through my body. I dropped to one knee with my hands to my head. It felt as if my head was about to explode.

"Hellsfire!" Serling said, reaching for me.

A red smoke floated from the shards. Its ghostly form wasn't as solid as Tashia's. "Serling, put the pieces down the hole, and quickly!" Kreezak said.

Serling limped from me and scrambled for the pieces of shattered jewel. While he did so, the green smoke receded out of me. I inhaled the precious air, gasping and coughing all the way.

"No!" Tashia said, but was too late. The bits of the broken jewel tumbled down the long rabbit hole. "Crosswalker, do you realize what you've done?"

The heart of the machine began to rot. The dark reds receded, overtaken by brittle browns and black. Tashia's construct swayed again, but this time without power. I had a brief moment of triumph, but soon I realized it wasn't over. We had to leave before the entire place collapsed, and I still had to deal with this demon.

I summoned my magic to me, raising my defenses. Tashia wasn't going to catch me off guard again so easily. Despite the blistering heat of the Burning Sands, I cooled the air in the chamber, focusing on the area around Tashia. With each breath, frost left my mouth, and tiny icicles clung around the edges of the wall. Yet no matter how cold I made it, the freezing spell didn't seem to affect her.

I caught a glimpse of a smile in Tashia's green smoke. "After all this time, I can finally have my revenge."

Her green outline turned toward me again, and I summoned a spell that would work on the ghostly head of a maleika. The lightning bolt fizzled from my fingertips. Instead of striking Tashia, it stopped when it was an inch from her.

Those spells, along with my wounds from earlier, had exhausted me. I needed more time—both to regain my strength, and to come up with something more powerful. It was me she wanted, not the others. I opened the door and scrambled out of the chamber, not wanting her to invade me again.

Outside the door were the crumpled bodies of the snappers. Standing near them were Ardimus and Wynna. They looked over my shoulder and saw what I ran from. Ardimus caught my signal, and when Tashia was in reach, he swiped at her with his enchanted scimitar.

A high-pitched screech rang through my ears. I paused briefly and looked over my shoulder, watching as Tashia's form dematerialized. Ardimus's scimitar had severed her bond to our world. If he could do it again, he might be able to get rid of her completely. Tashia reformed. Ardimus moved to strike her, but she swooped around his blow and glided toward me even faster. I ran, but it was no use. She quickly caught up to me.

I was fearful that she was going to invade my body again, but the demon flew underneath my clothes and tugged at my dagger, forcing it to fall to the floor. Tashia hovered above my dagger, speaking in a demonic tongue. The dagger glowed brightly.

Without warning, it tore a hole in the world. Bright light shone through it, illuminating the dim interior of the construct. There was a powerful pull, like a tide, and the energy moving between worlds tried to pull me in. Luckily, I was too heavy for it. My clothes and hair flapped wildly as the air around me was pulled in.

I stared at the hole, remembering the last time this had happened. My friend Jastillian and I were under attack by Will of the Wisps in a dead zone where I couldn't use my magic. The Will of the Wisps were pulled through the tear between worlds, saving our lives.

Ardimus rushed from behind Tashia, swinging his sword down on her. The demon laughed as her ghostly form was sucked into the portal. Piece by piece she went, until Ardimus's sword struck nothingness. The tear into our world sealed up and vanished.

"She's gone back to the Netherrealm," Serling said, with a wistful look on his face, staring at the place where the portal had been.

"She has," Kreezak said. "And we must stop her!"

"What do you mean?" I asked, staring at his fading form. "She's gone, and no longer our problem."

"If we don't return to the Netherrealm, she will resume her war and destroy every realm in the place that has ever wronged her. She has a long memory."

"What the demon says is true," Serling said. "They were lucky to have stopped Tashia the first time. This time, they will be ill prepared for her, for they never expected to see her again after Renak took her away. But it's your decision, Hellsfire. You owe no debt to those that reside in the Netherrealm, and the reason you came here has been swallowed by a sandstorm."

"Whatever you decide, you must hurry," Ardimus said. "The entire place is falling apart. One way or another, we've got to leave."

Debris rained down on us as the construct swayed. I leaned against a wall to steady myself as I thought about my decision. I hadn't released the demon, but I hadn't truly stopped her either. I was a wizard, and I had a responsibility and a duty. I hadn't forgotten it, even if Premier may had forgotten his.

May Krystal forgive me, but I had to help Kreezak and stop Tashia.

"I'll help you," I said to Kreezak.

"You're going to need a guide," Serling said. "I'll go with you."

"We're coming with you," Ardimus said. "I gave the princess my word nothing would happen to Hellsfire."

"No," Serling said. "You must warn the sultan. Tashia's power has grown. She shouldn't have been able to access the dagger's magic without a physical form, and she won't stop at the Netherrealm. She'll come here next. You must be prepared. I'm asking you to trust me like you once did." He gently laid a hand on Ardimus's shoulder.

Ardimus hesitated, and I watched the conflict in his dark eyes. Serling might have been right, but I would have welcomed Ardimus's sword and skills.

He nodded, but wasn't pleased with it. "Very well. When will you come back?"

"Hard to say, but we'll have to come back through the portal here."

"We'll send word and keep watch. Let's go, Firebird. Good luck to you. Hellsfire. Make it back for the princess's sake."

"I will."

"Let's go, handsome," Wynna said. "We've got to hurry before this place falls. Good luck." The two ran through the tunnel, dodging the debris.

"Hellsfire, let me see the dagger," Serling said. He smiled as he tapped into its power. The blade began to glow and his hair stood on end. "Yes. It's been awhile." Serling lifted the dagger and brought it down through the air, ripping a hole from this world to the Netherrealm.

Kreezak's ghostly form faded with each passing moment, as if he had trouble staying connected to our world. "Stay close." The demon left our world, heading for home.

Serling held out his hand. "Hellsfire, it's very important you hang on to me. If you don't, you can become lost in the Netherrealm. It's a very strange place compared to this world. Even time flows a little differently."

I took his hand and we entered the vortex together. The tunnel of light beckoned us, and we were pulled into another world.

CHAPTER 17

THE OUTLINES OF the crumbling construct faded from my view. Once my body was halfway into the portal, the magic began to suck the rest of me in. It was like my foot was caught in a thick bog and couldn't pull itself free of the muck. Serling grasped my hand tighter, and I let myself be pulled in.

Time itself froze in place. The construct's violent shaking ceased, and from the corner of my eye I glimpsed a piece of falling metal hanging in mid-air. That lasted only a second, until I was catapulted into the Netherrealm.

"Hang on!" Serling said. His high-pitched voice was bursting with elation.

I had ridden a dragon, so I knew how it felt to fly. This sensation reminded me of that, and our bodies weren't flying. We traversed an unseen path, with Serling leading the way. The light of the portal surrounded us, speeding up faster and faster, twirling around my entire body. It grew to blinding brightness, as if we were surrounded by a star.

The light faded as a night-like sky overtook it. My vision returned and as I gazed at the receding light, a piece of it broke off and flew toward me.

"Serling, do you see that?"

But he didn't hear me. His expression looked as if he wasn't even here.

The tiny star circled and glided around me. It stopped right in front of my face. As I stared into it, I glimpsed Krystal. She was lying on her bed, her skin pale and her breath heavy.

"Krystal," I said, reaching out. When my hand touched the star, the light scattered and the image vanished, but through my touch I sensed Krystal's warmth.

The star re-formed and Krystal returned. Her eyes fluttered opened and she gasped, "Hellsfire!"

I called out to her, trying to get her attention, but my words fell upon deaf ears. She glanced around, her violet eyes searching for me. She couldn't see me from her world. Suddenly, she jerked her head up and said, "Who goes there?"

I thought she was talking to me, but the image in the star pulled back and I saw a familiar face. He stepped from the shadows with a malicious grin. Premier. He must have survived the sandstorm and returned to Alexandria.

"Hello, Your Highness," Premier said. He gave her a mock bow. "It's good to see you again. You and I have so much to discuss."

Krystal reached for a hidden dagger near her bed, but Premier cast a spell to restrain her.

I might not have been able to touch her, but perhaps my magic could help. I summoned my power and fire left my hand, twirling through the Netherrealm.

"Hellsfire, what are you doing?" Serling shouted, finally remembering I was there.

When my spell struck the little star, it burst into flame. Its long tendrils of fire stretched toward me. Fearful of it hurting Serling, I let go of him. I raised my defenses just before it smothered me in a fiery cocoon. The pit of my stomach dropped, and so did I.

"Hellsfire!"

Through the fiery shield surrounding me, I glimpsed Serling far above. He stretched his hand out in vain, clinging to a walkway that was now visible to me. He got smaller with each moment, as I fell farther and farther away from him.

I gathered my magic inward, trying to slow myself down. I had no idea how long it would be before I hit the bottom. I cast a wind spell, but the flame around me darkened and smothered my magic. Its fiery touch wormed its way into my mouth. I gagged, trying to force it out. I was drowning as I fell. I fought against it, but the drowning lulled me into unconsciousness.

When I next opened my eyes, I sucked in my breath and flailed my arms. I relaxed and stopped when I realized I wasn't in danger of falling or drowning. I was lying on the ground. I started to pull myself up, but stopped, staring at my surroundings. The entire area was empty, like a blank canvas. Miles of vast nothingness surrounded me. Bright white light shone everywhere, even though there wasn't a light source I could see.

I got up and turned around. No matter which way I turned, the view didn't alter. I conjured my magic, making sure that it still functioned correctly in this strange place. It boiled up inside of me. I was thankful that it still worked. Immediately, I dispersed it. I didn't want to draw the attention of anything that might be attracted to my magic and use it against me, like that little star I'd seen.

I thought about the image I saw before I fell, and wondered if that was merely the Netherrealm preying on my fears, or if Premier had somehow survived the desert and reached Alexandria, or if Krystal had fallen ill again. I wasn't going to find out here. First, I had to find Serling, deal with Tashia, and leave this place alive.

I picked a direction and walked, hoping to find someone or something that would help me.

I was alone with my thoughts for over an hour, and the surroundings never changed. My mind drifted to Krystal, as it inevitability did. Before I had unwittingly cursed her, I thought of her often, mostly missing her. These days, I fretted with worry and guilt over what I'd done to her. With each step, that weight dragged me down.

Every decision I made seemed to be the wrong one. My intentions were always good, but the repercussions were disastrous. I had tried to bring peace, but all I brought was war and death.

I clenched my fists in anger, wondering where in the gods' names Serling was. He was supposed to be my guide, but he hadn't done anything but open a portal here. I had heard crosswalkers had great power, but he couldn't even save me from falling off that path. I didn't know Serling well, and now that he had returned home, would he even bother to do anything about Tashia?

As I thought of the question, the area around me changed. There was no shift or gradual motion, or passage of time. I blinked once, and in that second the white vastness vanished, replaced by a wilderness.

I paused unsure of what had just happened. I took a step backward and bumped into a trio of bright, colorful flowers. The three flowers were as tall as me, and their bright petals were as big as my arms. I leaned in to smell a blue one, and it leaned forward and smelled me. The other two did the same, then sneezed when they sniffed me. Despite my sour mood, I couldn't help but laugh.

I pushed past the sniffing flowers and waded through the blades of grass. They were almost as tall as an elf or dwarf. They brushed softly against my outstretched arms.

I didn't understand how the plants could even exist. There was no sunlight, and I didn't see any birds or bugs. It made no sense, yet everything around me was real to the touch. Even the dirt under my feet smelled real. I grabbed a clump of dirt and held it to my nose. It was moist, as if a previous day's rain had fallen upon it.

"It's real," I said, letting the dirt fall back to the ground.

While it was great to be in a place where I could get my bearings, I still didn't understand the Netherrealm. But that didn't matter. What mattered was that I was one step closer to Tashia.

I picked up my pace, renewed by the new scenery that surrounded me. However, I soon found myself having to push through all the foliage. It grew thicker with each step. I didn't have a blade to cut any of it down, and I didn't want to burn it.

As I walked, a slimy substance stuck to my hands and face. Each leaf I passed rubbed itself against me, smearing me in the stuff. Even my clothes became covered in it. I had more and more trouble walking through the plants, and my muscles strained with each movement. It was like something weighed me down.

I pushed past a large leaf and stopped when I saw a bare-chested, yellow-skinned man in front of me. He stood with a spear at his side, but didn't make a move to use it. He spoke in a tongue I didn't know.

"I'm sorry," I said, "but I don't understand what you're saying."

I tried to take a step forward but couldn't move. I strained my body, but remained stuck. I stared at the yellow man—the white slime hadn't touched him, but I was drenched in it. Something was off—the slime, the plants, this quiet warrior—it didn't feel right. I gathered in my magic, not wanting to hurt a native, but needing to free myself and be on guard.

The yellow man spoke again, but this time the words weren't directed at me—they were directed behind me. As I glanced over my shoulder, a sharp pain struck the back of my neck. I cried out in pain before I blacked out.

The world slowly came into focus. Eyes heavy, I rubbed the back of my neck, remembering the painful blow. I struggled to get up, realizing that I was in a large, soft, comfortable bed. I scanned the room until I saw something across the room that took my breath away.

A tall, naked, light blue woman rose from her bath. My eyes wandered up her legs and around the curvature of her two cheeks. I stared briefly at her back and the two long, transparent wings trailing down, before my gaze headed south again. Clear water clung to her body. There wasn't a blemish on her anywhere. I had never seen a body so perfect.

Her long, dark blue hair wrapped around her body as she turned. She smiled at me. "I'm glad to see you're finally awake." Her voice was as soft and smooth as her skin looked. A yellow, half-naked man wrapped a small sheer robe around her. Much of her flesh was still exposed, and I stared through the robe.

The woman sauntered over to me and helped me sit up. She sat next to me on the bed, and my mind fumbled for words. I couldn't take my eyes off her. She ran her fingers through my hair and shivers trembled down my spine. There were only two people in my life who'd ever had the power to do that.

"You're in great pain," she said.

I blinked several times and found words. "I'm…sorry?"

"I sense great loss and heartache in you."

"Who are you?" I whispered.

"Isn't it customary for a gentleman to introduce himself first?"

"I'm…Hellsfire."

"Hellsfire. An appropriate name." Her honey-filled breath wafted over me. "You may call me Alana."

"Alana...," I said, getting lost in her enchanting blue eyes.

"Yes?"

"You're...very beautiful."

Alana threw her head back and laughed. It sounded like music and warmed my heart.

I shook my head, feeling like it was full of clouds. I couldn't believe what I'd just said. I tried to focus. Something was wrong, but I couldn't tell what. I had seen beautiful women before without reacting like this, but my brain didn't seem to be working. It was as if I'd had one too many of the elves' Winter Chill drinks. "What do you want?" I asked, my voice barely a whisper.

"To help. I can cure your heartache." Her dark blue eyes studied me. "I see you've been afflicted by a terrible curse. It's rooted in you."

My eyes widened. I allowed myself to let hope seep in. "Can you help? I've been through so much."

Alana put her hand on my cheek and I instinctively nuzzled against its softness. "Yes. All I ask is for one favor. One tiny favor and you can be with your beloved again, the way you were meant to be."

"Name it," I said without hesitation.

Alana smiled. "Exactly what I wanted to hear. You must give yourself to me, willingly, as if you were with her."

"I...don't understand."

"Yes, you do," she said, laying a warm hand on my leg.

I was silent as I thought about her proposal. There were magics in the world I didn't understand, and there certainly was magic in the Netherrealm I couldn't even begin to comprehend. If Alana could help break Krystal's curse, then I wouldn't have to watch her wither away, and I might be able to be with her again. Yet that was only second to seeing her healthy and whole again. Krystal had had her whole life ahead of her until she met me. Ever since she came into my life, I had put both her and her kingdom at risk.

I glanced at Alana. I knew what she meant. But Krystal might never forgive me for it, and I would never forgive myself. I loved Krystal and I was committed to her with all my heart, body, and soul.

"I can't," I said, shaking my head.

"Don't you want to be with her?"

"More than anything."

"Then don't you think she would understand?"

I bit my lip. "I suppose." I looked up at her. "Why do you want to do this, and how can you cure her? You don't know me or anything I've been through."

She ignored my accusatory tone and moved even closer, until our bodies were touching. "I know more than you think. The magic lies in *you*, Hellsfire, not her. It is there where I believe I can fix your problem."

I was quiet as I considered her words. I had been checked out by wizards and so had Krystal. They believed that the problem was in her. I'd never suffered any ill effects from the curse, and while she did get worse when I touched her, she also got worse when I wasn't near her. But deep down, I'd always feared that I was the reason my beloved was suffering so much. I always said that I would do anything for her.

"I know you want me, Hellsfire," Alana said, her hand crawling higher up my lap.

I did nothing to stop her as I let out a sigh of ecstasy.

"I know it's been too long for you. Far too long. I can see it around you. Let it go and be with me," she whispered into my ear, before nibbling it. "She would understand. It's not like you would go through any pain. You'd be in a state of bliss. She wants you to be happy even if it's not with her."

I turned to look at her so I could refuse her again. That turned out to be a mistake, I got lost in those enchanting blue eyes of hers. I couldn't speak, and Alana took the opportunity to press her lips on mine. I couldn't resist—didn't resist. It had been far too long since I had any physical pleasure. Our mouths opened and our tongues mingled with one another. I'd thought I could only feel this way with Krystal, but there was something special about Alana. She tasted like the sweetest pastry and I wanted nothing more than to devour her.

Alana broke the kiss. I froze for a second, yet my body ached for more. A slow smile built across her face and her eyes glistened with desire, but she didn't make another move.

I cleared my throat. "I'll do it." I couldn't have said no. My body wouldn't have let me.

I leaned in for another kiss, but Alana pulled back and rose. She slipped out of her robe, letting it fall to the floor, once more exposing her perfect flesh. I couldn't take it anymore, and I grabbed her wrists and reeled her into me. She laughed as she fell, a delightful sound I ached to hear more of. I kissed her with fervor and she returned my passion by pressing herself against me harder. We rolled around on the lofty bed, my hands seeking out every part of her body. I yearned for her as if I was dying of thirst. Alana tugged at my clothes, but I didn't care if she ripped them off.

The doors at the far end of the room were flung open and someone yelled, "Mother!"

CHAPTER 18

ALANA GROWLED and her nails dug into my skin. Her calm, light blue eyes darkened and swirled about like little storms, and I pulled myself away from her. "Guards! Get her out of here!"

From the high rafters, more winged women I hadn't seen before emerged from the shadows. They dove down, their crystal-tipped spears pointed at the intruder, a pink-skinned woman with wings like Alana's.

I shook my head, trying to focus and think, but Alana wrapped her arms around me, pulling me closer. The storms in her eyes had abated. "Now, where were we?" She kissed me on the neck and I no longer cared about the interruption.

"Let go of me!" the stranger yelled. "Mother, we don't have time for this! We must—"

Alana peeled herself off me and said, "I know what we must do, child. I'm in the middle of doing something about it now."

The guards restrained the angry fairy, grabbing her and pushing her out of the room. But the intruder fought and strained against them. Her wings fluttered in frustration. Her eyes settled on me and she stopped fighting.

"Hellsfire?"

She knew me, but I didn't know how. I would have remembered meeting a light pink woman with wings. Her voice sounded very familiar, though. She had an unusual haircut—her hair was cropped short, was of a far darker pink than her skin. She looked a lot like Alana especially in the shape of her face. I shook my head, trying to clear the fog that filled it.

Alana wrapped herself around me, drawing me back to the bed. "Ignore her. She's not important right now, is she?" Alana traced my ear with her tongue while her hand crawled under my tunic.

"No," I said. "I suppose not."

"Hellsfire!" the pink woman said. "Think! Don't you recognize me, cutie?" A disappointed look crossed her face.

It was that playful tone and that word that triggered my memory. There was only one person who it could be. "Serena?"

"How many other pink fairies do you know?" she said, with a huge grin on her face.

I untangled myself from Alana and strode to my friend, ignoring the guards.

"Serena," I said, gawking at her. My eyes took in my fairy friend, from her legs to her round face. My eyes momentarily rested on her chest. "You look…bigger."

She giggled. "Bigger?"

The heat in my cheeks rose. "I didn't mean it like that." I was used to Serena being only a couple of inches tall. She had either hovered around me or rested on my shoulder.

"If you say so, cutie."

"Serena!" Alana said, storming over to us. She stood naked and was unashamed about it. Not that she had anything to be ashamed of, with her soft, unblemished body. I kept stealing glances at her. "What is the meaning of this interruption? We were in the middle of something important, and you know how I do not like to be disturbed during this time."

"I know what you were in the middle of, *Mother*. We have far more important matters to attend to than you seducing him with your magic." Serena turned toward me. "After all the things you told me about the princess, I can't believe you would do this to her."

I shook my head. "Alana said she could cure Krystal. She said the problem lay with me. You don't know the suffering I've caused Krystal and the pain she's been in. She's dying, Serena, and it's all my fault. I have to do anything I can to cure her."

My friend put a kind hand to my face and I took her hand in mine. "I'm sorry, Hellsfire, but you mustn't trust my mother. She would promise you anything to get you into bed. Once that happened, you would be hers—bound now and forever."

Her words piqued my anger. The fire within me boiled to the surface, evaporating the haze in my mind. "You dangled my love in front of me, and lied and tricked me!"

The fairies pointed their weapons at me, but Alana waved them off. She strutted closer to me, without a trace of fear.

"My dear Hellsfire," Alana said. "I wasn't lying. The problem is in you. There's magic there that shouldn't be there. I could get rid of it. And I could ease your pain. The suffering and heartache coming from you is intense."

"How could you break the curse if the entire Elemental Council couldn't?"

"I'm the Queen of the Fairies. There are magics in this realm I wield that you and your kind will never understand." Alana held her hands out. I took them and allowed myself to be reeled in.

"Mother!" Serena said, slapping Alana's hands away. "Stop using your magic on him!"

"Stop acting like a petulant child. We could use his power, especially now."

"You could always ask him for his help. That's the way decent human beings do things."

"You forget yourself. I'm not human and neither are you. You've been in their world for far too long."

"He's helped people before, and I know he'd do it again."

Alana gave a taunting smile to Serena while she slithered across my body. Her bare breasts rubbed up against my back. I gulped as her warmth seeped through my clothes. I tried to resist, but my body desired to be subdued by her.

"You're jealous, my daughter. You reek of it."

Serena narrowed her pink eyes at Alana. "Tashia's breached the Outer Rim."

Alana gasped. "Impossible." She stared at her daughter, then left me to grab her robes. I couldn't sense her magic, but she must have relinquished her hold on me because my knees buckled. Luckily, Serena caught me.

"Thanks," I said.

"No problem, cutie."

"Myla," Alana said, focusing her attention on a purple fairy. "Is what Serena says true?"

"Possibly. We've heard…rumors of the breach. I've already sent out scouts to confirm."

"Why did no one tell me?"

"You ordered that you not be disturbed, and I wanted confirmation first before coming to you."

"Not for something as important as this. Let's go. Leave these two alone. Hellsfire, I'll see you later." Alana gave me a tantalizing smile. For a moment, I lost my breath. Even though I now knew what she was doing, I still couldn't stop her. It was going to be hard to get used to this place and its weird magic. Everyone flooded out of the room behind Alana.

"Sure," I said. "I mean, no. What in the Inferno just happened?"

"Don't be too hard on yourself," Serena said. "My mother's magic is *very* powerful, and she's able to sense what your weaknesses and desires are."

My face soured. "I didn't sense any magic."

Serena giggled. "This is your first time in the Netherrealm, silly. Things are slightly different here than in your world."

I eyed her up and down and smirked. "I can see that."

Her face grew cherry red. "Oh, here, let me help you to the bed while the after effects of my mother's magic disappear. With her gone, your head will clear and your body won't be so…reactive to its desires. What are you doing here? Never mind. I *knew* you were eventually going to come here. I was right, and I'm not even a seer. I can't wait to tell Malik about this."

Malik was another wizard who was very close to Serena. He had once traveled to the Netherrealm and met Serena here. As much as Serena teased him about it, he didn't want to return here. He must have had to deal with the same problems I had when he first arrived though.

"How did Malik survive being here?"

"He…doesn't like to talk about it." Serena looked wistful. "When he first came here, he took pleasure and delight in this realm. Something happened to him that hardened him to Fairie."

"And you don't know what it is?"

Serena shook her head. "No, but I believe it had something to do with my mother. Whatever happened, her magic no longer works on Malik."

I nodded, thinking to be sure to ask him about it one day, if I survived this.

"I wish I could show you how beautiful our world is," she said. "I think you'd love it." She sighed. "But we're busy fighting a war against an extremely powerful and ancient demon. From what I've heard, she's stronger than before." She fidgeted with the blankets. "I'm not even sure if we can win."

"Tashia," I said.

Serena's pink eyes focused on me. "How do you know about her?"

"That's why I'm here. I came to warn the people of this realm and to stop her."

She beamed. "I knew it couldn't have been a coincidence that you were here. I can't wait to hear this story."

I relayed the entire story of what had taken place in the Burning Sands. Serena couldn't keep still, and flew around me while I talked. She did that back in my world, but it was far easier to handle there because of her size.

"Wow," Serena said. She lay on the bed on her stomach, with her legs kicked up. "You've been through a lot, Hellsfire. We should go and tell my mother that you'll help her. Even better if I could get credit for convincing you to. No matter what, make it seem like you're doing her a favor. Don't tell her you were coming here to help anyway. I'll help you find the crosswalker and the demon." She grinned. "But after we talk to my mother, we get something to eat, because I'm starving."

Serena led me from Alana's chambers. When we reached the doors, the circular symbol on them brightened before they split apart and opened inward. I was about to ask Serena about it when the bright light outside Alana's room struck me. I stumbled and grabbed Serena's shoulder, letting my eyes adjust to the light. There were no candles or torches, but the hallway contained a blinding, midday's sunlight.

The walls of the palace were built from a substance that reminded me of quartz. It looked clear, but I couldn't see through into the other rooms. I put my hand against the wall, feeling how smooth it was. Underneath it was a pulsating light and as I stared at it, I realized that was the source of the light in the hallway.

Serena couldn't help but notice my gawking. She told me how outside the individual rooms, the light was bright and always on, but inside the rooms a person could adjust it as they preferred. Her mother always preferred her room to be dimly lit, as it made things more comfortable.

The hallways were massive, both in width and length. The ceiling was fifty feet up, allowing enough room for dozens of fairies to fly over our heads. They zipped back and forth going about their duties.

Serena put her hands on her hips and stared at me. "Are you finished? We've got a war to prepare for. Come on!"

My fairy friend grabbed my hand and led me down the hall. She was right. We had to hurry. Serling and Kreezak could be anywhere in the Netherrealm and from what she'd told me, it was a bigger realm than I originally thought.

We passed through throngs of other fairies and Serena's wings kept fluttering as we went. Every few yards her feet lifted off the floor and I could tell she wanted to fly.

As we passed through the hallway, I noticed that all the flying fairies were women. They were the only ones with wings. All the males were very similar to the yellow one who'd ambushed me. They didn't wear any shirts, and most of them were very muscular. We passed by a group of male fairies jogging, and an orange one smiled and winked at Serena as he went by.

It was weird and wonderful walking in the palace. It was as if I was drowning in a rainbow sea. The fairies were frantic with activity, and I watched as weapons, troops, and supplies went back and forth. There could only be one thing on their minds—war.

I'd been through war before. I'd never fought for land, riches, or titles—I always fought for people. My life never mattered as much as theirs. Now, my friend had a war to fight.

"Why are you here, Serena?"

"Although I prefer your world to this one, this is still my home and I come back to visit. Although my mother would tell you that it's not often enough."

"You picked a bad time to visit."

She sighed and gave a wry smile. "Tell me about it. But that doesn't matter. I'm here now, and I will fight."

"I can see that. I've seen how Serling can cross over to the Netherealm, but how do you do it? Do you also need a ritual or spell?"

"There are a few weaknesses in the veils that separate worlds. We're able to spot them and come and go through them easily enough. My mother has her own portal. It costs us, though. For us fairies, it costs us our size and our Netherrealm magic, as you can see by my size. Demons can't go through those weaknesses. They have to be summoned into your world by another. Some of you mortals accidentally pierce a weakness in the veil and fall into our realm. It's rare, but it does happen." She smiled. "That's how Malik came here."

"I still don't understand how the war has already progressed so far. I got here less than a day ago."

She nudged me. "Didn't your crosswalker tell you that time works differently here? And you were in the worst spot for time to move—the fields of nothingness. Time speeds up while you're there, even though it doesn't seem like it."

I gritted my teeth. "I should have known." There were far too many rules to the Netherrealm. I had to learn what they were—and quickly—if I was going to have any chance of defeating Tashia.

"From what I understand, the fairies defeated Tashia last time."

"We did, but it was well before my time. From what I know, we had help, and the demon wasn't as strong as she is now." She sighed, the gloominess overtaking her bright eyes. "Tashia surprised us. She organized an army of demons and viciously attacked us before we knew she was there. We weren't prepared. Whatever Renak did to her, she's become far more powerful than before. So much so that the other leaders have accepted the ultimatum given to them. And with her victories, more have joined her."

"What ultimatum?"

"Stay out of the fight or die. I believe they're buying time. They want to see who will actually win. My mother has her fair share of enemies, but so does Tashia. There will be no outside help this time. We're all alone, and I'm not sure we can win."

I reached out and cupped her drooping head until her pink eyes met mine. "I'll fight with you to the end."

A smile slowly crept across her face. "I know you will. As powerful as you are, I can only hope that one wizard is enough."

I exhaled. She was right. I might not be enough. I had already faced Tashia's power, and it was intense even when she didn't have a body. Luckily, I was not alone. Now that we were back in the Netherrealm, Serling's power should be immense. Just how much he had, I needed to find out. But first we had to find him.

"If we find Serling, we may yet have a fighting chance," I said.

"Agreed."

Serena continued to lead me through the crystal palace. We went to the entrance hall, where Alana would be. Serena thought it best that I should talk to Alana first, and tell her that I would fight for her, because of Serena's persuasion of course.

The entrance hall had colored crystals dangling from the high ceiling. There were small ones and large ones, and they all sparkled. I craned my neck to see them all. The blue ones reminded me of a lake on a clear day, and the green ones were like a field of grass rippling in the wind. My eyes settled on the tiny purple crystals that clung to the wall like moss. The twinkling violet crystals reminded me of someone that I desperately wanted to hold again, and hear her laugh, full of life.

A gentle hand was placed on my shoulder. "Hellsfire, are you all right?"

"I'm fine, Serena. I was just…looking at the beautiful crystals. They're quite something."

She stared at me with suspicious eyes. "If you say so."

I tore my attention away from the dazzling lights and focused it on the back of the room. Alana was sitting on a throne, with half a dozen fairies around her. The throne was unlike any I had ever seen before.

It looked to be made out of the same material as the palace, but it must have been far softer. The throne contoured itself to Alana's every curve. Every time she moved, it shifted with her. It also changed color. It was a deep crimson red, until Alana spotted me and Serena. As she locked her gaze on us, the throne darkened to green.

Alana put a hand up and the fairies around her went silent as Serena and I approached. She smiled at me, and the pit of my stomach dropped. If I ever saw Tyree again, I needed to ask Malik how he was able to withstand Alana's magic.

The fairies around Alana parted, and I bowed. "Your Majesty."

"Mistress," Serena whispered in my ear.

"Forgive me, mistress," I said.

I was about to speak when the doors at the front of the room exploded open. I summoned my magic to me, getting ready to shield both myself and Serena from the immense power coming our way.

CHAPTER 19

AS THE INTRUDER entered Alana's palace, she sat motionless. Her people didn't, however. Two of the fairies took off flying toward the intruder. The debris from the fallen door finally cleared, and I was able to make out the person's silhouette.

"Serling? Stop!" I yelled.

Alana glanced my way, but didn't make a move to stop her people or Serling.

There was a cackle of energy around Serling. Did Alana notice? One fairy thrust her spear at him. He deflected it with his staff and when their weapons touched, a jolt of energy shot through the fairy. She was thrown back and crashed into the wall. The other fairy was a bit more cautious, sizing up Serling. But it didn't matter. Serling struck the floor with his staff. The Netherrealm magic surged forward and shocked the fairy. She froze in agony before dropping her sword.

Dozens of fairies had flooded into the chamber with weapons, ready to defend their queen.

Alana finally rose and said, "Crosswalker."

From behind Serling, flew a dark red creature. His rolls of squishy fat and round cheeks jiggled every time he moved. His thick wings were somehow able to support his wide frame.

"You dare to bring a demon into *my* realm?" Alana said.

All the crystals in the room grew crimson red. The ceiling seemed to shrink, and crystals around Serling and Kreezak lengthened.

Serling bowed and said, "Forgive me, mistress, for the intrusion and for trespassing onto your land. Your guards wouldn't let us in. They are fine, if a little sore."

"I recognize your power," Alana said, pointing a long finger at Serling. "I thought we banned you from ever crossing over into this realm again. Guards, kill the demon. I will take care of the crosswalker myself."

I looked to Serena, but she had already turned to Alana. "Mother!" Serena said. "Please let these two be. They came here for a reason."

Alana's blue eyes deepened like the ocean, and the storms within them rose. "You have no idea what you're talking about, daughter. These two were before your time. They're dangerous. *Very* dangerous. I've got enough problems to worry about without adding one crosswalker and one more demon to the list."

Serena moved in front of her mother, putting herself between them, in harm's way. "They're Hellsfire's companions. And they came here to help us stop Tashia."

Alana's eyes lightened until they became the color of ice. The fairy queen glared at Serling. "Is what she says true, crosswalker?"

Serling returned Alana's stare. "My help won't come without a price. My price is simple. Lift my ban, and I will fight for you."

The fairy queen sat back down on her throne. She leaned back and said, "And that's all you ask for?"

"Yes, mistress."

Alana was quiet as she considered his offer. Finally, she spoke. "There was a reason you were banished, crosswalker. I would have preferred your death over exile. Cross me again, and you will become bound to me. And what of you, Hellsfire?" Alana's gaze shifted to me. Her icy eyes regained color and in a sweet voice she said, "You were coming to tell me something?"

~ **190** ~

I grinned and said, "Yes. I mean, no." I shook my head. "I mean, Serena convinced me to fight for you and help defeat Tashia."

Alana raised her eyebrows. "Did she now? How did she manage that, I wonder?" She had a teasing smile on her face.

I took a step forward and opened my mouth. An overwhelming urge to tell the truth came over me. I clenched my fists, forcing my nails to dig into them. Alana was using her magic. While my mind fought against her, my body wanted to succumb to her. I couldn't use my own magic, as I would cause a scene in Alana's court. I didn't want to make an enemy of Alana, yet if I told the truth of why Tashia was in the Netherrealm, I might have one.

I latched onto the truth to overcome Alana's magic. "Serena's a friend, and I would do anything to help her."

Alana clapped her hands and laughed. "Delightful. I like you, Hellsfire. Serena, you must keep him. He's far more entertaining than that dour seeker of yours."

The crystals in the ceiling returned to their wondrous colors, and Alana rose. "Serena, be a dear and take care of our…guests. I have much work to do." Her eyes flashed. "Hellsfire, I'll see you later." She strutted away, and the rest of the fairies followed her.

Serling and Kreezak came up to me and Serena. Serling no longer had to limp like he did before. He stood proudly, his body empowered by his Netherealm magic.

"It's good to see you, Hellsfire," the crosswalker said. "I was afraid I'd lost you. I'm thankful the fairies found you."

"How'd you know I'd be here?" I asked.

He shrugged. "I didn't. I came here to offer my services to Alana. Count your blessings from the gods you were here. Because of the war, Kreezak and I ended up in a…not so friendly place." Serling took a deep breath. His eyes scanned the place. "I must say, it feels good to be home again, even if I am in the one realm that's probably worse for me than the demon one."

"And it's good to have a body again," Kreezak said, stretching his pudgy arms.

"I don't know if I've ever seen someone stand up to my mother like that before," Serena said with a baffled look on her face. "And live."

"There's always a first. Who might you be, young fairy?"

"I'm Hellsfire's friend, Serena."

"A pleasure to meet you," Serling said, and shook her hand. "This is Kreezak."

The demon held out his hand. Serena hesitated before quickly shaking it and snatching her hand away.

"What happened between you two?" I asked. "Why were you banished from this place?"

"That's a long story," Serling said. "One we haven't time for. Tashia's breaking through Alana's defenses like a bear eating honey. We must be ready when Alana makes her final stand. Let's get going."

"Where?" I said.

"To get help from an old friend."

Serling told us where we were headed. Serena gathered supplies for us while we waited in the audience chamber. The fairies that passed through eyed us all, but their coldest looks were for Kreezak. Serena came back with packs for all of us. She handed me and Serling ours, but simply tossed one at Kreezak.

"My mother wonders if you're going to flee again, crosswalker," Serena said. "But she doesn't have the time to deal with you right now. She's entrusting me to make sure you will help her defeat Tashia."

"I will. I would not want to return home to have Tashia ruling the realm."

"Good. Now what are we waiting for? We have a long journey ahead of us, and we don't have time to waste."

We exited the palace and ventured into the Netherrealm, with Serling leading the way. According to Serling, it was going to take three days to get where we needed to go. It would have been quicker had we had something to mount and ride, but Alana couldn't spare us any transport, no matter how much Serena had begged her. My guess was no matter how much Alana needed help, she still didn't trust Serling.

As we traveled, I still couldn't get used to the Netherrealm. The landscape changed at a moment's notice. Forests, plains, mountains, and even towns appeared in our path, or all around us, before quickly vanishing again. No matter how real the environment appeared, I couldn't help but feel that things were out of place. It was always the lack of sound that bothered me.

Growing up in my village, there were always sounds, whether it was birds taking flight from their branches, the crickets chirping, or the rain pounding on the roof. Living in cities the past few years, I'd learned they had their own set of noises—vendors yelling about their wares, guards patrolling the streets, hooves pounding against stone.

But there was no sound here except for us, and those made by the few souls we encountered. Those other inhabitants stayed further away from us, the closer we got to the edge of Alana's kingdom. Serena told me her mother had rallied all those within her borders that could fight. All that would be left were the weak.

I found it hard to keep track of time. During the first day, it was forever bright. The invisible light never dimmed nor darkened during that long day. Even when I slept, I had to bury my head in my bedroll, doing my best to block out the light. On the second day, I was extremely tired from the lack of sleep, but was awed by the lake we navigated around. The water was orange, making it look like it was on fire. The others warned me not to drink of it. Two hours after that lake, we were plummeted into pitch-black darkness. Serling illuminated the way with his power. Those three had no problem navigating the darkness or avoiding obstacles. I myself tripped over a rather sizable rock.

My companions felt at ease in this strange world, and I knew that I would never feel that way. Serling promised me that we were almost at our destination. As I stared at the murky sky and its spotty clouds, I didn't believe him.

As much as the landscape confused and depressed me, our trek did afford me time to think about what kind of spells I could use against Tashia. My elemental magic hadn't worked against her while we were in the Burning Sands, but Kreezak told me that like him, Tashia would have a body in this realm. She should be susceptible to my magic. But she would be far stronger and more powerful than before, and my spells would have to be just as potent to hurt her.

Serena was walking by my side, as she had been for the last three days. She talked to Serling asking him a lot of questions, as she had never met a crosswalker before. But she didn't speak to Kreezak unless she had to.

"Still don't like it here?" she asked me.

"It's...different from what I expected. It might take some getting used to."

"I hope I can show you around once this war is done. My mother's realm is a lot different during peacetime. It seems empty now, but that's because everyone is hiding or fighting. If you thought the Fiery Lake was great, it's nothing compared to what else is out there."

"I would like that."

Serena's looked straight ahead. "Serling told us where we were going, but I didn't understand why. I still don't. There's nothing of importance out here that I know of. I pray that mother was wrong about him, for all our sakes." Her look hardened when she glanced at Kreezak's back.

I lowered my voice. "What are you so cold to Kreezak?"

She breathed out and ran her fingers through her dark pink hair. "I suppose I am, aren't I? I don't mean to be. It's just...he makes my skin crawl." She rubbed her bare arms and shivered. "Fairies and demons are natural enemies, much like a wolf and a moose. Maybe more accurately, it's like when a human sees a spider crawling about their home. You want to squish it."

"So you want to squish Kreezak?"

Serena chuckled. "You know what I mean. I mean him no harm." Her hand went to her sword hilt. "Tashia, on the other hand, I do want to squish." Her voice went quiet. "I hope we get the chance. Before you showed up, things weren't going so well for us."

I reached out my hand and grabbed hers. With far more bravado than I actually felt, I said, "I'll do everything in my power to stop her. It's my fault she's here in the first place. We also have Serling and whatever crosswalker tricks he has."

Serena's thumb caressed my hands. "Thanks, Hellsfire."

She smiled and I returned it. The heat in my cheeks rose, and I was acutely aware of how warm her hand was. Over the last few months while I was in Tyree, Serena and I had gotten closer. But she normally fit in the palm of my hand or sat on my shoulder. That was no longer the case. My eyes traced her curves, wondering what else she could do at this size.

I cleared my throat, shook my head, and let go of Serena's hand. An aura rose up around her. The magic she radiated was similar to Serling's, but distinct enough to be its own thing. An urge to grab Serena and kiss her threatened to overwhelm me. I fought against it, and saw Serena's lingering look. Was she aware of the magic she cast? Despite what she believed, she was her mother's daughter.

"Hellsfire," Serling said, looking back at me. "We're here."

Serling and Kreezak stood at the entrance to a cave, one of many caves in the side of a small mountain range. The surface of the mountain was the color of molasses, but it shone like glass. No grass, dirt, or snow covered the sterile surface. The crosswalker and demon ventured inside one of the openings.

"The Endless Caves," Serena said. "But what could be of value in this place?" There was a tightness in her face.

I still couldn't trust Serling as much as Ardimus and Wynna did. There was just too much I didn't know about him, and he had committed a crime that was bad enough to get him banished.

"You'll always have me," I said. Serena briefly laid her head against my arm before we rushed to catch up to the others.

When we entered the dark eerie cave, the top of Serling's staff flared and a small, shining sphere of light appeared. The inside of the caves didn't have the same glassy sheen that the outside had. The rocky walls and ceilings were indistinguishable from one another. The ceilings and walls were far too close for my taste; the enclosed place made my heart beat faster. I hated small places—especially ones with the stale air of a coffin and no natural light. I closed my eyes and took a deep breath. Now was not the time to panic. I had to focus, and defeat Tashia.

"Why are we in The Endless Caves?" Serena asked.

"They may be called The Endless Caves, but they're not The Empty Caves," Serling said as he led us down a passage. "I promised I would find help, and this is where it is."

"People have gotten lost in here. There's a story of—"

"I know the stories, young fairy. Do not fear, I can guide us out once we're done."

"Why does your friend live here?" I asked.

"He has no choice."

We continued walking until we arrived at an even smaller cave. There was no exit in this one, and if I stretched out my arms, I could easily touch both sides. My heart sped up and sweat hung on my brow. I wanted to scream at Serling for bringing us here, and run off to get some fresh air. But I stood my ground and focused on the crosswalker.

Serling put his staff closer to the wall. "This is why we're here."

By the light of his staff, I could see the outline of a person on the wall, as if a child had taken a piece of charcoal and scribbled a picture of a body, twisted into an impossible position. But as I looked closer, I could see that wasn't it. It was as if the figure was a part of the wall. Everything was scribbled in black except for two bright red eyes.

"The story is true!" Serena said in a whisper, her hand covering her mouth.

"Story?" I asked.

"There was once a story about a corrupt crosswalker. For his crime, he was forever imprisoned inside a wall."

"What was his crime?"

"He stole gems from the Fairy Queen," Serling said. "And I imprisoned him for it. Alana learned as much as she could with her persuasions and torture, but the gems were never recovered."

"You put him like this?" I said. "Surely, there would have been a better solution?" I stared at the human-like painting.

"You don't know Brax the way I do."

"You want to free him?" I asked. "What makes you think he'd be in the mood to help us?"

"*This* was your plan?" Kreezak said, flying away from the man in the wall. He hovered near the entrance. "I can see why you didn't want to tell me *who* you were going to get. You realize that once you free him, he's going to want revenge on you and then—" Kreezak gulped "Me."

"That has crossed my mind, but we have little choice. Tashia's out there decimating the fairies, and Brax is the only one who might be able to stop her." Serling looked to Kreezak. "You spoke of revenge, and that's what I'm counting on. I'm hoping his hate for Tashia will eclipse any hate for you, me, or the Fairy Queen."

The demon snorted. "Hope."

We three retreated to the walls while Serling summoned his power. As the days passed, I had gotten used to his Netherrealm magic. He'd told me the powers he used were the links that bound the manas and the worlds. Now he chanted, and an electrical energy surrounded him. The purple and blue power sizzled, its crackling noise filling the low cave. Serling pounded his long staff on the floor. The energy shot out across the prisoner's cage. He did it again and again, and streaks raced across its smooth surface. Serling did it one last time, plunging his staff into the ground. The invisible cage shattered and the light from his staff was snuffed out, plummeting us into darkness.

Serling relit his staff. The shadow-like figure didn't move. It was still flat, carved into the wall.

"Did you do it correctly?" Serena asked. "It's been centuries since you've last done this. Has a person ever been trapped for so long?"

"You may be right," Serling said, taking a step closer and stroking his chin.

"If he is dead," Kreezak said, "we should thank the gods for small favors."

A dark hand peeled itself from the cave wall, stretching out and grabbing Serling by the throat. Two hate-filled red eyes flared to life. The sketch on the wall deepened, gaining more mass, until it became three-dimensional. The man extracted himself from his trap, his hand still on Serling's throat. The figure might have once been human, but he wasn't any longer. A black, thick armor like that of an armadillo covered him and his face was hazy, as if covered in a dark fog.

"Serling," he said, his voice dripping like venom and chilling the air. "You're not going to get Alana's precious treasure back, no." His hand tightened around Serling's throat, and the crosswalker struggled, trying to break Brax's iron grip.

"Leave him alone," I said, stepping forward with my dark flames surrounding me.

"Renak!" The man's red eyes dimmed and he dropped Serling. "Not Renak, no."

Serling gasped for air, his aged hand rubbing against his throat. "I'm…fine," he said, his voice raspy. "I had forgotten how strong Brax was. Is."

Kreezak and Serena came forward with weapons drawn. All four of us cornered Brax against the wall.

"Come to kill me, Serling?" Brax asked.

"I came here for your help."

Brax laughed. The harsh sound rang in my ears. "This must be another one of the fairy's tricks, yes. You'd be surprised at how good the desire-filled creatures are at torture."

"It's no trick," Kreezak said.

"Kree, what a nice surprise." Brax's fierce red eyes bore into Kree for several long moments. The demon squirmed under his gaze. Brax turned his attention back to Serling. "And what do I get in return for helping you?"

"Your freedom," Serling said.

"The fairy queen would never allow that, no."

"These aren't normal circumstances."

"What could be so important for her to free me, I wonder?"

"She didn't free you, *I* did. You would do well to remember it."

"So you say, yes." Brax narrowed his crimson eyes at Serling. "Name it, and we'll see."

"Tashia's back."

Brax's red eyes deepened. He balled his hand up, turned around, and punched the wall with his gauntlet-like hand. Pieces of rock tumbled down, though the hard wall didn't seem to hurt him. "That bitch!" He continued punching the wall until a hole appeared. He stopped and appeared to look to the heavens. "She is here. I sense her. And she is stronger."

The same magic that radiated off Serling began to emanate from Brax. Whereas Serling used his power to cast his spells, it seemed like Brax used it to enhance his body. Thankfully, Brax's power was nowhere near as strong as Serling's, but with each passing moment, it grew.

"Will you help us?" Serling asked, facing the bigger and stronger man.

Brax growled. "To kill Tashia, I'm going to need my sword."

"I destroyed your sword, remember?"

"Ahhh, yes, and I almost destroyed you. That's a lot of energy you're using to walk, Serling." In Brax's shadowed face, I saw the outline of a smile. "How's the leg?"

"We don't have time for this, Brax. She's breached the Outer Rim."

"What do I care if she destroys the pretty little fairies?" Brax said, leering at Serena. I stood in front of her with my magic at the ready.

"Brax!" Serling said, pounding his staff on the ground.

"How do I know Alana will keep her word and set me free?"

"She will."

Brax seemed to mull Serling's answer over. "At least for the time being she will, yes. We do have a common enemy. My bigger problem is, how do I know if I can trust *him?*" Brax took one long stride, closing the distance between him and Kreezak. He grabbed Kreezak by the throat, squeezing the fat out of him.

The demon squirmed, and slime and sweat oozed onto Brax's hand. Serling summoned an energy ball and slung it at Brax's hand. Brax grunted and dropped Kreezak.

"I had forgotten how much those sting," Brax said, shaking his hand. "How many of them do you think you can create before I tear your head off, Serling?"

"You'll have to contend with all of us," I said, summoning the fire and letting it dance in my hand.

"Yes," Serena said, her hand tightening on her sword.

Brax's laughter boomed. "Strange bunch, yes. All I ask is for one simple favor. Let me kill Kreezak. I'll even make it quick and painless—something I'm not prone to doing to my enemies."

"No," Serling said. "Considering the history those two have, we may need him."

Kreezak wiped the sweat from his forehead.

Brax said, "His feelings for Tashia are a liability. They were for me, yes. He already crossed me once."

"Feelings?" I said, raising an eyebrow.

"You don't know, wizard?" Brax said. "It's a rather important piece of information, yes, but I suppose the demon left that part of out. Serling should have told you never to trust a demon, especially this one. Kree's in love with Tashia. That's why he betrayed me to her. He was supposed to be on my side. He was part of *my* gang, and he betrayed me!" Brax's red eyes flared again.

"I didn't know!" Kreezak said, fluttering away from Brax.

"That makes it even worse, yes," Brax said. "You're either too stupid to be of any use, or you'll betray us to be with her. I don't want to be working with someone like that, no."

"So you're with us?" Serling asked.

Before Brax could reply, a loud, screeching noise rang through the caves. I cocked my head, trying to get a bearing on where it was coming from. It grew louder, getting closer to us. I raised my magic to get my defenses ready.

A portion of the cave wall exploded. I ducked as chunks of rock sprayed everywhere. A very large and jagged sword flew through the wall, soaring straight to Brax. He caught the handle with one hand and a surge of energy burst from him, nearly knocking us over.

"Ah, yes," Brax said, raising his mighty sword.

CHAPTER 20

I RELEASED MY gathered magic, using it as a shield for me and Serena. The air glistened with my energy as I prepared to deflect a blow from Brax's sword.

Brax paused, and I made out a shadowy smile on his featureless face. He strapped the massive weapon to his back and said, "What are you waiting for? We must move quickly before the fairies fall and we're fighting on our own, yes."

"You're going to help us?" Serling asked, lowering his staff.

"I have bigger concerns than either of you. But after this is done, we have a score to settle, yes."

"I know."

"Good." Brax turned his eyes on Kreezak. "You had better not cross me again, Kree, no."

Kreezak swallowed. "I won't."

"We shall see."

We left the confines of Brax's prison. Serling led the way out of the endless dark caves, the globe on top of his staff glowing. Kreezak stuck close to Serling's side, but constantly kept glancing back at Brax. Serena and I trailed Brax to make sure he didn't try anything.

"I thought I destroyed your sword," Serling said, ducking a low archway.

"You almost did," Brax said. "But it repaired itself. After all, I've been trapped for ages, yes."

I stared at the sword that was strapped to his back. The sword was enchanted, that much was plain to see, but there was more to it than that. Far more. I was only beginning to understand Netherrealm magic, but the sword was clearly linked to Brax. He had far more power than before. It was as if he stored his own power in the sword, like Serling had described when he was examining my father's dagger. While I had heard of people storing their power in objects, it always carried a risk. You could be separated from the object, or it could be destroyed, and then you would be powerless. If I was right, though, Brax had taken it even further with his magic.

I said, "As long as you live, your sword can never be destroyed, and vice versa."

Brax stopped and looked back at me. "You are a clever wizard, yes." Brax chuckled, which sounded disturbing with his deep voice. "If only the fairies had figured that out earlier, I might have been destroyed."

"I thought I severed that connection with your sword," Serling said. "I will not make that mistake again."

Brax's eyes bore into Serling. "There won't be a next time." He turned his attention back to me. "If you ever get bored with Serling, wizard, you should work for me. I could use you. You have power and aren't afraid. I can give you anything you can possibly want."

"You can't even begin to understand what I want."

Brax faced me. He was stouter and taller than me, and his magic was powerful. He drew his sword, and it hissed like a deadly snake.

"My sword is hungry, little wizard, yes. It needs to feed and it's time it had something to eat."

I stood my ground and summoned my own magic, continuing to stare into his crimson eyes. I wasn't going to back down from him. I was getting weary of people speaking empty promises and thinking they knew what I wanted.

"Brax!" Serling said, and grabbed Brax's sword arm. "We haven't time for this."

Brax tore his arm away from Serling, and I thought he might bring down his weapon on him. He paused and his magic subsided. "Not yet, no." He put away his sword and began walking again. "I want Tashia's blood on here, yes, but we're going to need help. The fairies were lucky once. Tashia's much stronger now. She'll easily defeat whatever pitiful army Alana has."

"What do you have in mind?" Serling asked.

"Time to bring the old gang back together, yes."

"You've got to be joking!" Kreezak said, fluttering around Brax.

"Was I ever one to joke?"

"Uh, no, but they're probably all dead. A lot of time has passed since you've walked the Netherrealm. Or worse yet, they joined Tashia's side."

"They'd never join her, no. They despised her as much as I did."

"How will we find them?" Serena asked. "We don't have time to go scouring the entire Netherrealm for them."

Brax's red eyes deepened. "Oh, I know where they're at, yes. They may be able to hide from Tashia, but there's no hiding from me. Isn't that right, Kree?"

Kreezak gulped and the sweat poured from him.

"Let's take a shortcut," Brax said, taking over the leading position from Serling. We'd reached a place where the caves had split, and Brax took us down the opposite way from where we'd come in. "If we have to take Serling's way, the battle will be over by the time we've reached it. We must hurry and help the fairy's mother after all."

"How do you know she's my mother?" Serena asked. "I never said anything."

He looked down on her. "You *reek* of her, young one, and not in the way most do after she's through with them."

Serena's jaw tightened, but she said nothing.

We left the confinement of the caves, far from where we'd entered. Dark clouds blocked out the haze of light. The ground we walked upon was hard and brittle, and broke with every step. A low mist clung to our ankles, blanketing the ground. In some ways, this place reminded me of the Wastelands, but worse—a lot worse.

"We're no longer in my mother's domain," Serena said.

"Stay close," Serling said.

"Yes," Brax said. "We wouldn't want anything to happen to you, now would we?" He glanced at both Serena and me.

The air was heavier, and colder, too, getting worse with each step. In Alana's realm, the weather was always a moderate temperature. Even when darkness descended, it was more a spring night than a winter one. Serena shivered and rubbed her hands against her arms.

"Are you all right?" I asked.

"I'll be fine," she said. "I've never been to this part of the realm before. If I had known, I would have worn something else. It's a bit cold here for me to be wearing what I'm wearing."

"I wish I had my robes to give you."

"Me too. Those always looked so comfy and warm."

"They are." I tried not to stare at the tight, short outfit that hugged her curves, but it was hard. She caught me looking and smiled. I turned away, feeling the heat rise in my cheeks. Instead, I focused on something else.

"Serling, how did you cast those energy balls?" I asked.

He stopped and asked, "You want to know how to create one?"

"Is it possible for me, or is it something only crosswalkers can do?"

Serling stroked his chin. "I suppose it's possible for an elemental wizard, although I've never given it much thought."

"A wise thought, wizard," Brax said. "But even if it is possible, the spell may only be cast in the Netherrealm."

"It doesn't mean I shouldn't try. I sensed a lot more power in those than in my fireballs. If we're going up against Tashia, we're going to need every advantage we can get."

"We'll need stronger spells than those to defeat her," Brax said. "I hope you're able to come up with something better, yes."

Brax was right. I needed to come up with a stronger spell, to not only defeat Tashia but her army. A ritual might work, but she wasn't going to give me the time to gather in energy or materials, or stand motionless while I cast it. Every person and creature had their weak spot. I just needed to find hers.

"Hellsfire," Serling said. "Would you like to learn how?"

I nodded. More knowledge of magic was never a bad thing.

"It's like creating a fireball," Serling said, "something you're very familiar with. But instead of using fire, you string together a piece of each of the elements in exactly equal parts. If one side is too strong or too weak, it'll collapse, or it won't have enough power to grow. That's all there is to it. If you can grasp onto the mana and the pieces that tie it together, you'll be able to do it."

" It sounds like an energy ball is equivalent to a web."

"I never thought of it that way, but then again, I can't do webs. Why don't you give it a try?"

I spaced my hands half a foot apart from each other. I summoned my magic, trying to do something I wasn't good at—be subtle. I had to force my fire magic to die down and not take over as it always threatened to do. I conjured tiny portions of each of the six aspects of magic. The colors swirled in my hand, and sweat dripped down the side of my forehead. It was like balancing on a rickety board over a deep crevasse.

Grassy greens and water blues overtook my hand at times, but it was mostly the fire and its strong red and orange color that I had to tone down. The hardest magics to grasp onto were the elusive life and death manas. I had never used all the magics at the same time before. All my previous spells only involved, at most, three manas at a time. More often than not, I only used one at a time.

My head pounded and my eyes wanted to burst. A drop of blood trickled out of my nose and onto the ground.

"Hellsfire, are you all right?" Serena placed a hand on my shoulder but yanked it back, feeling the energy I radiated.

I ignored her and fought through my pain, focusing on the task at hand. If I couldn't do this simple spell, then what hope did I ever have of defeating Tashia?

I held my magic strands, staring at the colors appearing and disappearing in my hand. Every part was equal. There was no more imbalance. As I wove the magic, the power of the spell flowed through me. While it wasn't as strong as the energy ball Serling could cast or my own fireballs, for the tiny amount of magic I used, it was potent.

As the spell coalesced together, the pain in my body eased. I smiled in triumph, watching as the wondrous magic swirled into shape.

"School's over," Brax said in his gruff voice. "We're here."

I looked up, and my spell was broken along with my concentration. I glared at his back, but relaxed when I realized that if I practiced this, I could do it. If I had enough time. I started to think about what other uses I might have for this magic. I might be able to strengthen existing spells with it, or come up with something entirely new. Unlike Serling and Brax, I was a wizard. I might be new to the rules of the Netherrealm, but I brought a different perspective.

I caught up with the others, and we stood at the crest of a hill. At the bottom was a large, very old building. The mist smothered it, yet through the mist, I spotted ancient cracks embedded in its walls. Muted light shone through the windows, and I glimpsed dark forms moving past them. Music, screaming, laughter, yelling, and even growling could be heard from the building.

I had expected a garrison, perhaps, or even a castle. But this was neither. "This looks like some kind of demons' tavern."

"Close enough," Brax said. "But in truth, it's a hideout and a place to get information, yes. Humans dare not come here. You had better be careful. I may not be in the mood for saving any of you."

"You're human," I said. "And you survived."

Brax chuckled. "Am I?"

"Ignore him," Serling said, peering up at his former friend. "But heed his warning and keep your magic close at hand."

Brax's long stride quickly took him to the building. He wasn't concerned about guards, and I didn't see any. The fingers of his sword hand twitched, and he seemed excited to return here. He didn't waste any time before flinging the doors open. An oppressive stench forced its way into my nose, making me want to hurl. I was reminded of when I journeyed into the Wastelands wearing the disguise of a goblin. Those unkempt, dirty creatures made me want to soak in a bath for a month. But I had grown used to those disguises. The goblin became a part of me. With all these creatures, there was little room for fresh air. The outside coldness melted from the heat radiated by all these creatures crammed together, and all of their attention was focused on us.

Most of the demons sat around tables and on chairs. The furniture was mostly made of hard stone, and was unevenly constructed. Not that that mattered. Their bodies were all different shapes and sizes. A monstrous glob of fat that passed as a demon licked its two lips, staring at us with beady eyes. One demon permanently leaned to the right. It had two elongated claws on that side, as opposed to one small claw on its left. Behind it, a shadow seemed to come to life and move, but it was a tall, slender demon. Its six eyes blinked simultaneously as it glared at us. My heart raced, and fear crept into me. It was like all my childhood monsters had come to life. None of them wanted us here. I remembered my training and focused on my fire mana. Its heat and power gave me strength.

A demon whose head nearly reached the ceiling was the first to approach us. "Humanssss," he said, his two sharp mouths snapping in anticipation. "Yummmmm."

Every demon in the place laughed. Their laughter was hollow, deep, and scratched at my soul.

Brax wasted no time in his response. His red eyes flashed as he drew his weapon. In one swift motion, he brought the hissing sword down on the demon. Everyone stopped laughing. Brax strapped the sword back unto his back as both halves of the demon fell on the floor, black blood oozing out.

"Who's next, yes?" Brax asked, peering around the room. The demons backed away from us, crowding into the cramped place.

A loud crash broke the silence as a rickety chair tipped over. A little bug-eyed demon, no taller than my knee, skittered out of the crowd.

"Strag!" Brax said. He pushed chairs, tables, and demons out of the way, his long legs carrying him toward his goal. The small demon had the body of a large leech, except with scrawny legs and arms. Brax seized him, picking him up by his skinny neck.

"Hello…boss," Strag said, barely getting the words out of his mouth.

"Is there a reason you were running away from me?"

Strag squirmed and gasped for air. He beat his hands on Brax's hands, but to no avail.

"I can't hear you, no."

"Leave him alone," Kreezak said.

Brax shot him a fierce look.

"Please," Kreezak whispered. "We may need him."

Brax released Strag and the little demon fell on the floor. Strag gasped for air. He didn't seem to fear Brax, because he ran up Brax's leg and settled on his shoulder. Strag craned his neck at the rest of us and looked back at Brax.

"I thought you were dead," Strag said. "That's why I ran away. I thought Serling slagged you centuries ago. I hate ghosts."

"My death has been greatly exaggerated, yes," Brax growled. "Where are the others?" His eyes flashed. "And don't try to hide them from me. I know they're here."

Strag's whole body shook as he pointed into the corner. "Over there, boss."

All the demons blocking our sight parted, illuminating the ones behind them. Brax strolled to the corner. The demons made no attempt to hide or run.

Brax stared at each of them. He didn't say a word.

"Boss, you're alive," one of them said. He was crouched low on the ground, his ten feet and hands reminding me of a millipede. His long, slender, dark green body straightened until he towered over Brax. His green eyes blinked several times. "It *is* you."

"Of course it is, Yetan. I see only four of you. Where are the others?"

"Dead," another one said. He folded his four muscular arms across his chest and bowed his head to Brax. If the two of us stood side by side, we would equal his shoulder width. There wasn't an ounce of fat on him, and I couldn't stop staring at the gold ring piercing his nose.

"What happened to them, Armal?"

A slender purple demon moved forward. The tentacles in her hair flowed as if they were alive. Her narrow face smiled, and her yellow eyes beamed. She put a tentacle to Brax's face. "Tashia killed most of us, beloved. Others were slain ages ago."

"Lasha," Brax said, gently laying his hand to hers.

"We don't have time for this," Serling said, stepping up next to Brax.

"Serling!" Lasha said. She stretched her tentacles and wrapped them around the crosswalker's throat. From his staff, Serling shot an energy ball at Lasha and she screamed. Brax thrust his arm into Serling and he crashed shoulder first into the wall.

I rushed to Serling, drawing in my magic, and Serena freed her sword.

"I'm fine," Serling said, rising. He rubbed his shoulder and stared at Brax.

Brax's four demons stood with him. Anger flooded their faces as they watched the crosswalker. But they did not make the first move.

"Looks like the old gang is back together again," Strag said. He scratched his head. "Uh, what's left of us, anyway."

"What's it going to be, Kreezak?" Yetan said. "Are you with us?"

"I'm with no one. I'm here to stop Tashia."

"Yeah, right," Strag said, sticking out his elongated, forked tongue toward Kreezak. "You just want to fuck her for all eternity."

The building boomed with demon laughter.

Serling's energy rose. I wasn't sure if we'd stand a chance if all the demons and Brax attacked us en masse, but I would back his play.

His energy levels dropped and he said, "Let's go." I glanced at him and he looked defeated.

That wasn't what I expected. "Go?" I asked. "What about them? I thought we needed their help."

Serling stared at Brax as he spoke. "It seems Brax wanted to be with his old gang again so he can hide from Tashia. We don't need a coward fighting with us. This was a complete waste of time." Serling turned his back to them. Serena, Kreezak, and I followed him, never taking our eyes from them or any of the other deadly monsters.

"Wait," Brax said, stopping us. "I said I'd help you and I will, yes."

"*Help* him?" the four demons all said at once.

"Yes, and the rest of you will too."

"But she almost killed us," Strag said, his eyes growing impossibly large. "And Serling tried to kill or capture us a number of times."

"Beloved," Lasha said, "you're the strongest man or demon I've ever known, but Tashia has gotten stronger." Her voice became a whisper. "She may even be stronger than you."

"And it's all because of Renak," Yetan said.

Armal grunted in agreement.

"It seems without me, you've all gotten weak, yes," Brax said, pulling himself away from them. "Just because a few of you died, you cower. Even Kree has shown courage, and I thought he had none."

"I did?" Kreezak asked.

"Yes, but make no mistake, I still don't trust you. Let us go. I don't want to be in the company of these weaklings, no."

We exited the building and walked fast. The Netherrealm's darkness overtook us once more. Serling lit his staff and we trudged on with him and Brax in front.

Serena looked to me. "What now? We were supposed to be getting help for the war. All we have is one old crosswalker, one corrupt crosswalker, one fat demon, and one wizard. No offense, Hellsfire." Her accusatory tone turned to those up front. "My friends and family are out there *dying*, and we're here exploring your old hideouts. I should be out there fighting instead of wasting my time here!"

Brax managed a little chuckle. "You're wrong, little fairy."

Serling's light dimmed, and I held my breath as shadows flurried around us. Heavy footsteps crashed on the ground and closed in on us. I stopped and turned, ready to burn the darkness with light. Through the thick mist, predatory red, green, and blue eyes glowed.

Serling put a hand on my arm and said, "Hellsfire, wait."

Brax's old gang ventured, cringing, into Serling's light.

"We're with you, boss," Yetan said, crawling forward as he shielded his eyes with five hands.

"Yeah, no matter how foolish it is," Strag said, climbing up Lasha. He leaped before she could slap him away. Armal snatched the little demon and placed Strag on his shoulder.

"You knew we were coming," Lasha said, and slithered her tentacles over Brax's shoulders and across his chest.

"There's nowhere else for you to hide, no."

"Revenge," Armal said, squeezing his head-sized hands. A malicious smile crossed his face.

"She'd come looking for us, sooner or later," Yetan said, skittering on all his feet, his body inches from the ground. "This is our best opportunity to take her out; otherwise she'll kill us one by one. And the pretty fairies are weak." Yetan looked up, baring his teeth at Serena. "They won't last long against her."

"What about the others?" I asked, glancing at the various silhouettes in the shadows that didn't dare stray into Serling's light.

Strag left Armal and hopped onto my shoulder. "Not everyone likes Tashia. A lot of us want her dead. Now's the best time, with our boss back and all. Everyone knows how strong the boss is. He's a natural demon leader, even if he is a human. Too bad a lot of these other demons are...unprofessional."

A growl erupted from a demon in the shadows, and a spike half the size of Strag flew toward him. He dodged it and it passed over my shoulder. Strag scrambled up my neck, perching on my head.

"Get off of me!" I said, trying to grab him. His body emitted a coat of thick slime when I touched him, and my hand slid off him.

Brax laughed and said, "To me, Strag, yes." I thought Brax was too far for Strag to reach him when Strag leaped. The little demon opened his arms, his thin, loose skin stretching between his limbs, and he glided toward his leader.

"Strag," Serling said. "Give it back."

Strag looked at Brax. Brax nodded. Strag sighed, then threw me my purse.

"Why, you little—"

"You have to watch out for him," Serling said. "He may be small compared to other demons, but he's just as dangerous."

"He's a thief," I said, glaring at the demon.

"He's more. If memory serves, Strag also specializes in spying, surveying, and getting into places where he doesn't belong."

"Don't forget finesse and skill, crosswalker," Strag said, wagging his finger. "Everyone else here has brute strength. I'm too small for that, but I get things done." Strag stood as high as his little body would allow and puffed his chest out.

"What would a demon need with coin?" I asked. "What could you possibly want to buy?"

"It's not the monetary value," Strag said. "It's the material. Gold is all right, silver's better, and copper's the best."

"They use it to make weapons," Serling said. "Depending on the creature, silver and even copper can be deadly."

"Plus some of us just like shiny things." Strag pointed to Armal's nose ring. The little demon grew serious. "Others come, boss."

"Just as I thought, yes," Brax said.

Emerging from the darkness, a demon rolled its body into the light. It was a gigantic worm whose dark, black body rippled with bright colors every few seconds. As he passed, he trained his white eyes on me for a bit too long. He shifted his body and with a mouth as small as a raven's, he spoke to Serling. I couldn't make out the gruff, guttural language, but I didn't like how the creature's eyes kept darting back to me.

I stepped forward and asked, "What's he saying?"

Brax chuckled. "She's saying she'd promise us a great army to help us. An entire batch of her children. They're quite the little darlings. If she wanted to, she could bring you to your knees with that luminescent skin of hers, yes. What do you see?"

I stared at the rainbow ripples. The colors danced until they melted together. A bright violet color I deeply missed was shown to me. I reached my hand out to touch it, but Brax's hand clamped on mine. I tried to tear it away, but his grip was like steel.

He released me and said, "I warned you, wizard. You do not want to touch her skin, no." I almost rubbed my sore wrist but stopped myself. He spoke to her. The demon's noise was very high-pitched for a moment. She looked at me once more before slithering off back into the darkness.

"She has a taste for wizards," Brax said. "She's survived a long time, and it's rare that she encounters one of your kind. I told her that she's never tasted a wizard with your power before, and that you might give her indigestion."

Brax chuckled and so did his demon followers. I even saw Serena crack a smile.

When her smile died down, Serena leaned over to Serling and whispered, "Think we can trust them?"

"For now. We share a common enemy. There's an old saying. How did it go? Oh yes, 'a demon's hate knows no bounds.'"

"But Brax isn't a demon."

Serling shrugged. "Technically no, but his hate is just as strong, if not stronger. When we're done, we'll sort things out, depending on who survives."

"I can't wait, yes," Brax said, never turning around.

"Neither can I, old friend. Neither can I."

We journeyed fast with Brax leading the way. He somehow knew where Tashia was and he needed no map. Serling, Serena, and I stuck together. As we drew more demons to our cause, Serling's staff light dimmed and weakened. He empowered it once more, and it blazed brightly around us. Not even Brax's gang was brave enough to cross the light's boundaries.

As the hours passed, more demons joined our army. Serena's wings kept fluttering and she looked to the skies often. I wanted to console her and tell her that we would reach her mother in time, but I couldn't lie to her. Brax said that Tashia was close, and Serena did feel us get closer to her people's realm. As much as Serena wanted to rush to help Alana, we needed the gathering demons around us, and I needed the extra time to prepare.

Brax and his gang of demons didn't slow as we grew closer to Alana's territory. I glanced at the dark shadows behind us. The space around us had grown, and there were gaps in the crowd. Earlier, deep in their realm, the demons were full of confidence with the legendary Brax to lead them. The closer we got to the realms of light, the more their courage left them. And I was sure the stragglers that had only come to see Brax would only go this far and no farther.

"Time to see what these demons are made of," Strag said.

We crossed the boundary, and it was as if the cloud of darkness was lifted. Light shone on the demons, and they hissed and growled in pain. All except for Brax's group. They were used to working in the light, but the ones that had joined us were not. Three demons went up in flames, their bodies bursting with fire. A trail of fire followed them back into the darkness. I watched as one demon's tentacles melted off before the rest of his body followed suit, and a pile of goo was left where he once was.

"Too many are dying or returning to their realm," Serling said.

"The strong will survive," Brax said. "That's all that matters."

I thought the light would reveal Brax's features, but his face was still draped in shadow. It blurred itself more, the more I stared at him.

Strag, perched on Brax's shoulder, rubbed his eyes. "I always hate coming here, boss. My eyes feel like they want to explode!"

Yetan twisted his long body. "Be thankful you don't feel like there's a scratch you can't itch."

"Minor inconveniences," Lasha said, standing next to Brax. The pair watched the last few demons attempt to cross. "Brax trained us for this."

"Coming here will weaken them," Serling said. "I doubt Tashia will have the same problem."

"We've no choice," Brax said. "If I had time, I could properly train and torture the demons into line and have my own little army, yes. Instead, I must settle for this pitiful bunch. This is where the final battle will take place. We better hurry."

"I'm going to fly up ahead to meet my people," Serena said. "Otherwise Alana may think she's being outflanked and attack us." She crossed her arms and glowered at all the demons in her realm. "She's not going to like this. *I* don't like this."

Serena stretched her wings. Before she could take flight, I grabbed her arm and said, "Be safe. Hurry back."

A smile overtook her face. "Of course, cutie." She rose into the air and sped away.

"Let's go," Brax said, turning and following the same direction as Serena.

I glanced behind us, staring at the scarred and disfigured demons. I couldn't tell if they had always been that way or if crossing into the fairies' realm had done it to them.

"Go?" I asked. "Don't you want to wait for your followers?"

"They're no followers of mine. My followers are right here. They'll either catch up with us or die in the attempt. These demons are far too raw. Tashia already took the strongest ones, yes."

"But strength isn't everything, right, boss?" Strag said.

Armal came up behind Strag and flicked him off Brax's shoulders. The little demon opened his arms, spreading his skin flaps to slow his descent before tumbling to the ground.

"Of course it isn't," Armal said. He almost crushed Strag beneath his feet as he walked by.

"Do not try to understand a demon's way," Serling said, pointing his staff at Brax. "If you understand it too well, you may wind up like him."

Brax looked over his shoulder at Serling and smirked.

We continued on our way, Brax's army dwindling with each moment. It might have been bravado that had fueled the demons to join us earlier. The light might have been forcing them to leave, or perhaps Brax was right. These demons were the leftovers—the cowards and weaklings—all we were able to get. I had been in my fair share of battles. But I had been with battle-hardened people, who had something to fight for. These demons might be more of a liability than an asset, and it worried me that they might switch sides. Still, they were all we had, and every bit helped. I just hoped it would be enough.

As we moved, the land shifted back to the fairy forest. The demonic army devastated the land beneath them. Their very touch wilted plants and corrupted soil. They reveled in the destruction and mayhem of their longtime enemy, and they cared nothing for the colorful plants.

After an hour, we were out of the forest and onto a vast plain. Off in the distance, I glimpsed the army of the fairies. Their scouts had already spotted us, and two dozen fairies flew out to meet us. Ten demon fliers started to fly toward them, but Brax called them off.

Serena landed in front of us, along with two soldiers. "I told you I'd be back." Her smile vanished. "My mother would have words with you, Brax. I suggest we hurry. We haven't much time."

"Lasha," Brax said. "Make sure the others don't get out of line while I'm gone."

"Madalyn," Serena said. "Try not to kill the demons unless they deserve it."

Madalyn fingered her spear. "I make no promises."

CHAPTER 21

SERLING, BRAX, SERENA, and I stood in Alana's huge command tent. There wasn't much room, because a few of Alana's advisors and a lot of her guards were there. Their entire focus was on Brax and Serling.

Alana's sensual robe had been replaced with armor. The armor was made from a material I had never seen before. Even though it was hard like a shell, it bent with Alana's every movement. In her hand, she cradled a thick wand that was three feet long. It looked like a transparent blue crystal, but would darken or lighten, triggered by her emotions.

The fairy queen loomed over Serling and Brax, her needle-like eyes focused on the pair. "*This* was your plan, crosswalker?" she asked Serling. "This is treason!" She struck Serling across his face with her wand, the blow amplified by her magic. Serling's magic wavered and he dropped to one knee, blood running down his chin.

I stepped forward, but Serena grabbed my wrist.

"No," she mouthed, shaking her head.

Serling tried to rise, but Alana struck him again and he collapsed. His magic flared and he grasped his knee in agony.

"Mother!" Serena said. "Stop this, please!"

"Why are you consorting with these—these beasts? You may be foolish at times, but I never would have thought you would sink so low as to release *him*." The fairy queen pointed her wand at Brax.

"It was not she who released Brax. It was I, Mistress," Serling said, forcing himself up from the ground.

"Do you think I do not know that?" The fairy queen took a step closer to Brax. "I want them back, and I want them back now." Her tone was low, but the menace dripped in her words.

Brax said nothing. He returned her fierce gaze with his own, his crimson eyes glowing brightly. The fingers of his sword hand twitched. I prayed it didn't come to violence because I had no idea what would happen or whose side I would choose. I'd come to the Netherrealm to stop Tashia, not to get involved in an old score.

"I can promise you that your little baubles are safe, yes," Brax said. "But I also promise you that you will never see them again, no."

The storms appeared in Alana's eyes, threatening to boil over with her powerful magic. Her eyes wandered past Brax and to the fairy that had just stepped inside the tent. She nodded and the fairy left. The magic in Alana's eyes dissipated.

"I must first deal with the more immediate threat," Alana said. "After this is over, you will return what you have taken from me. You've been gone a long time and over the centuries, I've learned a lot. This time, I will do far worse to you than have you imprisoned in that wall."

"We shall see," Brax said.

Alana strode out of the tent, but stopped next to Serling. "He's your responsibility, crosswalker. Brax and his...creatures better not interfere with me or my troops. I've got work to do. She'll be in range any moment now." Alana left the tent and all her people followed her.

"What did you steal from her?" Serena asked.

"You've seen her wand," Brax said. "Have you sensed how incomplete it is?"

Serena bit her lip. "I have. No one else has seemed to see that, though."

"I stole that portion of the wand from her, to suit my own purposes. She would be far more formidable if the wand was whole, yes."

"Then why don't you give it back? If you work together, you could defeat Tashia."

"I don't need her help, little fairy," Brax said. "I was imprisoned for far too long. Your mother tortured me during that time. I *will* make her pay for that. One score to settle, then another."

"With so many scores to settle, you'll never finish the game," Serena said.

"It's a game I plan on winning, yes."

She returned Brax's unwavering stare. "With your type, it always is." She looked to Serling. "Keep your dog on his leash, crosswalker. Let's go, Hellsfire."

I got ready to intervene in case Brax decided to settle his score with Alana by taking it out on Serena. Instead, what he did was laugh. His laughter trailed us outside the tent.

Serena took off and flew toward another tent. I chased after her and caught her before she entered.

"It'll be all right," I said.

"You know nothing, Hellsfire!" She turned, clenching her fists. "It's bad enough my mother has her own games and agenda, but those two are even worse! While I don't agree with my mother, at least I can understand her motives. That pair are after something, and I have no idea what it is. I just hope it doesn't interfere with defeating Tashia. That's why we're all here."

"Whatever happens, I'll fight by your side."

Serena's hands relaxed. Her eyes looked into mine. "Thanks, cutie." She exhaled and looked past me to the dark shadows of Tashia's demons. "Time to go to war."

We ducked inside the tent where three fairies rushed to gear up. Serena went to one of the piles of equipment, and chose one of the sets of crystal armor that would fit my tall, thin frame. She helped me to strap it on. The dirty white armor felt stiff as I tried to move around in it.

"I need to be able to move to work my magic," I said. "Stradus once told me that a wizard might have to rely on his speed and reflexes in the heat of battle, and I've learned that lesson well." I grabbed the top of my armor and pulled. "It's too restrictive and confining for me. I thought these crystals of yours would be lighter and more malleable than metal."

"They can be. The crystals you've seen at the palace and the armor my mother is wearing is far different from what you have on. Certain crystals are common place in my mother's realm, as you've seen. But there are common crystals and rare crystals. You can tell which ones you have on." She gave me a wry smile. "Unfortunately, I will have those same crystals. Even if we had access to your metal, we wouldn't use it."

"Why not?"

"Certain metals can be harmful toward us. The purer they are, the more they hurt. That's why the little demon wanted your coins."

"What metals?"

Serena cocked her head. "That's not important now. Aside from your dagger, you don't carry a weapon. Now give me a few moments while I get ready for battle. Unlike you, I don't have magic to protect myself."

I wondered if she knew she had some part of her mother's magic inside of her. Serena helped me take the armor off, and then I went outside the tent. I didn't have to wait long. Serena soon emerged. Black leather covered her entire body, contrasting with her light pink skin. I didn't know what kind of animal her leather had come from, though it certainly hadn't come from a cow. A crystal sword hung at her hip, and in her right hand she carried a spear.

"No crystal armor?" I asked.

She shook her head. "Not with this equipment. Mostly the males wear the armor, since they can't fly. Much like yourself, we fliers need to be able to move quickly. The better crystals are reserved for those who my mother favors...such as my dear, sweet sister. Hello, Myla."

The purple fairy I had met when I was in Alana's chambers flew down and landed in front of us. Her turquoise crystal armor and helm glistened in the sunlight. "Serena, mother has need of your wizard."

"What is it?"

"Since most of the demons can't fly, we were going to send a portion of our army to attack Tashia's army from above while our main forces engage from the ground. But the scouts we've sent ahead haven't been heard from. There's a darkness up there that's spreading forward. We can't penetrate it."

"Is it Tashia?" I asked.

Myla shook her head. "No. We don't know what it is." She pointed a finger at me. "That's where *you* come in, if you're up for it, wizard. My sister has told me all the things you've done in your world." She smirked. "I want to see if at least half of them are true. My sister tends to exaggerate her experiences in your mundane world."

"Then what are we waiting for?"

Myla took off and flew back toward her army. A portion of the fairies flew up and funneled together through the low clouds. As I glanced up at the sky, the white fluffy clouds darkened with each passing moment.

"The clouds aren't what you'll expect," Serena said. "You can see they're low enough for us to reach. They're also stable enough to stand on. Once we pass through, you'll be able to stand on top of them. It can be like standing on a bed, so watch your footing." Serena reached behind me and put her arms underneath mine. "You ready, cutie?"

I took a deep breath. "As ready as I'll ever be."

Serena's wings fluttered as she struggled to lift my weight. We slowly rose, and I watched as my feet dangled. The ground grew smaller until the troops beneath us looked like bugs.

"Could you stop squirming?" she said. "I don't want to drop you."

"Sorry."

"We're almost there. I'm just glad you decided not to wear any armor. I might not have been able to carry you."

As we hovered closer to the clouds, I caught sight of the demon army off in the distance. The black mass grew closer to the rainbow-colored fairies, but there was one spot of darkness that overshadowed all the others.

"Tashia," Serena said, as if reading my mind.

Tashia's shadow shrank as we flew higher. When we reached the clouds, the white mist closed around me, clinging to every pore of my body and cleaning my grimy face. I opened my mouth, hoping to alleviate the dryness caused by my nervousness over what I had to do. No matter how many battles I'd been in, the fear threatened to overwhelm me every time. I wondered if everyone felt like I did, or if it got easier with the passage of time? The refreshing chillness of the cloud energized me for the challenge I had to face, yet my heart beat louder and faster.

The clouds parted. White light shone everywhere, nearly blinding me. Off in the distance, I saw what Myla had talked about earlier. The white clouds were darkening like storm clouds, and the grim gray approached us.

Serena flew us through the fairies, to the front of the army. There were only a couple hundred of them. I had expected more.

"Here's where you get off," Serena said, and dropped me off in front of Myla.

I knew Serena had told me that I could stand on the clouds, but I still expected to fall through them as she let go. But my feet hit the clouds and stopped. It did feel like I stood on a bed. The cloud absorbed my steps as I walked, yet there was a lightness to it. When I pushed my foot through, there was some resistance, but the cloud gave way. I grabbed onto Serena for support and pulled my foot back up, steadying myself.

"Sorry," I said to her.

"Where are the rest of the troops?" Serena asked. "There's maybe three hundred here."

"Less, actually," Myla said. "This was supposed to be a sneak attack. Instead it's turned into a flanking maneuver against us, if we can't figure out what this is and stop it. I will only send for more troops *if* we need them. They're needed beneath us to engage the demons. The true battle is being fought there." The purple fairy turned to me. "Wizard, can you enlighten us to what's lurking out there, so we can best understand how to fight it?"

"Yes."

I sat down cross-legged on the cloud, my body sinking into it. I summoned my magic and willed it toward the dark clouds. My magic pierced the veil and met faces. Small creatures with no feet on their ghostly bodies.

They flew through the air toward us, and I knew them for what they were—maleikas.

They chanted as a group, and brought the concealing magic with them. My wizard's sight went to the maleika at the front. It only had one eye, as its other had been taken years ago. It stopped chanting and somehow saw through my magic. With its one eye glaring at me, it cast an incantation and banished me.

I opened my eyes, and my anger rose to the surface, thinking of the creature who had almost succeeded in killing me when I was an apprentice, and who had tried again to kill me when I was journeying to the Burning Sands. This maleika wasn't like any I had ever encountered before. It was malicious, and its intent was evil. The fairies, demons, and other maleikas all seemed content to stay in the Netherrealm. This one had plans. It had plans when Stradus took its eye all those years ago, and I was sure it had plans now. The fact that it was working with Tashia probably meant that it was using her for its own ends. Whatever those ends were, it didn't bode well for any of us. It had to be stopped, and I had to finish what my master began with its eye.

Serena put a comforting hand on my shoulder, seeing the expression my face. "What is it, Hellsfire?"

"Maleikas."

"This is bad," Myla said. "I expected more demons, not maleikas. I've got to relay orders."

"I don't understand it," I said. "They're only maleikas. They're only able to spy on people. That's what they were used for during the War of the Wizards and what I was taught to use them for."

"You're wrong, cutie," Serena said, helping me up. "You've been in the Netherrealm only a short time, and you've already seen how different things are here. The maleikas are different too." She stared at the looming maleikas hidden behind their spell. "Their form may be ghostly, but it also grants them the ability to adapt their bodies into almost any shape they wish. They need no blade, for their bodies are their own weapons."

"They sound tough to fight."

She nodded. "They are, but they can be killed. You've seen how their ghostly bodies are the size of bushes—some small and some large. When they change shape here, their body solidifies and they can't float or fly anymore.

With their body solid, it gives us something to strike, but they don't have the same weaknesses we do. They have no organs or blood in them. The crystals we wield can hurt and kill them, and so can magic. It's as if their bodies can't hold shape and dissolve into nothingness. If you ever find yourself without either of those, chop them into as many pieces as you can."

"I'll keep that in mind. How far do their shape-shifting abilities go?"

"They can stretch and change their body as far as the size of their bodies will allow them. The bigger they are in their normal form, the larger the shape they can assume. If, for instance, they try to shift into a huge sword and cut us all in half, there would come a point where their body will weaken. They won't be able to hold their form and will revert back to their natural, ghostly form. Think of it like stretching your arm to grab something just out of your reach. You might reach it, but stretch any farther and your arm might tear off."

I nodded, wondering how I would fare against the maleikas. I had thought of them as nothing but elaborate scouts I used for my own purposes, until now. And there was still the maleika with one eye.

"What about a maleika that can wield magic as if it was a wizard?" I asked. "Have you ever known one that can do that?"

She looked to me, and her pink eyes widened. "So it's true. I had heard stories of a maleika that could cast magic like that. That it first gained its powers by draining the magic of a wizard and transferring it into itself."

"I don't know if that's how it got its magic, but I do know it's extremely dangerous and powerful, and it leads the ones that face us now."

"Can you break the maleika's spell?" she asked. "You've seen how the light is everywhere in my mother's realm. The light strengthens us and the dark weakens us. The maleika's spell is going to fortify the demons below if we don't do something."

I stared at the black hole. The spell was enormous, covering the entire width of the cloud, dripping down into the world beneath us. The maleikas worked as a group, whereas I was just one wizard. I needed help, but I was sure Serling was busy down below with his own magic. I looked back at Serena, feeling her mother's magic flowing from her. It amazed me how she never seemed to notice she had it.

"I may have an idea," I said. "But I'm going to need your help to cast a spell."

"A spell? What can I do?"

I reached out with my hand. "Lend me your magic."

"But I don't have any magic."

I shook my head. "That's where you're wrong. You and Alana may have your differences, but you are your mother's child."

Serena bit her lip, but reached out to me with her hand. "All right."

The fairies were full of life, whereas the demons were full of death. Maybe that's why they were bitter enemies—they were polar opposites.

I reached out into Serena's aura. Her magic flared and through my wizard's sight, she radiated light. A blazing pink spark surrounded her. I caressed her hand and gazed at her, feeling the blood in my loins heating with desire. I reeled her in like a lover, drawing the magic into myself. As I let myself be carried away by her magic, my whole body felt more alive than it had in ages.

"What are you doing?" she whispered.

I opened my eyes. I hadn't even known I'd closed them. Her mouth was just inches away from my face.

"I'm sorry," I said. "I got caught up in your magic."

Serena's eyes shone with delight and she grinned. "It's all right, cutie. If we survive this, we can have fun later." She pulled away from me. "But first we must take care of the maleikas."

I nodded. I stared at Serena for a moment, surprised that she still had plenty of energy left despite what I had taken from her. My friend was full of life. Whether because she was a fairy, we were in the Netherrealm, or she was the daughter of Alana, I couldn't tell.

"You shouldn't be afraid of your power," I said. "You can go far with it."

Before Serena could say a word, I turned away from her, clasped my hands, and chanted. I used Serena's magic to strengthen what I already had. My magic drew a long, invisible, subtle line in the clouds, fueled by white mana.

I blocked everything out and held the spell steady. It was difficult to maintain something with that much power in it, while making sure the maleika wouldn't be able to detect it. I just needed one final thing for my spell to activate.

I waited for the maleikas to glide closer and closer to my spell. The magical energies backlashed against me, yearning to be released. Pain sizzled through my body, but I held it still. The maleikas seemed to be moving slower. The agony racked my body and I almost fell over.

"Are you all right?" Serena asked.

I ignored her lest I break my concentration. Through the dark veil, I glimpsed the maleikas floating closer to my spell.

"Tell Myla to get ready," I said through a parched throat. "They'll be visible soon, and that's when you should attack."

Serena flew off to find her sister, and I waited for the maleikas to cross into my spell zone. My hands shook and I couldn't hold the spell much longer. Just as the maleikas reached my spell, they stopped. That one-eyed freak must have seen it.

It studied my spell, no doubt thinking of a way to break it. Before it could counteract my spell, I lifted my glowing hands up and pushed them forward. I yelled with the release of magic shooting out of me. The line of light shot forward, dissipating the wall of darkness, revealing the maleikas. There were far more maleikas than I'd thought. I collapsed to the cloud, exhausted from holding the spell still for so long.

"Charge!" Myla said, the army of fairies sweeping forward.

The fairies' line rammed into the maleikas, breaking into them like waves and catching the creatures off guard. But unlike waves of water, the fairies were deadly. They attacked the stunned maleikas. Many ghostly forms fell against the sharp crystal of the fairies' weapons. Yet the maleikas were quick to recover. Not more than two or three dozen fell before their ghost-like bodies solidified and they transformed.

One maleika sprouted four legs, and two swords as hands. Wings bloomed from another and it took flight, slashing nearby fairies with its claws. But there was one maleika who towered over all. It tore through fairies in its monstrous form. Its quickness surprised me, as it constantly shifted shapes to suit its purposes. One moment it had spider legs and leapt onto a trio of fairies, crushing them. The next moment its legs disappeared and its body slithered on the cloud. With a pan-like hand, it swatted a pair of fairies. For a moment, it took its attention away from the battle and its one eye rested on me.

I rose from the cloud and from my all-too-brief rest. Battle had just begun, and this was no time to be tired.

A small group of three maleikas rushed at me, aiming their pointed weapons at my body. I stuck my hands out, summoning a steed of fire. It trampled them, their bodies burning and disintegrating into nothingness. They meant nothing to me. Only the cyclops leader did. I had to take it down because I knew no one else could. My former master had lost an apprentice because of this thing, and twice now it had tried to kill me. I craved revenge as badly as it did.

Five winged maleikas dove from the sky toward me like birds seeking their prey. I conjured a gigantic gust of wind and their bodies tumbled out of control, crashing them into their comrades.

Even though we were outnumbered, the fairies had swarmed the big maleika. I sprinted toward them, avoiding the blows of the other maleikas as I ran by. When I reached the leader, a litter of dead fairies surrounded it. One fairy's hand twitched and I bent down to her, trying to shield her from the battle and get her to safety. Her body went still as the life left her. I gently laid her back on the cloud and stared at my opponent. No more would die by its hand.

Its one eye glowed yellow as it stared at me. *"You!"* it said in Caleea. *"You shouldn't be in my realm, wizard."*

"I've come to finish what Stradus started. This time I'm going for more than your eye."

The maleika laughed. *"You have no idea what I'm capable of, wizard."* A huge smile formed on its face. *"You're in* my *world now."*

A surge of power blasted from it. All six elements of mana struck out at me. I barely had time to summon a shield, but the backlash knocked me off my feet. The maleika leaped into the air, its huge clawed foot aiming to crush me.

I rolled out of the way, but it brought its hand down. Instead of fingers, it had five sharp swords. I conjured a gust of wind to propel me away from it, dodging its deadly thrusts. Then I jumped up and unleashed a torrent of fire, smothering the creature with flames. I knew the fire wouldn't kill it, but I was still testing its defenses and needed to buy more time.

It leaped out of the fire far sooner than I thought, untouched and unharmed. It swiped at me with its large claws. My flimsy clothes tore, and when I put a hand to my stomach, it came back slick with blood. I stumbled, and it must have seen my weakness because it attacked with unrelenting fury.

The maleika assaulted me with simple spells. I deflected or dispersed them easily enough, but it also lashed out against me with its body. It tried to cut me down with its whirling blades. Without warning, one changed to a war hammer and nearly smashed me. I had been in battles and fought wizards before, but I had never been up against a foe who fought me with such skill as this, and who could shift its body to whatever weapon it desired. Just like it had planned, I had to split my focus between its magic and its physical attacks, and was unable to find an opening to attack it in return.

The maleika shot a funnel of fire. The raging heat brushed up against me and warmed my body. I lost sight of the creature in the roaring inferno, absorbing it into my mana. By the time my vision cleared, I barely had time to register a long tail swinging toward me.

I tried to turn away, but it still struck my face. The maleika's skin tore into me and flung me away from it. I went sprawling through the battle, my body careening out of control as I smashed into fairy and maleika alike. Each collision jolted me with pain, interrupting the magic I used to slow my flight. I was afraid I might never stop, or that one of the fairies or maleikas might impale me.

"Gotcha, cutie!" Serena said as she flew behind me and caught me. She grunted as my weight impacted her. She struggled to stop our momentum, her wings flapping hard.

I lifted my weary head up. Every movement racked my body with aftershocks of pain. "Thanks."

"Malik would never forgive me if anything happened to you." She stared at the maleika monster. "You were right. I've never seen a maleika cast magic like a wizard before. You're going to need a new plan of attack."

"I know, but I need time."

"You're far too used to being grounded," Serena said, glancing up at the sky. "I may have an idea."

She told me her idea, and while it was risky, it might work. The problem was, the battle wasn't confined to the top of the clouds. Aerial pursuits were being fought above them as well. I could feel how slow Serena was because she had to carry me, and I wore her out more with each second. The maleikas weren't going to leave us alone, especially with such a burdened and tempting target. I was the only wizard and human amongst fairies and maleikas.

"Can you do it?" I asked her.

Grim determination was etched into in her face. "I must."

Serena flew us away from thick of the battle, climbing higher into the sky. The plan was for me to come at the maleika from above. Unlike its brethren, the monstrous maleika wasn't flying. With its size and magic-wielding abilities, it didn't need to. I was hoping it wouldn't notice me until it was too late.

I gathered in magic while Serena flew us away. The battle's roar dulled, and I thought I might have enough time.

"Hellsfire," Serena said, looking over her shoulder. "We've got trouble."

I peered back and saw a group of five maleikas break away from the thick of the fighting to chase us.

"Can you outfly them?" I asked.

"Only if I drop you. Can you cast a spell at them?"

My fingers twitched with power. "I could, but this power isn't meant for them."

She nodded. "I understand. Now hold on!"

Serena grunted and flapped her wings harder. Since we couldn't attack our pursuers, she had to fly as fast as she could. It didn't matter. The maleikas crept closer with each passing moment. She veered hard right, nearly dropping me. It slowed them down momentarily, but they adjusted and continued toward us.

Another group of three maleikas appeared in front of us, cutting us off. They flew straight at us, their sharp claws and blades preparing to slice us.

Serena's breath became ragged, and the moisture from her panting dripped down my ear. Her wings flapped slower and slower.

"Hellsfire…" she said in a raspy voice. Sweat dripped down her face and landed on my own. She stopped and hovered in midair.

I knew what I was going to have to do. All the magic I had built up was going to have to be used to kill these maleikas. The fairies weren't prepared for such an assault up here. As valiantly and skillfully as they fought, they were just outnumbered. I waited until they were almost upon us, yearning to release my magic. I hated that it was going to be used on them, instead of the one I had hoped would be destroyed by it.

A purple blur flew on to meet our enemies on our left, flanked by an orange and blue fairy. Four more sped up from beneath us, clashing with the maleikas on our other side. They dispatched the maleikas quickly and then flew off again, except for Myla.

"You must hurry," she said. "I was only able to grab three dozen fairies from below. Mother can't spare any more forces from fighting the demons." She stared straight at me. "This needs to end, wizard. Whatever you're going to do, you need to do it now!"

Myla left and Serena continued to fly me until we hovered well above the one-eyed maleika. The magic I had been gathering crawled inside of me. It seeped through my skin, begging to be released. I kept it at bay while I performed the spell Serling had showed me earlier. The crosswalker magic was at my fingertips, but instead of creating one of Serling's energy balls, I wrapped it around my own elemental magic.

"Hellsfire," Serena said, her hands trembling.

I looked up and her face was racked with pain and I realized I was the cause of it. Her body wasn't trained to handle the amount of magic she was now holding in her hands. Magic sizzled up her arms and her grip loosened.

"Now," I said.

Without hesitation, Serena let go of me.

I plummeted toward my enemy, guiding my descent with air magic. A subtle or skillful spell wouldn't suffice with this maleika. I was going to have to cast something strong, powerful, and sloppy. I had wanted to save most of my power to use against Tashia and her demon army. But if this maleika and its army weren't stopped now, the fairies here would be slaughtered. Even with the combined power at my command, the dark flames whispered in my mind, promising to imbue me with their power.

As I roared toward the maleika, the energy in my wake made me look like a falling star. Every maleika I passed, I merely touched them and they vaporized from my power. My opponent loomed closer and I remembered Serena's words. I was going to try to squash this maleika from existence with my magic.

Just as I was just about to slam into it, it looked up, and I saw fear in its eye. I thought I would finally avenge Tara, Stradus, and all the fairies. But just before I slammed into it, it shielded itself with magic and strengthened its body with its physical ability.

My spell and I rammed into the maleika. I unleashed all my pent-up magic, the colorful, shimmering spell slamming into the creature's body. Instead of killing it, it clashed against the creature's shield. I roared, fighting the shield. Its magic buckled and bent but wouldn't break.

I cut off my magic when I realized that. I slid down onto the cloud and gasped for air, my arms hanging down at my side. It rose through the smoke. The color in its body had drained away, and its size had shrunk by a quarter. It still dwarfed me, though.

It raised its claw-tipped finger to fling a spell at me. Nothing happened. I smiled. My spell might not have destroyed it, but for the moment it could no longer summon any magic. Though, in my weakened state, I wasn't sure what kind of spells I could manage.

I pressed my attack, falling back on a simple spell I could conjure at any time—my fireballs. I strengthened them with the magic Serling showed me. My fireballs were electrified, the sparkling rainbow energy surrounding the fiery glow. They sizzled and splashed against the maleika's body, and I watched as the hapless creature crumpled to the ground. With each blow, my magic tore against its body and it shrank in size.

The maleika rose and bellowed. It brushed off my attacks and grew long wings. In one swoop, it covered the distance between us, raising four sharpened claws at me. I was exhausted from using so much magic earlier, but the dark flame within me roared, threatening to consume the monster.

I had unleashed it in Tyree because I wanted to stop their war from entering Northern Shala. I did, but at a great cost. So many people died, and Krystal and my friends had been put in danger. If I freed my dark fire, I knew all of the maleikas would be killed, but so would all the fairies up here. I would bring destruction onto Alana's army as surely as if I was in league with Tashia myself. Serena would die.

But I couldn't let myself be killed. I had to do something. The dark fire wouldn't let me make a choice. Its power seeped out of my skin and a black aura surrounded me. The magic wanted to be used, and it didn't care who it had to hurt to save me.

"No!" Serena said. She flew to intercept the maleika and rammed a crystal-tipped spear deep into the maleika's form. The maleika lashed out at her, trying to kill her. Instead, its claws ripped into Serena's wings and she cried out in agony as she was flung away.

Serena's crystal flared and a bright green light enveloped us all. The maleika roared like thunder, its body flashing back into transparency. It exploded and vanished with the light.

After seeing the defeat of this maleika, the fairies redoubled their efforts and charged. The rest of maleikas changed back to their original shapes and floated away in retreat.

I didn't care about any of that. I rushed over to Serena's body. She was so very still. I held my hands over her and began gathering in white mana. Her wings twitched and she moaned.

"Serena," I said.

"Hey, cutie," she said faintly. "Is it over?"

I nodded. "You did it."

"But I don't understand how. Others dealt it worse blows, but they did it no harm."

"I must have shattered its magical protection enough for you to strike the killing blow."

Serena smiled. "Good." She tried to get up, but yelped in pain and collapsed back on the cloud. "My wings."

I reached into my purse and took out my last rejuvenation potion. There was a moment of hesitation before I put it to her lips.

"Drink this. It won't heal your wounds, but it will restore your strength."

"But you need it. Even with my strength returned, I can't fight with my wings like this. There's still the demon army below."

"I know, but you saved my life. Take it."

She nodded and let me pour it into her mouth. I helped her up and she leaned on me. "Thanks, I feel better." Serena laid a hand on my stomach, and I winced. Her hand came back with blood on it. "We need to get you looked at."

"Later. When we have time."

Myla flew over. "That was quite impressive, but we're not done yet. While we may have stopped the maleika advance, we still have to contend with the demons. I'll fly your wizard down, and Eliza will take you."

The purple fairy reached behind me and lifted me up while an orange fairy did the same to Serena. Before we took off, Myla said, "Take Serena down below, safe and out of harm's way. She's done enough for today. We must try to win the day without her." She looked to Serena and gave a small smile. "Mother would be quite proud of you. I know I am, little sister."

Myla took off and all the fairies above the clouds followed us down. Now that I had a moment of respite, my body ached from fatigue. All the magic I'd cast and the wounds and bruises I'd suffered were keenly felt now. But like the fairies who had survived the battle on the clouds, I knew I would have to push all that aside. The reason I'd ventured into the Netherrealm waited below.

CHAPTER 22

AS WE FLEW ACROSS the battlefield, I stared in horror at all the bodies on the ground. Hundreds of bright-colored fairies were strewn across the battlefield, their bodies twisted in impossible positions. Dark clumps of dead demons were intertwined with them, but not enough of them. I glanced up to where the living were. I expected the fighting to be thick there, and the bright and dark armies to be clashing against each other. Instead of killing each other, the fairies and demons were pulling back. All except for one figure. At the front stood Brax, his large sword easily recognizable from here. In front of him was a gigantic demon that I knew was Tashia.

"What in the seven realms is going on?" Myla said. She didn't need for me to tell her to fly us near where Brax was.

Tashia was a lot larger than I had originally believed. She was almost the size of one of Alexandria's piercing towers. The bottom half of her was slug-like, even having the same dark olive color and slimy texture. I thought that must be her weak spot since there was no armor or even skin to protect it. Blood was splattered across her, yet I didn't see any gashes on that underside. There was something I did sense around that portion of her body—magic. It was far more potent than what the maleika had wielded. It must have shielded her from harm.

The top half of her body was covered in thick black scales like a beetle's shell. The armor plating overlapped and was christened with scars and scratches. Four arms stuck out from her sides, with claws attached to the ends, snapping in anticipation. In place of hair, a nest of snakes writhed on top of her head. The six snakes hissed and danced from side to side. They stared briefly at me, with yellow eyes that shone as bright as the sun. They all blinked together before focusing back on Brax. She snarled, exposing rows of pointy teeth.

Myla landed us out of the way, but still within earshot. Serling and Brax's gang were nearby. So were a couple of other fairies. What surprised me was that Alana wasn't there. I finally found her watching from a distance, surrounded by guards. The fairies gathered their wounded, while the demons left theirs for dead.

"You dare to invoke the Demons' Right of Dispute?" Tashia asked Brax. "You're nothing to me."

Brax's red eyes flashed. "Then why did you agree to this parlay, yes?"

"Mere curiosity. I didn't believe the rumors that you were still alive after all these years. But then I glimpsed that ridiculous oversized sword of yours."

"You feared it once."

Tashia chuckled, her deep laughter reverberating in my stomach. "My power has grown since then."

"So has your size, yes."

Tashia's yellow eyes glared at him. "I've never understood you, Brax. You've always been an enigma to me. A crosswalker who fancies himself a demon."

"You interfered with my carefully laid plans," he said, pointing his sword at her. "I've come to collect."

The demon smirked. "Honor is such a *human* notion. The Demons' Dispute only applies to demons. You are no such being."

"Do you refuse, then?"

Tashia stared at Brax, but I glanced at the demons around them and to Brax's gang. They waited in anticipation of what she would say. While Brax wasn't a demon, I was sure a lot of the demons here considered him to be one of them. What would happen if Tashia declined this challenge? Would her army falter?

Tashia slithered closer. Brax didn't move, even though she could crush him with her body. "Very well. The gods must favor me, as I get to slaughter two of my enemies today."

"We shall see, yes."

Tashia stayed where she was, but her gaze slid over to the group where I was standing. At first I thought it was to watch Brax's companions or even myself, but her eyes wandered to Kreezak. The fat demon fluttered higher, straining to get closer to her.

"Restrain him," Brax said. Kreezak stopped as Armal moved closer. "Fly over to her and I will strike you down, yes."

"I wasn't going anywhere. I was just trying to get a better look. It's been ages since I last saw her in a body."

Strag grinned. "I'll bet."

"Can you defeat her?" Serling asked Brax. "She's far more powerful than before."

Strag crawled up Serling's staff, resting on top of it. "The boss can slag her. She's no match for him one-on-one. No matter how fat she's gotten."

"Tashia has grown more powerful, yes," Brax said, "but she's still a demon. Disrupting the maleika's magic has ruined her plans. She will be weakened from fighting in the light. There's a reason demons don't force their way through the Outer Rim."

"If you win, Tashia's army will be broken," Myla said. "If you lose—"

"I will not lose, little fairy, no."

"In either case, this will buy us some time." Myla took off with the other fairies, flying toward Alana.

"To kill her, you'll have to destroy her heart," Kreezak said in a low voice. He stared at his hands as if he had given up a great secret.

"I know how to kill demons," Brax said.

Kreezak shook his head and fluttered around Brax. "You don't understand. Renak imbued her with too much power. Now that she has a body again, it will be the *only* way to stop her."

"Then where is the heart of your beloved?"

Kreezak hesitated.

Lasha wrapped one of her tentacles around his neck. "He asked you a question."

Kreezak squirmed, trying to break free from her suffocating grip. "I don't know!"

"I think you do. You've always known Tashia intimately."

"She has a different body!"

Yetan stretched himself and rose, freeing a blade from his side. "Let's see how much you truly know."

"Enough!" Brax said. "We don't have time for this. Destroying the heart isn't the only way to kill a demon. That I do know, yes."

The other demons let Kreezak go. Brax walked away and conferred with his gang of demons. Even Kreezak followed on his heels.

"Do you think he can actually defeat her?" I asked Serling.

"Hmmm…I'm not sure. Brax is more demon than man, and his power is incredible, but Kreezak's right. Renak has empowered Tashia. Thank the gods she can't fly. But if Brax succeeds, our task is over. If he fails, it falls to us." Serling looked to me. "How are you?"

I took a deep breath, feeling my aches and pains. The blood on my stomach had dried, but the wound still hurt every time I moved. "I've been better, but I'll get through it."

"Let me see if I can help." Serling's staff glowed. As he walked around me, his magic seeped into my body. My wounds closed and my energy returned.

"Thank you," I said.

"No matter the outcome, I suggest we gather in our energy. Things rarely go as planned on the battlefield."

I nodded.

Brax strolled away from his demons and drew his massive sword. Its loud hiss hung in the air, growing louder with each step.

The enemies stared at each other. Everyone was silent as we watched the two opponents size each other up. There were no bold words, threats, or taunting. Neither made a move, yet magic radiated from them. It intensified and grew in strength. Brax's red and Tashia's yellow eyes brightened until I thought the light would blind us all. I blinked, and when I opened my eyes, it had begun.

Brax charged at Tashia, baring his huge sword. Tashia sneered and flung daggers of energy at him. They flew out of her claws, glittering with the same magic Serling had showed me. Brax deflected the ones closest to him back at her with his sword. Two hit her, the energy dispersing across her body, yet they dealt her no damage. When Brax was in range, Tashia struck out with her claws. Despite his bulky frame, he was fast enough to block every blow with his massive sword.

Tashia screamed as his jagged blade sliced through her rough, bug-like armor. Brax pressed on, attacking everywhere he could, trying to make his way to her soft underside. Even though she had four claws and he had only one sword, his strikes were fast enough to keep her on guard. His strength seemed to match hers, despite her monstrous size.

Tashia brought her tail down, its stinger aiming to drill a hole into Brax. He rolled out of the way at the last moment, and she left a gaping hole in the ground. Brax sprinted toward her, no doubt wanting to carve out a huge chunk of her flesh with his sword. Tashia fired more energy bolts at Brax but he moved with such inhuman speed that they never touched him.

The demon roared an incantation and a beam of darkness encircled Brax. He crumpled as if a great weight was pressing upon him. His body sank lower and lower, nearly to the ground. Tashia spaced her claws apart in concentration. A flurry of energy daggers shot out of them and toward Brax. He yelled in agony as they struck him, lightning racking his entire body. Tashia slithered closer and grinned in a moment of triumph.

"No," Lasha said and covered her mouth.

Tashia brought her deadly stinger down, hoping to end this battle.

Brax roared, and the energy Tashia had cast around his body dispersed. Right when she brought her stinger down, his eyes flared red. He swept his hissing sword in an upward arc, slicing Tashia's tail off.

Thick, green blood spurted as Tashia swayed. Brax leaped up, stabbing his sword in one of her claws. He drove it down, pinning her to the ground. Brax ran up her arm. She frantically tried to force him off, casting a cone of cold around him. His body was unfazed by the magic, and he kept running until he jumped for her massive head.

"To me!" Brax said.

The sword obeyed its master, tearing out from Tashia's claw and soaring back to Brax. He caught it in midflight and raised it, ready to strike through her head.

The demon caught Brax, her pincers squeezing him like a walnut. With the magic surging from her claw, pieces of his black armor-like skin cracked. Dark blood oozed out from the cracks.

Despite the fact that he couldn't move, Brax never let go of his sword. He aimed it at her like a crossbow and did something completely unexpected—he laughed.

Magical energies poured into Brax, but he didn't use them to counteract Tashia's magic or even break free from her death grip. His red eyes leaked power and a dim glow of intense energy surrounded him. The magic left him as he transferred all of it to his sword.

Tashia realized her fatal mistake. But it was too late to let go. Brax unleashed all of his magic, blasting it directly into the demon's head. The beam of light shot into the clouds, taking Tashia's head off. Tashia's limp body dropped Brax and they both crashed to the ground. He rose, pushing her heavy claw off him, his sword ready to strike. After a few tense moments, her body twitched and that was all.

The entire battlefield had been quieted, except for Brax's gang. The collective cheers of the four boomed out into the silence.

"I knew he could do it!" Strag said, perched on Yetan's shoulders. "The boss always knew how to kill demons."

Serling continued to gather in energy, and so did I. I prayed Kreezak was wrong about Tashia's weakness. This wasn't over.

Brax strapped his sword onto his back and limped back toward Lasha.

"Brax!" Kreezak yelled. "She's not dead!"

Brax freed his sword and faced Tashia. Green sparkling energies surrounded the demon. Her wounds sealed up and her body shook as it rose. Her neck jerked and her head began to grow back.

"Find her heart!"

Brax gathered more magic and unleashed his sword's blast of light against Tashia's chest. This second attack was far smaller than the first, but it still created a huge gaping hole. Her body collapsed once more. A moment later, showers of magic returned around Tashia, healing her. Instead of shooting her, Brax raised his sword and charged.

He chopped at her, doing his best to find her heart and finish her before she re-formed. Green blood splattered everywhere, drenching him and the ground around him. Yet as much as Brax sliced, there was just too much of Tashia. His attacks lessened with each blow, and the slower he moved, the faster she grew back.

"Hellsfire," Serling said. "When the time comes, you and the fairies must attack Tashia. Find her heart and finish her. I will immobilize the other demons. Understood?"

I nodded. "Shall we attack now?"

"No. If we interfere, Brax will kill us. He wants to do this on his own. He needs to."

So we watched, and I continued to gather in power. The fire leaked out of me and surrounded my entire body in a fiery aura. It swayed and burned hot. Underneath its surface, the dark fire yearned to test its power against the monstrous demon. I itched to set my magic free, but the time would come when Brax fell. I wouldn't have to wait long.

Tashia rose up, fully formed. Her wounds were gone, yet the magic I sensed from her had diminished. Brax faced her, barely able to grip his huge sword. His red eyes dimmed, yet he showed no signs of quitting.

The corrupt crosswalker charged Tashia once more. This time, Tashia easily grabbed him and ripped his sword away. Magic surged through his body. The shadow that draped his face began to vanish and the red light in his eyes lessened. The black armor that encompassed his body shredded away and fell to the ground. Brax tried to call his sword, but it could only drag itself on the ground in spurts. Brax's two red eyes came out of their sockets and tumbled to the ground.

Tashia held his body up and bellowed, "This is a man! He's not one of us, and never was! Now, he is no more."

She squeezed and her claws ripped Brax in half. She flung his body far away and laughed.

"Hellsfire, now!" Serling pounded his staff three times. Electric bolts shot out from the ground, paralyzing every demon, even those on our side. The fairies took the hint and attacked and slaughtered the frozen demons.

I sprinted toward Brax, and Tashia turned her yellow eyes toward me. She tried to cast magic on me, but it was slow in building. She had used far too much energy in facing Brax. As soon as I ran into range, I unleashed the flame, summoning a thermal blast on her lower, weaker half. My magic breached her defenses. Her body caught on fire and her skin sizzled and burned. She rolled on the ground, crushing fairies and demons alike as she tried to douse the flames.

The flames beneath her died out and the magic within her flared. She summoned enough power to shower me with a flurry of energy daggers. As they flew closer to me, I could feel the intense might in them. How did Brax manage to survive them? I knew if they got past my magic and struck me, I would be killed.

But they wouldn't get past my magical defenses. Brax might have been a sword-wielding crosswalker and she a monstrous demon, but *I* was a wizard. When her energy daggers were almost upon me, I reached out with my magic and yanked at them. For the moment, my power was far stronger than hers, and they stopped in midflight, hovering inches from me.

I flung them back at her, strengthening the daggers of energy with my fire. Dozens of them exploded when they smashed into her. Those that remained, I pushed, forcing them to dig and tear into her. She slowed, but the magic Renak imbued her with started to heal her wounds. Like Brax, I had no idea where her heart was. I was going to need time to find it.

I reached into my pouch and pulled out the last potion I'd made under Stradus's tutelage. I threw the small vial at her and it exploded on the ground. An energy cage shot out from it, materializing around the gigantic demon and trapping her. I stepped closer, but warily, as if I was approaching a dangerous animal. I looked to see where her heart was but it could be anywhere, and she was so gigantic. I didn't know or understand demon anatomy. All I knew was that her heart wasn't in her head or chest.

She pounded in fury against the walls, and each time, the cage electrified her. She howled and continued to beat against it. With each blow, the cage weakened. She stopped and stared at the cage. When Tashia smiled, I worried. Instead of fighting the magic of the cage, she began to absorb it. The power flowed into her, strengthening her until the cage disappeared.

My time was up. I was going to have to find her heart.

"Tash!" Kreezak said, flying in between us.

Serling's spell had broken. The crosswalker leaned on his staff, gasping for air. He had used all his power to immobilize the demons. He would be no help to me now.

Tashia halted her movement and her face lit up with a beaming smile I found eerie. "My little Kree. How good it is to see you in a body again." He flew to her and she reached out and put a gigantic claw under Kreezak's chin, stroking it. "I've missed you. All that time together in the jewel, yet we couldn't do anything."

"I've missed you too."

"Then stand by my side. I'll forgive you for turning against me in the first place."

"Only if you stop this madness."

Tashia's six eyes narrowed. "Madness? The fairies would imprison me. Kill me, if they could."

"I know, but I won't let them."

Tashia growled. "Wouldn't you? You helped them last time."

Kreezak flew around her. "I was trying to get them to see reason. I was making headway when Renak freed you."

"This is what I think of fairies."

Tashia slithered forward and snatched a fairy from the air. She plucked the fairy's sword aside, then pulled off her wings one at a time. The fairy's screams were agonizing. My power rose up in me, the flames coming out and surrounding me. I wanted to smite the beast that tortured the fairy. Yet I still didn't know where her heart was. And was one fairy's life worth what Kreezak was trying to do?

Tashia tossed the fairy aside and stared at me, challenging me.

Brax had the right idea. Instead of chopping her to bits, I would unleash that dark fire, incinerating every part of her body. I walked forward, letting the darkness rise to the surface.

But Kreezak stopped me. The little demon huffed and puffed, his face contorting in anger as he hovered inches from her face. "Don't you want us to be together? That's all I've ever wanted! Your quest for power and revenge will destroy you!" He waved his chubby finger.

"I cannot be destroyed!" Tashia roared, sending a shiver through me.

"But Tash—"

"But nothing!" Tashia slapped Kreezak and sent him tumbling through the air.

With the demon army decimated, the fairy army turned most of their attention to Tashia. They attacked her with renewed vigor. If she was defeated, the rest of the demon army would break. I almost joined them, but instead I ran to Kreezak.

The blow hadn't been strong enough to hurt him, but he seemed defeated all the same. "Are you all right?"

Kreezak lifted his fat head up. He never looked at me, but just stared at Tashia with longing and pain. In a weak voice he said, "You've...got to stop her. She can't be reasoned with. I can see that now. Her anger is too great—far greater than our love. Renak's power must have corrupted her."

"Maybe she was always like that."

Kreezak's angry eyes met mine, but then the anger faded into sadness. "Maybe."

"Where is her heart? You've seen me, Brax, and the fairies fight her, but to no avail. You know her best."

He glanced toward the ground.

I grabbed him hard by the shoulders and raised my voice. *"Where?"*

"We've always had a connection. It was why Shala sought me out. When we were younger, I used to lay my head upon her heart. I loved the way it sounded. *Thump, thump; thump, thump.* I heard it now." He finally looked up at me. "Her heart is located deep in the middle of her lower back. You'll have to get under her armor to reach it. Can you do it?"

I glanced back at Tashia. The carnage of fairy bodies kept piling up around her, no matter how many fought her. "I'll have to."

"Good."

I thought of the maleika I'd fought above, and thought the same strategy might work here. My magic was a beacon to Tashia. She would sense me well before I got anywhere near her back, and she was too huge to hold down. I whistled down a lime-green fairy and had her carry me up above the battlefield, gathering in magic as we went.

We were hovering well above Tashia when the fairy said, "Revenge my sisters."

"I will."

"Good."

The fairy let go of me and I plummeted into the fray. The wind pushed against my body and face, flapping my cheeks and nearly blinding my eyes. I forced myself to remain calm as I accessed the wind's magic and used it to guide my descent. I wove between the fairies, aiming for Tashia's back. As large as it was, I had to get it right, and more importantly, I had to find a way to cut through her armor.

I pushed my hands through the wind and summoned all the fire I could. A long streak of fire trailed behind me. I fired the blast, hitting her with its full force. The flame engulfed her entire back side, the backlash slowing me down and pushing me back.

Tashia's howl deafened me, and I landed with a loud thump on her lower back. Her entire back was set aflame, and I drew the fire to me. I chanted and channeled the power, creating a shield of fire and wind. I tapped into the earth mana to anchor myself onto Tashia so that I wouldn't be flung off.

She slung her body around, trying to throw me off, but my magic held firm. Her stinger bashed against my shield, sizzling with every burst. She amplified her strikes with magic and my shield buckled with each blow.

I didn't have much time. I whipped out my father's dagger and tapped into the crosswalking energy. I cut and sliced my way through her beetle-like skin. Green blood squirted out, landing in my eyes. My mind nearly buckled from the constant chanting and her attack on my dying shield. Sweat carried my strength away, and my heart felt like leaping from my chest. But I kept going. Serena and the others counted on me and I wasn't going to let them down.

I sheathed my dagger and dug through her wound. Slime and guck wormed its way underneath my nails. I had to hurry, because the wound was beginning to heal. The muscles grew back, and dark veins twisted and resealed themselves. I tore through her flesh like a madman. Finally, I reached her heart.

The thick black mass of flesh beat like drums, but I couldn't hear what Kreezak had heard. Familiar black mana radiated from it. I had felt that power before—when I was in Renak's old stronghold deep in the Wastelands. The ancient wizard's power swirled inside her heart. Instead of killing her or draining her, Renak had twisted his magic to bestow more power on her.

Renak's power crept up my arm, but it didn't attack me like I expected it to. His power added to my own, and it called the dark flames from within to the surface. I yanked her heart free, thinking that would be enough to destroy her.

The roaring of my fire wall ceased. Tashia had broken through, and she still lived. I realized that even if it was separated from her body, as long as her heart beat, she could never be killed. The backlash of the shield tore into me. It severed the magic I had cast to anchor myself, and I started to slide off her.

"Die, wizard!"

As I slid off Tashia, her tail lashed toward me, its sharp stinger imbued with potent magic. I couldn't summon magic fast enough for an adequate defense. There was only one thing I could think of. The only thing I had strength enough to do. I lifted the monstrous heart and put it in the path of my destruction.

The stinger pierced Tashia's own heart. My hands shook from the magical force that was released. Black magic emanated from the heart and traveled up my arms, into my body. My body welcomed the ancient rush of power. Tashia's heart shriveled in my hands, until it crumbled to dust. I lifted it in my hand, and a puff of wind carried it away.

The shadows under my feet grew larger. I glanced up and barely had time to register Tashia's massive body swaying. I scrambled out of the way, running to escape her gigantic shadow.

The impact of her body crashing into the ground caused me to stumble and fall. When the dust settled, I clasped my hands over my ears. I turned back around and stared at Tashia's body, waiting to see if she would attack again.

Kreezak sputtered past me to his former love.

"I'm sorry, Tashia," Kreezak said, petting her face as the great demon lay there dying.

"There's no reason to be sorry." She struggled to smile. "You were right. Wizards cannot be trusted. At least I shall devastate the fairies."

"What do you mean?"

"Renak bestowed a final spell on me in case I should be defeated—a demon's death spell."

Tashia laughed, green blood gurgling out of her mouth.

The demons and fairies closest began to run, crawl, slide, and fly away. A huge build-up of magic emanated from within Tashia. Her body glowed and wisps of magic flowed out of her like mist. It wrapped around her, spinning faster and faster, becoming more powerful with each second. Kreezak never left her side, clinging tightly onto one of her claws.

"Hellsfire!" Serling said, limping toward me. "You must—"

The magic bestowed upon Tashia erupted. The searing magical energy yearned to annihilate everything in its wake. Tashia and Kreezak evaporated into nothingness. Then it headed for me.

I raised my defenses, but Tashia's and Renak's mystical energies shattered them. When the power touched me, the flames were extracted from my body. My magic roared like a storm, yet I had no control over it. My magic clashed against Tashia's explosion, sparks sizzling as each one tried to be the winner. The angry flames continued pumping from my body. Tashia's final spell repelled them, straining my mind and body and consuming my life force to fuel its need to destroy everything.

I finally listened to the voice and its whispers, and gave in to the power that had beckoned me for years now. My flames darkened and raced out of me. My weariness vanished, and I was stronger and more powerful than I had ever been before.

My magic no longer combated the deadly spell. Instead, it consumed the black mana Renak had used. It drew it inside of me until Tashia's spell ran out of fuel. The dark magic funneled back inside my body.

Its icy cold touch shivered my soul, and the black mana smothered the flames both without and within.

With the fire inside me gone, I blacked out.

CHAPTER 23

A GREAT FLAME *roars high into the sky, stretching to the heavens. I gaze at the light show, letting its warmth comfort my body. Yet with each passing moment it gradually wanes and wavers. Bit by bit, it withdraws.*

The fire looks injured. I rush to it, trying to catch it before it burns itself out. The small fire fades in my hand and I concentrate to keep it going. Nothing happens. I can do nothing but watch it disappear as the light vanishes. The darkness overtakes me.

A soft hand wakes me, caressing my face. I let myself nuzzle against that familiar hand. I open my eyes and see it's Krystal. Her face is hovering over mine as I lie on the ground.

I flinch away from her and say, "What are you doing? You know you can't touch me. You'll die."

Krystal smiles—that special smile that's for me and me alone. "But I just did."

I open my mouth to reply, but say nothing. She's right. "How—?"

Krystal puts her long finger to my lips. Without thinking, I kiss it, remembering her affectionate touch. "Shhhh. Sometimes you talk too much, hero."

She leans in closer until she brushes her lips upon mine. I return the passionate kiss, moaning. It's been ages since I last kissed her, touched her, made love to her. Before it can go any further, Krystal releases the kiss. The shadows crawl up her legs, beginning to embrace her.

"Krystal!" I say as I scramble to get the shadows off her.

She's calm and her violet eyes fill with worry. Not for herself but for me. "Hellsfire, I'm fine."

"But—"

"Trust me."

"You know I do."

"It's you who should be worried."

I give her a quizzical look. "What do you mean, angel?"

Krystal's lower body disappears, but it doesn't perturb her. She puts a hand to my face and I snuggle against it. Her hands disappear and her face begins to fade in and out. I look through my transparent love.

"I love you, Hellsfire. Just because I'm not with you doesn't mean I won't always be with you. Don't let the darkness overcome you, hero. Remember that."

"Krystal!" I say. I reach out to the empty space that was once filled with her light. Painful tears threaten to spill over. "Please don't leave me again!"

Without her or the fire, I succumb to the emptiness.

I opened my eyes to the real world and found someone's soft lips on mine. I broke the kiss, seeing a familiar, cute, pink face.

"Hellsfire," Serena said, putting a hand to her chest. "I didn't mean to. It's just you were having a nightmare and the next thing I know, you reached out and—"

"It's all right," I said. "I don't blame you."

I found myself lying in bed. The dim lighting told me where I was—Alana's palace. Even though blankets covered me, I found the air chillier than normal. That's when I realized that there wasn't a strand of hair on my entire body. I had no hair on my head, no chest hair, not even any eyebrows. My fire must have singed everything. That had never happened to me before. I hugged the blankets closer to me for some warmth.

Serena gawked at me, her pink eyes piercing into me. "The princess is…she's a very lucky woman."

"What do you mean?"

"When you kissed me, you kissed as if I was her."

"I did?"

Serena nodded. "And that was…I don't know how to describe it. Powerful, magical, breathtaking, and more. I've never felt anything remotely like that—here or in your world." She paused. "I believe now I understand why my mother does what she does. It is magic she can use for her own purposes, but she's also trying to capture what she's missing. It's…quite enticing."

Serena sat on my bed. "You should see my mother. She looks truly happy, a rare sight indeed for the Queen of the Fairies. A mortal enemy has been destroyed, and she got her stones back."

"Brax's eyes," I said.

"Yes." Serena chuckled. "Mother was quite displeased at being fooled so. Though she said she checked his eyes." She paused. "They never found his body."

"Whose body?"

"Brax's. After the battle, his body was missing, along with his demons and his sword."

I thought about when I first met Brax. Tashia might have destroyed his body, but she hadn't destroyed his sword. Brax and his sword were linked. A lot of magic was forged into it. I had no doubt that Brax was still alive, but would he be as I knew him, or would he be just a man?

Serena stared at me with a quiet fascination. "How did you save us? You protected everyone from Tashia's death spell."

I was quiet, thinking about her words. I had used hellsfire to shield us, and Renak's dark power from Tashia was added to my own. I had no idea what it meant, but it couldn't bode well for me.

"I'm not sure. I had no control over it. It just…happened."

"Happened?"

"Yeah," I said, forcing a fake smile and shrugging. I didn't want to tell her the truth—how the magic might affect me in ways I couldn't understand. How it might already be affecting me.

Serena stared at me with accusatory eyes, and I held my breath. Would she believe my lie? Her eyes softened and she giggled. "As much time as I've spent in your realm, I'll still never understand you wizards."

I stared at Serena's bandaged wing, wanting to change the subject. "How are you?"

Serena grunted as she tried to lift her wing. "It'll be months before I'm able to fly again, but our healer reassured me there's no permanent damage."

"That's good. I'd hate for something to happen to you."

"How are you feeling? Malik always feels exhausted whenever he uses so much magic. Though I've never seen him use as much as you."

I reached out to the flame to comfort me. The fire was my consort, my power, my blanket, and next to Krystal, my everything. I expected it to be weakened, like it was all the other times after I nearly died doing something foolish, but what I found stunned me.

There was nothing.

I looked down, bending my neck until my chin touched my bare chest. "No," I whispered.

"What's wrong?"

"Quiet! I need to concentrate."

I closed my eyes and slowed my breathing in meditation. I encased my mind in quietness, ignoring Serena's nearby breathing and how her eyes studied me. Sweat dripped down my neck and my face. I searched deep within myself, and I couldn't find or reach any sort of magic—not inside of me, or even from Serena, sitting next to me. I had been exhausted countless times before, pushed myself to the edge, but I had always been able to sense the magic that was in all life—to feel that something was there. This time, it wasn't coming to me. It wasn't around me. It wasn't in me.

My magic was simply gone. There was only a void of deep darkness.

I trembled as I looked at Serena, trying to say something. My hand reached out, grabbing her pink flesh, my fingernails digging into her skin. My heart pounded in my ears and I choked on my own breathing.

"Sit back and relax, Hellsfire," Serena said. "Deep, calm breaths."

Serena pried my fingers off her. I breathed as best I could.

"Good. I'm going to go get some help. I'll be right back." The little fairy ran out of the room, yelling into the hall.

I receded into my mind, searching frantically for mana, energy, something, anything! The only thing I found was the emptiness that now dwelled inside me. I couldn't find a trace of my magic. What was wrong? Without my magic, who was I? Was I still a wizard, and why had this happened? What did this strange place do to me?

"I don't know what's wrong with him, Serling," Serena said, barging back into the room. "He just started panicking."

Serling came over and placed a hand on my shoulder. "Hellsfire, what is it?"

In a barely audible voice, I said, "My power...it's gone. I can't feel any magic."

"Gone?" Serena said. "Is that even possible?"

"I'm afraid it is," Serling said. "It's...rare, but it can happen. Are you sure about this, Hellsfire?"

I nodded.

Serling sighed. "I know how you feel."

I glared at him. "You know how I feel?" I burned with anger, but the fire didn't threaten to come out of me like it had so many times before. "You know nothing, crosswalker!" I grabbed him by his thin white robes. "I've lost everything! I've lost my father, my master, my woman, and now my power! I have nothing! Do you hear me, crosswalker? Nothing!"

Serling put his staff to my head. Power flowed from it and into me. I let go of his clothes and plopped onto the bed. "Rest," he said.

"What are you going to do now?" Serena asked.

I blacked out before I could hear his answer.

I woke up to a snoring Serena, slumped over in a nearby chair. There were sheer, light clothes lying on the dresser next to the bed, along with my pouch and dagger. I dressed and secured my belongings. I was tempted to wake Serena, but I wanted to be alone with my thoughts. My powers still hadn't returned to me.

As I wandered the bright corridors, I tried to ignore how happy the fairies were over their victory. I glared at one couple as they walked past me. The man had been injured and the woman was clinging to him, smothering him with attention. I knew I should have been happy for them, but I wasn't. I couldn't help but feel that they were responsible for me losing my powers, even though that was a foolish and selfish notion. Countless fairies had lost their lives and shed their blood to stop Tashia and her demon army. I was only thinking of myself, when it was my fault she'd been here in the first place.

My feet eventually found a balcony. I leaned against the railing and stared at a nearby forest. Its red and orange canopy glistened, and a blue, sparkling haze settled on it.

"There you are, cutie," Serena said, yawning. "Up early, I see."

I didn't acknowledge her.

"I'm sorry; did you want to be alone?"

"You can stay," I said. "I'm alone enough. Now more than I was before."

"Serling worked his magic while you were sleeping. He couldn't—"

"Find anything. I know. I would have felt it."

"He also said that it may come back to you if you leave the Netherrealm, or that it may just come back on its own in time."

"Really?" I raised an eyebrow.

"Yeah, but he also said not to get your hopes up."

"Of course."

"I asked my mother to help you. She said there might be some ritual or spell she can try. She was waiting for you to wake up."

"Thanks."

"No problem."

The deafening silence didn't bother me as I continued to stare at the view, but my fairy friend wasn't content to let me admire it in silence.

"Hellsfire?"

"Yeah?"

"If things don't work out, what are you going to do?"

I sighed and stared into the empty sky. "I…don't know. Maybe without my magic, I can go back to Alexandria and to Krystal."

I reached into my pouch and pulled out a vial of Krystal's blood. This was the first thing I had thought of, but I hadn't wanted to get my hopes up. Over the last few months, my resounding lack of success had taken its toll on me. Without my magic, I prayed that the curse within her had cleared up. I would gladly trade my magic for her health. I put a drop of her blood on my finger. It fizzled as if my finger burned it.

I exhaled. "The gods must hate me."

After a few minutes of my self-loathing, Serena pulled my face toward her until we stood face-to-face, inches away from each other.

"Serena—"

"Don't worry; I'm not going to kiss you. I doubt it would be even half as good as when you kissed me thinking I was the princess." Serena turned my head to the side, inspecting my face. "You *are* different."

"What?"

"Your eyes. They always had a certain spark and fire to them. That's gone. Instead of that light, they seem to be darker now."

"Thanks."

"I'm sorry." She let go of my cheeks. "I didn't mean to say that. You've got to get your magic back, Hellsfire. The magic really is a part of you wizards. I see that now. If you don't find a way, you can stay here for as long as you like."

"I can?"

Serena smiled in glee. "Of course. I'll be your tour guide and show you around. You'll get to love the Netherrealm. It's not that bad of a place."

"I'll think about it." I didn't know if I could ever call the Netherrealm my home. It was tempting to stay while I sorted things out. But I might allow myself to give in to its carnal pleasures. It was a chance I couldn't risk.

Serena's face sagged. "You're not going to stay here, are you?"

She read me before I had even made up my mind. I breathed deeply. "No, I suppose not."

"If you ever change your mind…"

I leaned over, embraced her, and kissed her on the forehead. "You're really sweet, and a true friend. Thanks for being there for me."

She sniffled in my arms. "Any time, cutie." She pulled away from me, holding me by the hand and dragging me away from the balcony. "Let's go see if my mother can finally be of some help."

Serena led me to Alana's chambers. The queen was leaning back in her huge bed. A wide smile spread across her face as she twirled her wand, admiring it. The stones that were once Brax's eyes were on top of it. If I still had my magic, I would certainly have sensed how much more powerful she was now.

The fairy queen's light blue eyes fixed on me. She rose and my eyes immediately focused on her body, which her loose, transparent clothing made no attempt to hide. She glided to me and brushed her long fingers against my face. Without my own magic, her magic took me right there. My body shivered and would immediately obey her.

"My dear Hellsfire," Alana said. She took my hand and the feeling of loneliness, emptiness, and exhaustion vanished. Pleasure and lust took its place.

"Mother!" Serena said, tugging me away from Alana, nearly causing me to fall. "Leave him alone!"

"Oh, you're no fun."

I stood there, bewildered, trying to get some kind of bearing. With each heavy blink I took, I tried to focus.

"Don't be jealous, my dear," Alana said, grinning. "You can join in if you like."

Serena's whole body turned cherry red. "I can't believe you! I need you to help him, not manipulate and use him! He saved our lives, Mother! He defeated your mortal enemy; he got your precious stones back. Now in his moment of weakness, you try to seduce him! What kind of person are you?"

"Who said I wasn't trying to help him?"

"Don't give me that. Look at you, Mother! You're a whore!"

"You've never understood," Alana said, shaking her head. She kept her composure and didn't explode at her daughter like I thought she would. "And your time in the mortal realm has clouded your judgment. It's always been a give and take thing. I give them what they desire, what they need, and in return, they give me what they can. Hellsfire would understand the balance in it."

I vaguely shook my head.

"He has done much for me, daughter. I owe him. He does not owe me. I promise you, I shall not enslave or trick him."

"Then help him get his powers back."

"I will try, but not even the crosswalker is sure I can." Alana walked behind me and wrapped her arms around my chest. She blew into my ear, sending chills through me. Alana took a quick nibble and my knees buckled. "Serena, I can give Hellsfire intense pleasure for as long as he can stand it. Days? Weeks? Months? Years? I sense this one can last quite awhile. All that energy he's contained from not touching that precious princess of his. I know you care for him, my daughter, but if I can't get his powers back, what then?"

Serena slumped her shoulders. "I don't know."

I looked up at Alana with a questioning face. Was she right about all of those things?

"These humans are not like you and me," Alana continued. "Though they're loathe to admit it, they're all ruled by their emotions. I can make him forget about all of the pain and guilt he feels." Alana stroked my cheek. "Can you say the same?"

"He won't stay here."

"Already asked?" Alana laughed, and it sounded like music to me. "Just because he turned you down doesn't mean he'll turn me down." Alana ran her hand down my chest. "See?"

I let out a sigh of pleasure.

"Hellsfire," Serena said. "You must fight." Her fists clenched in anger but her eyes were heavy and sad. If I continued on my course, I would lose Serena too.

"I...can't." I was so tired of it all. If I didn't have my powers or Krystal, I at least had this. Alana was right. Our emotions threatened to destroy us and I needed some kind of release—or at the very least, an escape from it all. I reached up and ran my hand through Alana's long hair.

"Sure you don't want to join us?" Alana said before she sucked on my neck.

Serena turned and headed for the door.

"Children. Now, where were we?" Alana slithered in front of me and kissed me.

I returned the kiss, getting lost in the moment as the magic and passion overwhelmed me. I was free and my head was clear. Nothing mattered. Not Serena, not my magic, not even Krystal. The only thing that mattered was Alana's touch. Her every caress and kiss soothed me in a way I desperately needed. Gods help me, I was going to let myself drift away in it. And I didn't care.

I tore off Alana's clothes with a frenzy I didn't know I craved. She laughed in delight as I slammed her on her lofty bed. I took a moment to admire her perfect, naked body. I grabbed it, aching for my lust to be satisfied. I might not have had my fire anymore, but the warmth of her body beneath mine was more than enough.

"Stop," Alana said before I entered her.

"What is it, Mistress? Did I do something wrong?"

"No. It's that spoiled, ungrateful daughter of mine." Alana's face was somber and thoughtful as she pondered her words. "I realized if I do this, she will never forgive me. Of all the things I've done, it's *this* she won't forgive. She would deny me, the Queen of all Fairies, my very nature!"

Her eyes darkened and the storms reappeared in them. But I didn't move. Not out of fear or arousal. I just didn't care. I would do whatever Alana required of me.

The small storms in her eyes vanished. "You may go, Hellsfire."

Part of me found I didn't want to go. "Are you sure?"

She made a face. "Now this is interesting. What do you want?" She made no move to pry her soft body from mine.

She must have released her magical hold on me, because my head was clear. "I think I don't want to betray your daughter's trust."

"Very well." Alana slid out from underneath me.

I hurriedly dressed, desperately needing to get out of the room before my body betrayed me.

"Hellsfire," she said when I reached the door. "Be gentle."

I bowed. "I shall try, mistress."

I left Alana's chambers and ran down the hallway, looking for Serena. I found her at the end of the hallway and grabbed her shoulder, "Serena!"

"Hellsfire! What are you doing here? Shouldn't you still be with my mother?"

I told Serena what had happened between me and Alana. Her mouth hung open and her eyes were wide.

I put a hand to her frozen shoulder. "Serena?"

"I can't believe *I* got my mother to stop. That's a big deal!" She came out of her shock and grabbed me. "I also can't believe you said no when given the chance. This is huge. I've got to tell Myla. She won't believe it."

"Your mother loves you."

She sighed. "I know she does. I love her too, but she can be so frustrating at times. I suppose that she would say the same thing about me." Serena was silent as we stood in the hallway, letting fairies pass by us. She locked her arm in mine. "Now let's see if she's able to get your powers back, or at least find a way for you and the princess to be together."

But Alana wasn't able to, and neither was Serling. It was weird being probed by them and to have magic cast on me without being able to feel it. I had gotten used to being able to feel how magic moved, how it was alive, how strong or how subtle it could be. I now felt nothing, and realized I had taken my abilities for granted.

They told me that the place where my magic had been was like a vacuum. But it wasn't empty. Something had replaced my power, but they couldn't tell me what. I wondered, did it have to do with Renak's magic? A week passed before they finally gave up. Alana believed that while they might not be able to summon my magic, she could break Krystal's curse.

That frustrated the Queen of the Fairies even more than my lack of magic. She had experience with that type of magic. I thought her magic was very similar to it. But try as she might, not even she could break Krystal's curse.

Throughout the entire time of failed tests, magics, and potions, Serena stood by my side for support. However, the legacy of Renak had beaten me again, and there was nothing I could do. Stradus was right. The things done during the War of the Wizards had left repercussions for years to come. I was through with the Netherrealm.

It was time for me to go.

Serling explained to me that while a person not born of the Netherrealm could crosswalk to the Netherrealm from our world anywhere, they would end up in designated places. Crosswalking was like a network of tunnels in that aspect, and all those tunnels ended in the same points. However, leaving from the Netherrealm back to our world, a person, whether fairy or human, elf or demon, had to leave from those points. Along with accessing the Netherrealm's magic and opening a portal, a crosswalker could navigate those tunnels.

Serena, Alana, Serling, and I stood crowded together in a small room that barely contained the four of us. The chamber was located deep in Alana's palace. It was guarded and well away from anything vital, but close enough that it could be accessed in a hurry if need be. At the end of the room there was supposed to be a portal, but it was closed now.

I stared at the walls of the room, trying desperately to feel any sort of magic that made it stand it out. I sensed nothing, and that was going to take some getting used to. It was as if the world was now dead to me.

"I'm going to miss you, Hellsfire," Serena said. Her eyes were sad, and tears trembled in them.

"You're going to see me in Tyree, aren't you?"

She sniffled. "Yeah."

"Then what's the problem?"

"Because I'll be a small, little sprite. Not my normal self."

"You are who you are. No matter what your size is." I smiled. "I'll see you in a couple of months when you're fully healed."

"It won't be all bad," Alana said from behind Serena. "Maybe we could get better acquainted and you could tell me all about that world you left me for. I would very much like to know about it, if there are people like Hellsfire there. And I've...missed you." For the briefest of moments, I saw Alana's blue eyes waver with sorrow.

Serena's face stiffened.

"Don't look so surprised. I may not understand your fascination with the dull mortal realm, but you are a daughter of mine." Alana faced me. "Goodbye, Hellsfire. I hope you find what you're looking for."

"I hope I do too."

"If you ever change your mind, find a way back here. My offer will always stand." Alana smiled, and it melted me. Her smile vanished as she addressed Serling, towering over him. "Thank you for your assistance, crosswalker. Now that the ban has been lifted, stay out of my way and out of my realm."

"As you wish, Mistress," Serling said, bowing his head.

Alana spun away, taking her leave of all of us as she exited the room. I stared at her rump while she went.

Serling went to the front of the room and summoned his magic. His hair went wild and his whole body lit up as if electricity ran through it. The crosswalker transferred that energy to his staff and he tore a hole into our world. The bright, swirling light hypnotized me.

I tore my gaze away from it and asked, "Are you going to be all right, Serena?"

She looked back at the door her mother had left through. "I'll be all right. I might have been wrong about my mother. Maybe she's not as selfish and manipulative as I thought. All this might have changed her. Don't worry, cutie, I'll be in Tyree soon enough."

"Come on, Hellsfire!" Serling said from the portal. He waved me forward.

"Are you going to be all right?" Serena asked me.

I exhaled. "I honestly don't know."

"I think it'll be all right. Now go. Serling's waiting."

I placed my hand on her waist and reeled her in close.

"What are you—?"

I silenced her with a kiss. I owed it to her. She had stood by my side in battle, and in Tyree when I had been wallowing in guilt and worry. This little fairy had become one of my closest friends. The kiss was soft and sensual, with a little bit of passion. She moaned out loud and returned it. I let it linger on for a little too long before I broke it.

"Thank you, Serena, for everything. I don't know what would have happened to me if you weren't here."

I went to Serling and he took my hand. "Hang on to me this time, and we shouldn't have any problems."

I nodded, hoping that Serling would lead me back home.

MARC JOHNSON

CHAPTER 24

THE HOT, DRY AIR filled my lungs as soon as we exited the portal. I scanned the fallen debris that surrounded us, realizing that we were in the ruins that Tashia once inhabited. Serling laughed at having the ability to seal up the portal, this time without my dagger.

I was glad that Serling had his powers again, but I felt no joy. Even with all the failures in the Netherrealm, I thought returning to my world would bring a rush of power. I was wrong. Serling only needed to look into my eyes to assess this. I was quickly running out of options. Every failed attempt was bringing me closer and closer to despair. And without my power, breaking Krystal's curse was going to be even harder.

With Serling out of the Netherrealm, his limp had returned, and without my powers, navigating the ruins was a difficult journey. The metal that had made up the ruins had collapsed in many places, blocking multiple hallways. We had to dig through high piles of sand to get through.

We climbed and dug our way out of the ruins toward day's end. I shielded my eyes from the blinding sunlight and steadied myself as the heat threatened to smother me. When my eyes focused, I saw thousands of people on the horizon.

"The sultan's army," Serling said.

A dozen of them broke off and rode to meet us, with Ardimus and Wynna at the front. The pair, along with another man who I didn't recognize, jumped off their horses as soon as they reached us.

"What happened to the demon?" one of the sultan's men asked.

"You may tell the sultan that Hellsfire took care of her, Kasib," Serling said. "The sultan has no need to fear any threats from the Netherrealm."

Kasib glared at me, no doubt thinking that I was the reason for the disturbance in the first place. And he would be right.

"The demon would have destroyed the Burning Sands, like in the stories of old, if Hellsfire hadn't stopped her."

Kasib's stony face didn't relax. "I will convey your words to the sultan, and I will spare you a pair of horses and supplies."

"Our many thanks."

"However, we will stay and make sure the threat is neutralized." He turned to Ardimus and smiled. "It was good to see you again. Try to visit more often."

"I will. You still owe me money from our wager. I'll report to the sultan as soon as I can."

We four rode out, bypassing the army, heading back to Falak. Serling relayed most of our story, but I filled in the blanks when I could. My mind kept wandering back and forth between what I'd lost. I don't know which pained me more: Krystal or my powers. Both were such a huge part of me it was like losing parts of my soul. Stradus's death weighed on me from time to time, but whenever I performed my magic, I always felt as if he was with me.

There was one last idea I had. One that I would need to try at Mina's house. Otherwise, I would head back to Tyree and maybe ask the council for help.

When we returned to Mina's home, I rushed to where my robes were. I prayed to the gods before putting the thick fabric over my head.

My former master once told me that a wizard's robes become part of the wizard. While I never quite understood what that meant, I did always feel as if my robes were a part of me in some way. Fighting in the Netherrealm, I had felt unprotected without them, even though they were just cloth.

Yet when I put my robes on, they did not help restore my powers. I had no idea what, if anything, could. My mind searched for any piece of information

I might have heard or read, where a wizard lost his powers and regained them, but I couldn't recall any stories.

I took off my wizard's robes and cradled them in my hands. "Maybe this wouldn't have happened if I had you with me," I said. "I'm going to miss you, but until I'm able to get my powers back, I shouldn't be with you. *If* I get my powers back. Don't worry; I'll leave you in good hands." I folded the wizard's robes.

We ate dinner and I spent the rest of the night writing a long letter. What was left of me, I poured into that letter. I told the others that I planned to leave the next day and head back to Tyree. I wanted to go alone, but Ardimus insisted that I take a couple of guards with me; otherwise he would ride with me to Tyree. We settled on two guards, who would do their duty and leave me alone.

The next day I said goodbye to Mina, and we got my supplies, and hired the guards. Not long afterward, we were on the outskirts of Falak. Serling and Wynna had come along to see me off.

I reached into my pack and pulled out my wizard's robes, handing them to Ardimus. "Give these to the princess. Tell her…"

I had no idea what to say. There were so many things that I wanted to say that were for her ears alone, and there were so many things I wanted to apologize for. I was giving her my robes because I knew she would keep them safe, and I wanted her to have something to remember me by.

"Tell her I'll be back for these," I said.

"Understood."

"It was a pleasure meeting you," Wynna said, hugging me.

"You too," I said, returning it. "Take care of Ardimus. He needs you."

Her face lit up when she glanced at him. "I will. It will be hard, but I know you'll be with the princess again."

"I hope so."

"And thank you for allowing me to be whole again," Serling said. "If it weren't for you, I wouldn't be able to return home."

"I'm glad I met you and was able to learn about your kind of magic…when I still had it." I pulled Serling aside. "I need you to do something for me." I took out the sealed letter and handed it to him. "Can you make sure this gets delivered by a messenger you trust? I'll pay you."

"I won't take your money." His brow furrowed. "But why don't you just give it to Ardimus? He'll give it to the princess when he sees her."

"It's…not going to her." I lowered my voice as far as humanly possible. "I need it delivered to a woman named Kathleen Awel. She lives in my hometown of Sedah, south of the elven city of Sharald."

He opened his mouth to say something, but then saw the look on my face and thought better of it. "I'll make sure this gets there. You have my word." He hid the letter on his person.

"Thank you."

We went back to the others. Ardimus had a questioning look on his face. I was going to have to lie to him, but Serling interrupted me.

"We had some unfinished business to discuss regarding the Netherrealm," Serling said.

"Nothing bad, I hope?"

Serling shook his head. "No, just clarifying some things."

I looked away as Ardimus scrutinized me.

"Very well," Ardimus said. "Ride well, Hellsfire."

"Hellsfire," I said. "I'm not even sure if I should be called that anymore."

"It's your name. You were born with it. It's who you are."

I mounted my horse. "Is it? Take care, all of you."

Not waiting for my guards, I spurred my horse underneath the bright desert sun, heading into parts unknown.

To be continued in...

ETERNAL DARKNESS

The Passage of Hellsfire, Book 4

Author's Corner

Email: *marcanthonyjohnson@gmail.com*

Facebook: *https://www.facebook.com/MarcJohnsonAuthor*

Goodreads: *http://www.goodreads.com/marcjohnson*

Twitter: *http://www.twitter.com/Hellsfire*

Website: *http://www.marcanthonyjohnson.com*